Advance 1

"David Carter gets everything right in this tender evocation of adolescence on the North Carolina coast: the landscape (physical and emotional), the idiom, the smell of fried seafood and salt in the breeze. *From the Edge of the World* takes us to a time and place familiar but entirely new, rendered lovingly by the sensibility of an attentive and assured storyteller."

— Michael Parker, author of *The Watery Part of the World*

From the Edge of the World

For Becky! From one southern writer to another! Can't wait to read your work. Looking forward to seeing you sometime soon and catching up..

Love,

"David with the earrings" :)

From the Edge of the World

David L. Carter

Apprentice
House Press

Loyola University Maryland

The author wishes to thank Jennifer Heap Bouchard for the generous use of the lyrics to her song 'Salt On a Sore'.

First Edition

Paperback ISBN: 978-1-62720-185-8
E-book ISBN: 978-1-62720-186-5

Printed in the United States of America

Design by Julia Joseph
Marketing by Taylor Garrison
Development by Andrew Mann

Published by Apprentice House

Apprentice House
Loyola University Maryland
4501 N. Charles Street
Baltimore, MD 21210
410.617.5265 • 410.617.2198 (fax)
www.apprenticehouse.com
info@apprenticehouse.com

For my father, John T. Carter, Sr.
April 27, 1938- March 12, 2011

Summer 2005

It was the smell that woke Victor up. It was a smell as familiar as it was unpleasant; it was the creeping funk of unwashed clothes and hair, mingled with intermittent gusts of stale tobacco breath, and beneath it all, the creeping, overpowering odor of an alcoholic's sweat. Anyone who has ever shared close quarters with people who do not take care of themselves will know the smell, or one similar to it, and Victor was not only someone who had shared close quarters with the unwashed, he himself had at one time gone weeks without bathing simply because it seemed pointless to do so.

Victor pressed his nose and mouth against his duffel bag, but that was no help. The choice was between breathing or not. Slowly, carefully, he drew a breath through his barely open mouth, queasy with the sense that he was admitting something unwholesome into his lungs. The bus was full. He was stuck with this smelly bum beside him. Forgetting his predicament, he sighed, and as a result gagged.

He knew from experience that a person's own filthiness is never as annoying to them as it is to those around them, so he coughed to disguise the gag. He lifted his head from the duffel bag and rubbed his face. Through the corner of his eye he glanced at the man that had sat down next to him. A typical drifter, in filthy denim clothes and a dingy white ball cap, out of the back of which a long, uncombed grey and white ponytail hung. This drifter looked to be about middle age, although such types tended to look middle aged as soon as they turn thirty. He had about two weeks' worth of moth-eaten beard on his face and neck and bright blue eyes set in red streaked whites. His face, though pale within the creases was on the whole toasted from exposure to the elements, and he had the ancient, seam lipped expression of a man with no, or very few, teeth. He was bobbing his head and patting his fingers against the Hefty bag he held in his lap in time to some tinny arena rock that seeped from the headphones in his ears that were attached to a device in the breast pocket of his denim jacket. While Victor watched, the drifter reached into the bag on his lap, felt around in it, and then pulled out a pair of cheap aviator sunglasses, with which he shaded his bloodshot eyes. Good. The old bum would listen to his music and leave him alone. Victor relaxed again with his temple against the warm, grimy window.

He did not sleep, but he dozed. The warmth of the window, the rumbling, humming, and jostling of the bus as it made its way due east on the interstate all served to lull him, despite his seatmate's aggressive smell, into that smooth, sunlit, pleasant semi-consciousness that was not quite the oblivion of sleep and not the hassle of being awake. This was the rest he sought and sometimes found when he slept in his classes at school; this aimless mental drifting, in which dreams merged with memory and longing to give him, at least in stolen, fleeting moments, some respite from his constant sense of dissatisfaction with life. These semi-sleeps were worth even the embarrassing pools of slobber he tended to leave on his desk or the cradle of his own arms when the bell rang for him to move on to the next period. Here on the bus, as in school, he did not dream, for in dreams one retains one's identity. He dissolved; he was the bright burning orange sunlight against his closed eyes, he was the slow rise and fall of his own breath, he was the woman in the seat just behind him, complaining to her seatmate about her daughter's boyfriend, he was the fox in a red white and blue striped sweater on the billboard he noticed as the bus pulled onto the highway from the bus station. He was conscious, but only slightly, and that slightness made all the difference. Nothing mattered when he was in this netherworld.

Nothing mattered until the drifter suddenly burst into song. In accompaniment to the tinny strains of his headphones, he began to

2

hum, then sing, in a croak without any sense of volume or key, some rusty metal ballad.

With every note the drifter's ragged voice grew more high pitched, cracked and lusty. Victor rolled his closed eyes, then sat up and looked around. The terrible singing was drawing attention from throughout the bus, the two black women across the aisle were staring at him and winked at Victor, and from behind and in front and all around them people were rising in their seats to get a look at whoever was making such a fool of themselves. Victor wanted to crawl into his duffel bag.

The drifter's singing became louder, until from behind them an empty wadded up Doritos bag arched over the headrest of the seat to land on the garbage bag in the drifter's lap. The drifter sat bolt upright and crowed "Fuck you!" and then tossed the chip bag over his head in the general direction from which it came. Muttering, he reached into the breast pocket of his denim jacket and the music stopped. Leaving the headphones in his ears, he turned to Victor. "People ain't got any goddamn manners any more, do they boss?" he said. The alcohol on his breath was as sickly sweet as a rotting magnolia. Victor guessed it was not even eleven o'clock in the morning, and this man was already as drunk as if it were past midnight. If he ignored the man, maybe he would fall asleep and leave Victor in peace. But as drunks will, he took Victor's silence for shyness, and assumed a kinship. "Ahh, fuck 'em, right?" he looked at Victor with such a searching, sleazy expression that Victor had a sudden repellent image of the man kissing him. He looked past the man at the two black women across the aisle, who now watched him with expressions of amused sympathy. He hated them. The old drunk followed his glance and leered at the women. They clutched one another's smooth, brown, gold braceleted forearms and cackled with laughter. Encouraged, the drifter leaned across the aisle to engage them in conversation, but they rolled their eyes at one another and drew in their lips and withdrew into a sotto voce discussion between themselves. The drifter leaned back in his seat and looked at Victor through his cheap sunglasses. "Mornin' boss," he said. "Didn't mean to wake you up there."

Victor shrugged.

The drifter cracked his knuckles. "Ain't it a pretty day? Too pretty to sleep! Just look at the country. This here is God's country," he indicated the landscaping passing beyond the window Victor had been sleeping against with one grimy finger. "Lookit it. God's country. I'm a traveling man, boss. Been all over the USA, but I like callin North Carolina home, like the sign says. Where ya headed, boss?"

The drifter waited so patiently for Victor's answer that Victor had no choice but to reply. "Morehead City," he said, in a tone one might use to indicate that one was going to a prison.

"Down East!" the drifter crowed. "Down East! Lucky you, boss, lucky you! Whatcha got goin on down east, brother? You got an old lady down there?"

Victor nodded, forgetting himself. In a way it was true, he had an old lady in Morehead City with whom he was going to stay, his grandmother, who he had last seen when he was too young to remember. He knew that his grandmother was not the kind of old lady the bum meant, but that didn't really matter. Victor was only seventeen, and had never so much as kissed a girl, and he found himself shamefully flattered that this old drunk would assume for a moment that Victor would have a woman.

"Watch out for those island girls," said the drifter with mock authority.

"Where ya coming from boss?"

Victor was being sent to work in his grandmother's restaurant in Morehead City because his mother refused to have him mope around their apartment in the capital city of the state all summer. But until he was six years old he and his mother and father had lived on Long Island near his mother's Italian family, so he mumbled 'New York' in a casual way.

"New York City!" the drifter crowed again. "A New Yorker, huh! A New York Yankee. You're a long way from home, boss. Ain't on the run, are ya? They always get their man, believe you me," the drifter nudged Victor with a sharp denim elbow.

It had been weeks? Months? Years? Since Victor had smiled, but to his astonishment a reluctant grin lifted one side of his mouth, even though he had no idea what the man meant. The drifter, missing nothing, began to wheeze with appreciation for his own wit. Victor shook his head, slightly, looking at his feet, like a shy child.

"Just making tracks, huh," said the drifter. "So am I, kid. So am I," he held his grubby, thick-fingered hand out to Victor. "I'm Lewis. Everybody calls me Shorty, though. Betcha can't guess why," he winked.

Victor shook his hand. Without any forethought, he said "I'm Steve," in a voice so clear and strong he couldn't believe it was his. Unsettled by his unplanned lie, he blushed.

But the drifter did not notice. "Nicetameetcha, Steve," he said, and released Victor's hand. Victor turned to the window and willed the warmth and color in his face to fade. Steve. Of all the people to claim to be. Steve. Steve had been a methhead in the treatment center that Victor's mother had sent him to the year before when he refused to leave the apartment for school or for anything. Steve had been at times floridly psychotic, and sometimes violent, but popular with the female patients for his long blonde hair and effortless charm. Victor had shard a room with Steve and had hated him, hated his manic methhead ways, his contempt for the girls that adored him, the unabashed conceit with which he preened in front of the mirror screwed to the door of their room. Steve had made no secret of his disgust for Victor's lack of hygiene, and to some extent it was an effort to at once impress and thwart Steve that motivated Victor to bathe and groom himself and in general at least appear to be less subhuman, at least for as long as he was in the treatment center. His therapists and his mother were overjoyed, but no one else really noticed. He was discharged with the feeling that he had somehow been bested. So now why was he pretending to be someone he despised and feared?

Shorty was rummaging in the plastic bag in his lap. He pulled out a little round container, opened it, and pulled out a wad of tobacco that he prodded into his cheek. He held the container out to Victor, who shook his head.

"Ya don't chew?" said Shorty.

"No."

"Smoke?"

Victor nodded. Though he could go days or even weeks without a cigarette and not even notice, he considered himself a smoker. His mother, who was an intensive care nurse until her diabetes and weight gain became so disabling that she had to take a desk job, smoked two packs a day. Victor's father had smoked too, until Victor was eight years old. Victor recalled the day that his father quit smoking as the day he realized that his parents could only barely tolerate one another's company.

"A smart kid like you?" said Shorty. "Aww, that's too bad. You know you'll stunt your growth," he emitted a series of phlegmy cackles and Victor thought he'd better smile. Victor was six feet tall and with his lack of muscle and long thin neck seemed much taller.

"I been smoking since I was 8 year old," said Shorty. "My daddy give me my first carton for my tenth birthday. Lucky Strikes. Back then we didn't think nothing of it. I grew up in Johnston County, tobacco all over the damn place, I picked it, cured it, drove it to market, smoked it, chewed it, spat it, did everything but fuck it from the time I was in diapers. Too late to do anything about it now, I got bigger problems on my back as I'm sure ya noticed. But, that's the way it goes. You don't drink do ya, Steve?"

It took a moment before Victor remembered he was Steve. Did he drink? He would if he knew how to get hold of any alcohol. His father drank. He could remember his parent's arguing once over the fact that Victor's father was in the habit of offering Victor the head of the beers he would treat himself to after mowing the lawn or completing some other task about the house on the weekend. "A little," he said. Victor was quite sure he would drink all the time if he had friends he could drink with.

"I'm a alcoholic," said Shorty. Victor wished he would lower his voice. "It's a disease. It's a allergy. There is no cure, only abstinence," he settled himself back in his seat with an air of having performed some duty. His voice became singsong. "But I ain't never touched nothing too ghetto," he said. "Stay away from those ghetto drugs, Steve," he said. "A little weed… that's nothing. God put it in the ground for a reason. Takes the edge of things. But all that crack, that meth, that her-on…" he looked over his cheap sunglasses at Victor like a schoolmarm. "That's for the scum of the earth, ya hear me? I hate to see a nice young white boy get mixed up in all that. Before you know it he's running around with a rag on his head and his britches hanging down off his ass like … you know what. God I hate to see that. You know what I mean, Steve?"

Victor gave a wary glance past the drifter to the two black women across the aisle, mortified that they might be overhearing the drifter and assume that he was like 'Shorty,' but if they heard 'Shorty's' rant it didn't seem to bother them. Still, Victor sat back in his seat as far as he could. He wished that the drifter would put his earphones back on and start singing. As it was he was liable to say anything.

Shorty indicated Victor's duffel bag. "That's a coast guard sea bag, ain't it!" he said.

Victor nodded, relieved. "It was my dad's," he said.

"Aww," murmured Shorty. "He still with the guard?"

"He's dead," said Victor, without a twinge. His father ran an auto insurance company in Conway, South Carolina, and had just fathered a daughter with his new wife, who was seventeen years his junior and who dotted the I in Victor with a heart in the birthday card she had sent Victor signing both her name and his father's.

"Aww," the drifter murmured his sympathy. He looked at Victor as if to invite further details, but Victor didn't know what to say. He didn't really wish his father dead. He just didn't want to talk about him. The drifter patted Victor's forearm.

"That's too bad. It's a shame to lose your old man. My old man died six years ago, age sixty-six, I remember it like it was yesterday. He had the big C, had it for years, but it finally took him out. He was a fighter though, my god in heaven you better believe. A holy fucking terror even when he was on his damn deathbed, you just ask one of them nurses aids that had to wash him. He was as big a bastard as you'd ever want to meet sometimes, treated my mama like a dog, but he was my daddy and I loved and respected him as such. You can't hold nothing against anybody when they're gone, can ya Steve. Seems like when they're gone, they just seem better and better. You want em back even if it means everything you couldn't stand is gonna come right on back with em. I'd give my left nut just to have my daddy clip his toenails on the coffee table one more time. Know what I mean, Steve?"

Victor hazarded a glance at Shorty, who was drumming his fingers lightly on his garbage bag. Behind the cheap sunglasses the drifter's expression was strangely thoughtful. "But now you take someone you're really crazy about… say your ex-wife… and you can get tired of 'em and for as long as they're livin' you'll move heaven and earth just to keep away from 'em cause they get on your ever lovin' nerves so G-D bad, excuse my language. It's a funny thing in this world, it really is. I could go weeks, months, years, without giving my daddy a second thought, 'fore he got real bad off. I couldn't stand the sight of him, tell you the truth… but it's something about when people are getting ready to leave this world… I swear something comes over em, something changes. It's like they're little babies again, I reckon, they just get easier to love. And just when you start to want em around again, they're gone…" the drifter's voice narrowed and ceased, like the stream from a faucet being turned off. He sat silent for a moment, and his fingers stilled from their soft drumming. He drew in his lips and then blew them out again with a sputtering, equine exhalation. "Oh, me," he said. Then, like a sky suddenly swept free of clouds, his countenance brightened. He nudged Victor with his bony elbow, "Listen at me. Sound like a preacher."

Victor shook his head. The drifter's thin shoulders underneath the denim jacket shook and his phlegmy laugh sizzled out of him like hot grease. "I just like to run my mouth. I talk to everybody. I'd talk to the devil," he said jauntily.

And yet for the next half hour or so they rode on together in an easy silence. The bus jostled over the rough old highway. Their bags - Victors canvas, Shorty's garbage - bounced in their laps. Victor gazed out the window, grateful for the lull in this treacherous conversation. For no reason the he could discern, he had denied his name and his father. So now he was Steve. He searched his mind for some motive for this disguise. There was none. He could call himself Steve, he could say that he had no father, but the facts remained, his name was Victor, and he not only had a father, but in addition to that a four-year-old step-brother as well as an infant half-sister whom he had never seen and was not likely to ever see. And he was traveling, not to his 'old lady', but to a literal old lady whom, as far as he knew, was as likely to be as impossible to please as his mother. The likelihood of this was in fact high, given the fact that the old lady and his mother seemed to like one another even though their family ties to one another had ended with Victor's parents' divorce. Victor's mother talked to this North Carolina grandmother every few weeks on the phone, but she never spoke to her own mother up in Long Island. Victor didn't even know if his mother's parents were even still alive. Victor remembered his mother's family from his preschool years in New York, but only vaguely. What he remembered most vividly was their volume, they shouted, they laughed, they were extravagant in their expressions, their outrageous claims, like monkeys fighting over a clutch of bananas. And they were chubby, his mother's parents, chubby and swarthy and soft bodied, like loaves of dark bread. He remembered that their

9

house, like those of all his countless aunts and uncles and cousins, was always full of fights and food and children running in and out. Why wasn't his mother sending him to them?

The bus slowed. The sunlight and the yards they passed and the storefronts and the people ambling down the sidewalks were all plunged into oblivion as the bus pulled in underneath the awning of a station. The interior of the bus was suddenly cool and dim. People began rustling in their seats. Shorty turned to Victor and once again held out his damp, hot hand. This time Victor shook it without a wince. "Goldsboro, Steve," the drifter said. "Welcome to Goldsboro, North Carolina. Home of Pope Air Force Base and my ex-wife Donna. I gotta get on the bus to Norfolk, if it ever shows up. I got a buddy up in Norfolk's got some work for me. If the bus ever gets here," he grinned. Despite the smell of his breath the grin was winsome, like that of a scrappy little boy, with all of its missing teeth. Take care, Steve. Don't do anything I wouldn't do, hee, hee, hee. Listen, Steve..." he leaned forward. "...Can ya do me a little favor?"

There was a hiss from the front of the bus as the doors opened. Several people stood, stretched, reached up into the compartments above their seats for their belongings, and got off the bus. The drifter, with his plastic bag in his lap, lingered. He gazed with shameless supplication through his cheap sunglasses at Victor.

"I ain't had a bite to eat since yesterdy," he said. "Think you could let me hold a couple bucks till... till we meet again?" he clasped Victor's shoulder and palpated it. "I'd be much obliged, boss. It'd help me out a lot..." His hand rested on Victor's shoulder, a gentle, warm, but unmistakable pressure.

For the first time since... since when? Since he was a child, Victor felt tears spring to his eyes. Was this what all the friendliness had led up to? He could not look at the drifter, whose hand still gripped his shoulder. When he had left the treatment center, he'd become so aloof from the months of irritability and not bathing and then the total remove from outside society that he'd wandered the halls of his school like a ghost, recognizing but not being recognized by his peers with whom he had at times been friendly, if not close. The only people who ever spoke to him then, aside from teachers and the guidance counselor, had been those clean cut, smiling types of either sex who would introduce themselves to him as he sat by himself in the cafeteria, or as he moped around the edge of the woods during his free period, or as he drifted off into one of his paradisiacal dozes during a study hall, and who invariably ended by inviting him to come along with them to their church, or their bible study. He felt now as he felt then, like a pawn. The drifter's hand slipped off his shoulder. The old man stood, then, looking sheepish. He shrugged.

"Don't worry about it," Shorty said amiably. "I'll figure something out. I always do. You take care, Steve."

Victor had quite forgotten that he was Steve. Somehow, being someone else took the sting out of being touched on. "Hold on," he said, and reached into his pocket. He pulled out a five-dollar bill and pressed it into the drifter's hand.

The drifter's grin was like that of a child who had just reached under his pillow and found a bill left by the tooth fairy. Clutching his plastic bag to his torso with one arm, he grabbed Victor in the other and pulled him to, pressing his bristly cheek against Victors smooth one and ended, incredibly, with a wet kiss to Victor's temple. "God bless, you, kid. It'll come back to you. Trust and believe on it, Steve,"

Victor felt inexplicably, uncomfortably warm. He sat back down in his heat. "See ya," he mumbled, and he looked out the window as the drifter shuffled down the aisle and off the bus. After a few minutes the bus was moving again, due east toward the edge of the continent, and Victor closed his eyes against the bright sun, but he could not get back to the peaceful doze out of which the drifter had roused him with his terrible but then bearable odor.

Outside the cool dark cocoon of the bus the sun was bright and the air was moist and hot, and there was a faint briny tinct to the air which reminded him that he was in a new atmosphere. While the bus hissed and groaned behind him, he set his duffel bag on the concrete and stretched up his arms and brought his hands together and cracked his knuckles, squinting up at the cloudless blue sky. It seemed that no one was there to meet him, and he stood aimlessly in the parking lot until the driver of his bus disembarked and passed him on his way into the depot. Victor picked up his duffel bag and followed, and once his eyes adjusted to the dimness of the interior, he saw two women, the older one small and rather dry looking with closely cut and curled gray hair, dressed in lavender sweatpants and an untucked blouse. With her was a much younger woman, a girl really, short and thickset, her hair was a fountain of dark yet sun-streaked unkempt curls; she was dressed in a man's white V-neck t-shirt and a long loose skirt with embroidery at the seam. As soon as the women saw him they rose from their seats near the glass door and approached him, the older woman holding out her arms, and the younger girl smiling slightly and taking him in through the huge lenses of red plastic framed glasses which, along with her round, cheeky face and explosion of curls made her look like a bewigged owl.

"Victor?" the old woman said. Her voice was nasal. He looked down at her, struck by how tiny she was, the top of her crest of pale thin waves of hair came up only to his shoulders. She reached up to clasp her arms around his neck and he had to bend his knees to accept her embrace. "Well, my Lord honey…" she said as she quickly let go to peer up at him through her sun tinted bifocals. "I never would have recognized you. Last time I saw you you didn't come up to here on me, and now look at you. Tall as a stork. It sure is good to see you," she reached forward and took his right hand and squeezed it. "My Lord," she said again, softer, as if she were talking to some invisible companion of her own age.

12

The old lady dropped his hand and reached behind herself to push forward the younger girl who allowed this, lifting one eyebrow. "You've never even seen your cousin Shelby," the old lady shook her head in wonderment. "First cousins, and you've never even laid eyes on each other. Now that is a shame. That's the world we live in today, though. Shelby, help Victor with that sea bag."

The girl grinned at Victor and reached for the strap of his duffel bag, but he bent to grab it before she could. "That's okay," he said. "It's not heavy. It's just clothes and stuff. I've got it," he hoisted the strap over his shoulder and felt as if he'd averted some obscure danger. Shelby shrugged, still smiling inscrutably, and stepped out of his way.

The old woman circled him like a moth around a light bulb. "Well, it looks mighty heavy to me. You sure you don't want any help? Well, I guess you know what you're doing. You don't have any more bags on that bus do you? Shelby, ain't you going to say hello to your cousin?"

"Hello to your cousin," said Shelby. Her voice was surprisingly low and smooth, like a woman on the radio, with no trace of the nasal accent of their grandmother. Victor nodded at her. Behind the glasses her eyes were large and strikingly pretty, a dark, greenish hazel that seemed to hold within it some of the gold of a sunrise. The color of her skin was quite dark, the shade of copper, but with a rosy undertone. Her jaw was soft but square under a wide mouth, and there was a slight gap between her two top front teeth. She caught him staring and her smile contracted a bit, and she turned away. She was not exactly fat, but her boxy shape, unmitigated by her loose clothing, seemed more masculine that his own, and she moved like a tugboat as she led them out of the depot to the front parking lot where the car was waiting.

It was an old LTD, dark blue and dingy with road dust. His father, Victor remembered, was an aficionado of sports cars, and would hate to own such a commonplace vehicle.

"You let Victor sit in front, now, Shelby," the Grandmother said as she let herself into the driver's seat.

"I was *going* to, Gum," snapped Shelby.

Gum? Victor looked at the old woman beside him, who looked as diminutive as a doll with her hands on the steering wheel. Was he supposed to call this person Gum? He was sure he could not. He'd always wondered why the cards he'd received over the years at Christmastime and on his birthday, were signed with that silly, baby name, rather that Grandma or Nana, and now he saw it was because of Shelby. He looked up into the rearview mirror. Every slight move Shelby made was accompanied by the faint clatter and jingle of thin silver bracelets on her arms. Even though she was his cousin, he'd hoped against hope that she'd be pretty. She wasn't, but there was something about her that made him want to stare, as if he couldn't take enough of her in to remember her by. She wore no make-up, at least not then, and her features were not so much plain as they were strange; very full lips, a tiny blunt nose, wide eyes, the light, indeterminate color of which were so striking against her rose-copper complexion, the boxy, curveless body.

"How is it that Victor's so tall, Gum?" Shelby said from the back seat.

The grandmother kept her eyes on the road as if it might drop off into oblivion at any moment. "From ya'lls granddaddy, I reckon."

"Daddy's tall," Shelby says. "But I think Victor's taller. But Uncle Eddie's short. Is your mother tall, Victor?"

Victor has never thought about it. "No," he says after a moment. "She's shorter than my father. But I think her brothers are all tall. I don't know."

"You don't know?"

"I don't remember. They all live in New York."

There is a long silence. Shelby leaned back against the back seat. "Genetics fascinate me. I read that some of the most crucial traits skip a generation. So there's a sense in which we all get more from our

14

grandparent's than from our birth parents. God forbid!" she says and poked the back of the driver's seat headrest with her index finger.

"Quit that," the old lady said mildly.

The house was smaller than he expected, one level, a modest structure of brick and cream-colored aluminum siding, with an open carport tacked onto its left side. It looked, with a few minor differences, exactly like all the other houses on the street. Several thick spreading trees rose out of the square flat front lawn, and a walkway branched off of the driveway to lead to three steps and a place to stand before the front door. Victor realized he had all along unquestioningly expected a house standing on stilts that lifted it over the edge of the ocean, and he felt a vague disappointment. The only hint that there was water anywhere nearby was in the sharp tang of the air, and for all he knew the ocean was miles away, and might as well not be there at all for all the good it would do him.

When he stepped inside the house, he shivered, as the air conditioner was turned up high, and all the curtains in the front room were drawn. When his eyes adjusted he could see, by the inconstant light of a mute television set, a tiny living room inhabited by a sofa and easy chair, both upholstered in a blue and green tartan pattern, a low, round wooden coffee table, and walls peppered with framed photographs, decorative shelving, and one large print over the sofa of a woman in eighteenth century dress playing a harpsichord. A hallway led from the right side of this room to the rest of the house, except for the kitchen, which could be entered through a wide space in the wall just before the hallway. Into this space a shadow, then a more substantial figure appeared, it was a man, dressed in what looked like pajama bottoms underneath a plaid bathrobe, holding what looked like a half-sized soda can.

"Hey, Daddy," said Shelby.

"Hey." the man said in a faint, somewhat raspy voice. He looked at Victor and lifted his free hand in greeting, and his robe gaped open to reveal the shadow of ribs and one nipple surrounded by sparse,

15

light hair. The man's face was pale and his high forehead was wrinkled. He had very short light colored hair and a receding hairline, a square jaw and a stringy neck. Even in the dim light Victor could see that his eyes were the same bright light blue as the Grandmother's, and like hers, lightly shadowed underneath.

"You must be Victor," the man said. He stepped forward and held out a hand. Victor shook it, and was struck by how limp and damp and warm the man's hand felt. "I'm your Uncle Buzz. I reckon you figured that out already."

Victor nodded.

Uncle Buzz looked at the can in his hand as if he'd forgotten all about it. "This here's my lunch," he said. "I didn't know ya'll would be back so soon. I would've got dressed," he took a sip from the small can, and grimaced. "It ain't too bad. It's all I can keep down, lately."

The grandmother laid her purse on the arm of the sofa. "Did Dr. Patel call, William?"

It took Victor a moment to realize she was speaking to Uncle Buzz, who shook his head.

"I'll call him after lunch," the man in the bathrobe said as the old lady harrumphed. "Let's get Victor settled," she said, "and then we'll have something to eat. Victor, honey, I don't know how much your mama told you, but your uncle's going for some physical therapy over in Beaufort when a space opens up for him this weekend, so for a couple of nights, I'm afraid you'll have to bunk out here in the living room, if that's all right. The couch pulls out, so you ought to be pretty comfortable. I know it ain't too private, but..." she holds out her hands in a helpless gesture. "I wish we had more room, but we don't."

"That's all right," said Victor.

"I suppose for right now you can just lay your stuff out over by the window..." she indicated an open space of floor underneath the blinded east window, "And then when William gets settled you can move everything into his room."

Victor nodded and put one foot on top of the other. He could sense everyone looking at him.

Shelby walked over to her father and butted her head gently against his frail shoulder. "I can't wait to come see you, Daddy," she said. Uncle Buzz nodded and lifted his free arm, as if with enormous effort, to drape heavily across his daughter's shoulders. She turned to Victor. "He gets his own private room, and they have hot tubs and a massage therapist. It's not a rest home. It's more like a damn health spa."

"Nice," said Victor, uncertainly.

"Well, I don't know why we're all standing around," the grandmother said after a brief silence. "William, let Shelby show Victor your room before you go back in there. Shelby, go on and show Victor the rest of the house, and I'll get some lunch ready. I'm just going to have a tomato sandwich, it's too hot for anything else. Victor, what do you want? I've got peanut butter, I can grill some cheese..."

For some reason, Victor wanted one of the supplemental milkshakes that Uncle Buzz was drinking, the same sort of thing they made all the anorexic and bulimic girls in the treatment center drink. His stomach was so tense that he could think of nothing less appealing than a peanut butter sandwich. "Peanut butter's O.K," he said. He picked up his duffel bag and followed Shelby down the hall. The first door, on the right, was the bathroom, small and dark and clean smelling. The next door, to the left, was the door to Uncle Buzz's room, the room that Victor would soon inhabit. He peeked in for a moment and saw an unmade twin bed, a window overlooking the front yard, and, opposite the bed, a tall dresser. The doorway down the hall a bit and to the left was shut tight. "That's the master bedroom," said Shelby. "The old lady doesn't like anybody going in there, so we won't go in. There's not much to see, anyway. It's the biggest room in the house, though. There are a couple of pictures of you when you were little on the wall. They look like school pictures. I guess your mom must have sent them."

At the end of the hallway there was another door shut tight. There was a laminated magazine picture of James Dean tacked to it and a knotted string with tiny copper bells attached hanging from the doorknob. "You want to see my room?"

"Sure."

She opened the door and immediately the intermingled scents of candle wax, incense, and menthol cigarette smoke wafted out. She stepped inside and Victor followed, and the musky air made him sneeze three times in a row. The walls and ceiling were painted a smoky shade of lavender, the bed in its antique metal frame was heaped with stuffed animals and pillows of all shapes, colors, and sizes, and thick hot pink velvet curtains were drawn across the two sets of windows. Pictures framed or simply torn from magazines were pinned or hung haphazardly on every wall, and there was a vanity with an enormous round mirror and a tiny television atop a French provincial dresser. A wooden framed rocking chair upholstered in an incongruous brown sat underneath one window, its arms and back draped with clothing. Shelby put her hands on her hips and looked questioningly at Victor.

Victor had never been in a room so feminine or so thoroughly fragranced, and yet he was overcome by an eerie feeling of familiarity. It was as if not so much the room itself, but some invisible presence within it, was welcoming him back to a place he couldn't quite remember. He smiled at Shelby. "It's cool," he said.

She snorted. "Gum hates it. She says it looks like a whorehouse in here. As if she has any idea what a whorehouse looks like."

Suddenly Shelby's expression became stern. "I'm glad you like it. But please don't ever come in here without my permission. If you do, I'll be pissed, and I have my ways of knowing if my space has been invaded. I don't want to be a bitch, but I want to make it clear that I can't live in a house with someone who doesn't respect my boundaries. Everyone has to have their own space, and this is mine, for now. I know we don't really know each other, but we are cousins, and I'm glad you're here, believe it or not, because I've always wondered what

18

you're like, but I don't want you- or anyone- in my room without my permission. Okay?"

"Okay," as Shelby spoke he felt an initial rush of fury, as if he'd been offered something that was suddenly, tauntingly snatched away, but almost as instantly he wanted to assure her that he could be trusted. "I need my own space, too."

Shelby smiled. "You'll like Daddy's room. It's good," she said obscurely. "Do you smoke?"

Victor hoped she meant tobacco. "Yes."

"Menthol?"

"If that's what you have."

She held out a pack. "Take the whole thing. Gum gets them wholesale for the bar at the restaurant. I never have to buy my own," she walked over to her vanity table and picked up an ashtray. They settled themselves on the carpet, Shelby leaning against the side of her bed, and Victor leaning against the closet door. For the first time Victor asked a question. "So, are you my only cousin?"

Shelby rolled her eyes. "There's no telling, with this family." l

Uncle Buzz did not join them for lunch, having enjoyed his nutritional supplement earlier he retired to his room, presumably to sleep away the sunny afternoon. It struck Victor as odd, and rather comforting, that the women in the house behaved so casually about his own sudden arrival as well as the uncle's illness and immanent departure. From what Victor's mother had told him over the past few days about this side of his family, it appeared that Uncle Buzz was or at least always had been, until he got sick, a very heavy drinker, and his drinking was to blame for his disease. Victor's mother had mentioned all this in the context of explaining that his uncle and cousin lived with his grandmother, and not the other way around.

"Buzz has never been able to take care of himself," she'd said. "He went into the military right out of high school, just like your father, but he got kicked out as soon as he met poor Shelby's mother." 'Poor Shelby's mother' was the only way Victor's mother ever referred to Shelby's mother, and she would only say that she was 'unfit,' but not why. She must be a monster, Victor figured, given that his mother seemed to consider Shelby's alcoholic and apparently unemployed father to be more fit than this absent, enigmatic female figure.

He looked across the round kitchen table at his cousin Shelby and tried to conjure up the image of the monster that gave birth to her. Shelby didn't on the surface resemble her father, but if one really looked one could see that they shared the same square, pointed chin and they both had slim, delicate looking fingers. It was hard for Victor to imagine Shelby having any other mother besides their grandmother, who, having eaten half of her own tomato sandwich was now standing by the sink smoking a cigarette and peering at the label on one of Uncle Buzz's cans of nutritional supplement.

Shelby seemed to detect Victor's scrutiny of her, and looked up. He blushed and looked down at his plate, which, with its half-eaten sandwich lying in nervous pieces upon it, seemed horribly unappreciated. Shelby's plate was clean. She pushed back her seat, stood, and the bracelets on her arms jingled as she smoothed back her wild mass of hair and twisted it into a loose, but steadfast knot at the nape of her neck. "I'm going to my room to write in my journal," she said pointedly, and took her plate to the sink. "I'll be out when it's time to go to work," she spoke to their grandmother, but it was clear to Victor that he was the one being told to keep his distance for a while.

Victor left the house with the vague notion of figuring out if it would be possible to find, and walk to, the beach, but as soon as he stepped out of the cool darkness of his grandmother's house onto the white hot concrete stoop that served as the front porch, it was obvious to him that to walk far would be to risk not only getting lost, but getting sick. The sky above was clear and pale, and the sunlight bore down on the crown of his head like a heavy hand. He didn't want to go back inside, though, so he looked to the right and to the left, and, finding that there were children playing in a yard a few houses to the right, he headed to the left. Through the soles of his sneakers he could feel the heat of the road's surface, and he hadn't walked a block before all of his clothes were damp with sweat. There was a relentlessness to the heat here that he couldn't recall ever experiencing before, for one thing, it seemed that all the trees here were thick and short and scrubby, and there were only a few of them scattered among the yards along the street, whereas back in the city, particularly in the suburbs near his apartment, there were tall cool pines everywhere.

He came to a side street and looked up at the street sign, noticing for the first time that the street his grandmother's house was on was called Blackbeard Lane. This brought to mind a distant and long forgotten memory that made him pause in his aimless tracks, of a morning long ago; it must have been a weekend morning, because his father was never around on weekdays, back when they lived in New York. He could not have been more than four or so, and he was complaining to his father, as they drove somewhere on some errand, that he did not like their last name, Flowers, because, evidently, some other child had taunted him on account of it. Other children, he had realized, had last names that were words in their own right, names with complicated sounds that meant nothing other than to indicate the family that shared it. But his last name, he was now abashedly aware, meant something besides his family, it meant flowers, and to his mind this had an embarrassingly girlish connotation. He had suggested, riding in the car alongside his father, that they change their name to something better.

"Better!" his father had bellowed, in exaggerated indignation. "You want a name that's *better*? Well, I'll tell you boy, there is no finer name than that of Flowers! There have been Flowers' in this country since before it was a country! I'll have you know that the very first Flowers, your great, great, a million times over great grandpappy, sailed with Blackbeard the Pirate!"

Victor wiped his brow, remembering. That had been his father's way, and still was, for all he knew, of dealing with troubles, he made light of them masterfully, with his easy manner, and compelled you to take lightly whatever it was that distressed you. Only his mother, Victor thought, could withstand his father's insistent levity, and she did so, he knew, with a consistency that was just as impressive to behold. Victor stood now on the corner of Blackbeard Lane and some other street, and wondered if and how his parents ever got along with one another.

He turned right, down the street that branched off of Blackbeard Lane, a long dead end called Shackleford Drive. One yard down on the left a shirtless old man wearing loose yellow shorts and a dingy fisherman's cap on his head with a bandage over one eye was watering his front lawn with a hose. The man lifted his hand to Victor, and Victor lifted his in return, caught off-guard. He looked down to the dead end of the street and knew he would have to pass the old man again in order to get back home. He foresaw the ordeal with disproportionate dread. The simple gesture of friendliness seemed too strenuous to repeat; yet it could not be escaped. He might even be obliged to speak, if the old man spoke to him. Victor was suddenly seized with a longing so sudden and fierce that it nearly doubled him over and caused his heart to race, for the regimented anonymity of his high school, for the torpid misery of his life with his mother, for the clinical scrutiny of the treatment center, for all those suddenly inaccessible areas of his life where it was not expected or required of him to be civil. When he got to the dead end of Shackleford Drive and doubled back, the old man in the yellow shorts and the fisherman's cap had gone inside, or had taken his hose to the backyard. Along with the sensation of relief, the thought of suicide came to Victor and coursed through his consciousness like a balm. The relief it brought him was in exact proportion to the sense of abandonment he felt. For the first time he realized he would not shrink from death, if his life continued on its pointless course inward. It was with this secret strength that he returned to the house where he was a stranger, yet family.

Close to the corner of the house, where the fence began, there was a gate. Victor lifted the latch and let himself into the backyard. A medium sized dog dashed out from the darkness under the back porch and gave voice to such aggressive barks that Victor felt his heart in his throat. Before he could get the gate back open the dog stopped short in front of him and began to sniff his feet, legs, and behind. Once he realized he was not going to be bitten, Victor offered his hand again to be sniffed, and at the same time squatted to come face to face with the dog. The smell of the animal was strong and rank, and that along with the matted state of the fur around her belly and tail suggested that if the dog had ever been bathed, it hadn't been recently. And yet while the smell was unpleasant, it was not overpoweringly so. The dog's breath was hot and meaty. "Phew," whispered Victor, "You're a smelly old mutt, aren't you? But you're nice," the dog blinked and panted, as indifferent to Victor's remarks as a queen to the mutterings of a peasant. But his attention seemed to please her, or at least interest her. She circled him, snuffling, paying particular attention to his hindquarters until finally Victor had to laugh and push her away. Though there was no one but the two of them around, it was embarrassing, to have one's ass investigated by a dog in broad daylight. Still squatting, Victor reached to pat the dog's head, which was warm and hard, then he ran his palm along the length of her body. Her coat was so invitingly warm with the stored heat of the sun that despite the heat of the day, Victor let his hand, then his whole forearm, rest against her. A lump, then a tickling sensation, arose in his throat. He let his arm drop. He had not had such prolonged physical contact with a living being in years.

He stood, but the dog, it seemed, was not prepared to relinquish intimacy. As soon as he rose she lay down on her side and presented her mottled pink and black, obscenely furless and nippled underside to Victor, and he regarded it for a moment with an intense, if fleeting distaste. The dog's four paws motioned in the air like beckoning fingers and she whined encouragingly. Clearly, she expected him to rub her belly. This old dog cared for nothing but that he should make contact with that area of herself that she could not reach. Kneeling, Victor tentatively put his hand to her belly, which was surprisingly cool. He rubbed in circles until the flesh was as warm as that of his own hand, and the dog wriggled in ecstasy. Victor couldn't help laughing. After a minute he stood, groaning, and the dog, after a few more moments, clambered to her feet and trotted away in the direction of the doghouse, her mission accomplished. Victor let himself out through the gate and stood for a while in the driveway, feeling better than he had in many years, though the feeling lasted only a moment.

Once he got inside the house, he found that his grandmother and Shelby were waiting for him in the kitchen. "Honey, it's ten till," his grandmother said, with an edge to her voice, "We've got to get going."

Victor didn't even know what hour it was ten till, but he realized he'd forgotten completely that he was there mainly to work at the seafood restaurant his grandmother owned. She was standing in the kitchen, having changed her clothes, and a large canvas purse hung by its strap from her shoulder. Victor looked down at himself in his T-shirt and jeans. "Do I need to change clothes?"

"Naw," his grandmother said. "Wash your hands, though. You've been out in back playing with Lily, haven't you? She's a sweet old girl, ain't she?" her smile was thin and quick, but real.

Lily, then, was the dog's name. Victor washed his hands in the kitchen sink.

"Shelby!" the grandmother stepped out into the hallway and screeched down its length, "Let's go!"

In a minute they were all congregated in the living room, where Uncle Buzz lay covered up to his chest on the sofa with his gaunt head against the armrest. He was watching a raucous talk show on the TV.

"William, call me when they nurse comes, I want to talk to her," said the grandmother to Uncle Buzz, who looked at her as if she'd appeared out of nowhere. He nodded.

"Let's go," the grandmother marched out the front door and down the steps to the driveway. Shelby rolled her eyes and nudged Victor. "She freaks out if we're not there by three sharp. But it doesn't really matter. Right, Daddy?"

Now Uncle Buzz looked at Shelby as if she'd appeared out of nowhere. "Do what?" he said.

"Bye, Daddy," Shelby said.

Uncle Buzz nodded at the television.

Outside, the LeSabre honked. Shelby giggled and nudged Victor again. "She was worried that you'd gotten lost when you went out. She acted like you were gone for hours. Just make sure from now on you're ready by quarter of three, and she won't get in a tizzy. Do you have a watch?"

"No," Victor had not had a watch since he was a little boy.

"Tell her you need one. She'll get you one. She won't mind."

The Le Sabre honked again, a long, sustained, impatient honk.

"Jesus Christ Almighty," said Shelby. "See ya, Daddy."

25

Uncle Buzz lifted his hand. "Bye," he said. His voice was very soft, and Victor wondered if this is as a result of his sickness. That along with his pronounced drawl made his goodbye sound remarkably like the bleat of a lamb. As Shelby opened the front door, introducing a gash of sunlight into the dim room, Uncle Buzz spoke again. "He can borry mine."

Shelby turned, "What?"

"My wristwatch," Uncle Buzz raised his head a bit from the back of the sofa where it rested. In the shard of sunlight across his face he squinted. "He can borry my Timex with the gold stretchband. It's old, but it runs as good as ever. It just don't stay on my wrist no more. My arms is got so thin…"

Shelby looked at Victor. Her face was calm, set, unreadable. Victor blushed.

The horn honked again. Shelby pushed open the screen door and belted out; in a voice so loud it made the hairs on the back of Victor's neck stand up, "Just a minute! I'm talking to Daddy! Calm down!"

She tried without success to slam the pneumatic screen door, "That's nice of you, Daddy. But I doubt your watch'll fit Victor. Look how skinny *he* is. Gum'll get him one that fits."

She looked hard at Victor, "Let's go before she honks at me again and I have to kill her. See you, Daddy."

Uncle Buzz had turned back to the talk show on the television. Shelby marched out and down the steps, and Victor stood frozen in her absence. After an interminable moment he lifted his hand to Uncle Buzz. "Thanks," he said, hardly loud enough for anyone but himself to hear. Uncle Buzz nodded, however, and Victor then hurried to the car.

The restaurant had been in the family ever since Gum's late husband, Victor's grandfather, bought it upon his retirement from the

Coast Guard in the late nineteen-seventies, and Victor's own father had worked there throughout his childhood until he, and shortly afterwards Uncle Buzz, entered the Coast Guard themselves. All this was explained to Victor as his grandmother showed him around the empty restaurant, pointing out the various things that would be relevant to his position as the sole busboy and dishwasher. He would have help with the bussing on Fridays and Saturdays, when, his grandmother whispered; a Mexican boy would be in to help him. "But don't count on him too much," his grandmother said conspiratorially, "they work hard when they come, but they don't always come when they're supposed to. They're on their own time…"

Not long after his tour, the other employees began to wander in, first three blonde waitresses who all looked like the same person at different ages, a couple of bikers who did the cooking, and one small, muscular young Latino who, Gum whispered to Victor, was the one who worked hard, but only when he wanted to.

For a while there was nothing for him to do but sit at the bar and drink a coke out of a Styrofoam cup as everybody else scurried about the restaurant, getting things ready for the evening. Besides managing the place, Gum served as bartender, and she mentioned to Victor, as she set up the bar while he drank his coke and watched her, that if it weren't for the regulars who came in every night, on season and off, to drink, she wouldn't be able to stay in business. Shelby parked herself on a stool behind the cash register by the front door and read from a paperback book, every now and then putting it aside to chat with the waitresses, who peered curiously over at Victor.

After his grandmother finished setting up her bar, she called the waitresses over from their various stations. "Jean, Dottie, Kelli, come on over here and meet Victor, my other grandbaby. Victor's Eddie's boy; he lives in Raleigh with his mama. He's going to be working here while William's in treatment. Victor, this is Dottie, she's been with us about ten years now, and this is Dottie's daughter Jean, and this is

Jean's daughter Kelli. Dottie is my first cousin. So she's family, too, all three of them are. Isn't that something?"

"Not really," called Shelby from the cash register, "just about all the white people down here are related. So be careful who you sleep with."

Gum ignored Shelby. The waitresses all smiled and offered their hands to Victor one at a time. "We're pleased to meet you," said the oldest one, Dottie, who was short and looked like a plumper, softer, more relaxed version of Gum. "Your grandma has always said she wished you would come visit."

All three of the waitresses were dressed identically in short black skirts and blue and white checked blouses with sailboats embroidered over the right breast. The two younger ones, Jean and Kelli, smiled at Victor with the gentle condescension of older women over young boys, then went about their business. When they had gone, his grandmother turned on the television that perched on a shelf above the beer cooler and refilled Victor's Styrofoam cup with coke. They watched the muted television for a while, and then suddenly his grandmother turned to Victor and looked him directly in the eyes for what seemed like the first time.

"You've been here before!" she said. "Lord, I just remembered. We came here after your granddaddy's funeral, me, you, your daddy, and William, and you sat here at the bar and drank a coke just like your doing now, and you were such a little thing you couldn't even see the TV, so I had to put you in my lap. Do you remember that?"

Victor did not. To imagine himself or for that matter anyone else in his grandmother's lap was difficult.

"Well," his grandmother shook her head and smiled in that peculiar way he noticed she had, of smiling a smile that drew in her lips and pulled the corners of her mouth downward like a frown, but which was somehow unmistakably still a smile. "Well," she said again, and Victor noticed that her accent was such that when she prefaced a statement with the word 'Well,' which she often did, it came out sounding like "whale."

"Whale, we enjoyed having you."

Victor had never really worked before, and he was astonished by the sheer physical and mental relief with which he took to the tasks of gathering the dishes, washing, and storing them. He had no contact with the other workers in the kitchen aside from brief and soon forgotten introductions and every now and then a curt nod, and once the dinner hours were underway, he moved from task to task at a steady pace that was almost comfortable. At one point, while he was making the rounds of the dining area to pick up the bus pans that were full, he caught a glance of his cousin Shelby perched on her stool behind the cash register/display case peering, with her glasses off, into a paperback book which she held with one hand just a few inches from her face. Not for the first time, Victor wished that he could read the way Shelby was reading, with an obvious lack of effort. To read for any amount of time, unless he was reading something sexy, usually put him to sleep. He moved on to collect the overflowing bus pan behind the bar, and with a surge of pride he could not help but feel, he overheard his grandmother say to one of the aged, overweight patrons of the bar, that he was turning out to be a good, steady worker.

It was only when the pace slowed that Victor felt a craving for a cigarette. Having left his own pack in his sea bag, he rinsed his hands and went up to the cash register to ask one off of Shelby. She looked up as he approached and smiled her broad gap-toothed, lofty grin. "Having fun?" she says.

Victor nodded. "It's all right. Can I bum a cigarette? I left mine."

Shelby smirked. "You can always just take a pack from behind the bar," she paused. "But not while there's customers. It doesn't matter. Here you go," she rummaged around in the big black vinyl tote she used as a purse and held a nearly empty pack out toward him.

"Thank you," he said, putting it behind his ear. "What are you reading?"

She picked up the book from where she laid it down on the display case beside the cash register and held the cover out for him to see. It was yellow, with the stylized silhouette of the face of a genderless figure with full features. The single word *Cane* was printed in stark brown letters across the top of the book.

"Oh," he said, "I've never heard of it. What's it about?"

"It's not *about* anything. It's poetry," she said.

Victor grimaced.

Shelby laughed. Her laugh was silent, a soft rocking of her body from deep inside. "What's the matter?" she said. "You don't like poetry?"

Victor shrugged. Not being a reader, he hadn't read much poetry outside of bathroom graffiti.

Shelby rocked again. "You're a boy," she said. "Boys don't develop any sensibility until they're in their twenties. If even then. I'm not even going to bother reading this to you. What kind of music do you like?"

Shelby looked at him, then lowered her brow like a gorilla, thrust out her chin, and pretended to shove her hands into pockets. It was only when she spoke, though, in an unnaturally low and gruff voice, that he realized she was mimicking him.

"Uh, I don't know..." she said. "I like, gangster rap, I guess, and metal..." she laughed and pushed her glasses back up into her viper's tangle of curls.

Victor blushed. Her pose, when she was mimicking him, was a pretty accurate reflection of how he was now standing, and yet it was

30

not just him, it was an absolute caricature of the archetypical sullen disaffected teenage boy. She could have been portraying any of the younger white guys in any kitchen, in any restaurant anywhere. With an unpleasant sensation, like that of a cold shower, it occurred to Victor that he was not unique.

Shelby poked him in the chest with the corner of her book. "Move. They're trying to pay," Victor turned and sure enough, an ancient couple wearing matching sun visors totteringly approached the register. "Let's go to the beach tomorrow," Shelby said to him as she reached for their bill, "then we can talk."

Victor nodded and went back to work with a feeling of lightness that he could not put his finger on. It was only a little later, while bent over the sink scrubbing a burnt spot off the lip of a frying pan, that it came to him that, for the first time in his memory, he was looking forward to the next day.

The day's, or rather, evening's work, ended with the three of them, Victor, Shelby, and their grandmother, seated in a booth across from the bar, in the absolute silence that the grandmother demanded while she counted the day's proceeds. When this was finished, all the coins rolled and all the bills banded and zipped into a bank bag, the grandmother leaned back and lit up a cigarette.

"It was a good night, for a Monday," said Shelby.

"Not too bad," says the grandmother. "We could always do better," she hung her cigarette in one corner of her mouth and spoke out of the other one to Victor. "What did you think, honey? You seemed to keep up pretty good."

Victor nodded.

"It's a lot busier on the weekends," his grandmother said. "We'll have Oliver, the little Mexican boy help you with the dishes then, take him off the line. I don't know, though, you might be able to handle it yourself."

Victor could feel Shelby stiffen beside him "Gum, Oliver is not a little Mexican boy. He's Salvadorian, for one thing, and he's almost twenty-five years old. Why do you have to be so ignorant?"

The grandmother tapped the ash of her cigarette into a tray. "Little Oliver? He can't be no twenty-five. He's as twenty five as I am," she says. "Did he tell you he was twenty-five? Lord, help me."

"He showed me his green card."

The grandmother snorted. "My Lord honey, you know as well as I do you can't go by that! They make them things themselves so they can get jobs here and not have to go back where they came from. For all I know, his name ain't even Oliver."

"If that's what you think, then you have no business letting him work here. You're taking advantage of him."

"I'm paying him, ain't I? And just as much as I'd pay a real American. Don't talk to me about taking advantage, when I was his age, I was getting less than a nickel for every oyster I'd bring into the Beaufort market from Core sound. Everything I do here with my Mexicans is on the up and up, not under the table like a lot of places around here…"

"Blah, blah, blah," says Shelby. Her indignation seemed spent. The next question she asked was without judgment. "Are you paying Victor under the table?"

"'Course I am," the grandmother winked at Victor. "He's family. He ain't going to turn me in. Are you, son?"

Victor smiled and shook his head.

Shelby rested her chin in her hands. "You don't pay me under the table," she said. "I'm family."

"You'd turn me in," the grandmother said, and lit another cigarette.

The three Flowers returned to a dark and silent house. Uncle Buzz had gone to bed, leaving vacant the living room sofa, which the grandmother immediately stripped of its cushions and tugged into the shape of a bed. This was to be Victor's accommodation at night until the end of the week, when the bed Uncle Buzz was waiting for at the nursing facility would be available.

Although Victor dreaded the prospect of sleeping out in the open like this, he went immediately to sleep, and woke up early in the morning to the sound of a deep and persistent bark. A pale, pearly sunlight seeped in through the closed curtains of the living room and the doorway of the kitchen. Victor rose, padded down the hallway as quietly as he could to take a piss, and then let himself out the front door to sit on the concrete stoop and smoke the first cigarette of the day.

Though it was only just past dawn, the temperature outside was already swiftly rising, and Victor returned with relief to the cool darkness of the living room. He was torn between relishing this time to himself and wondering how soon it would end. He was afraid that turning on the television would disturb the women, so there was nothing to do but pad around the living room and look at things; the living room walls were covered with pictures and tiny shelves that held knick-knacks and samplers and such. There were framed photographs set atop a large white doily that draped over the top of the entertainment center shelves, and Victor crossed the room to look at these. The largest picture, a 5x7 school photograph of a chubby little girl was clearly Shelby at the age of about six or seven, recognizable from the tiny mole on her chin and the striking, yellow-green coloring of her eyes, but in all other respects the picture looked nothing like the person she was today; the little girls hair was parted severely and braided into two stiff pigtails that hung down to her chin, her glasses were missing, and her gap toothed smile was anxious, not at all like the present Shelby's open grin. Beside this there was a larger color picture, this one a studio photograph, of a slightly younger version of his grandmother, her

33

hair thicker and thoroughly dyed an unnatural chestnut color. She was posed beside a broad-shouldered, unsmiling man with iron gray, slicked back hair and formidable grooves in his face from the corner of his nose to the line of his jaw. Both his grandmother and the man, whom he assumed must be his dead grandfather, were dressed as if for church, his grandmother in a plain, light blue shapeless dress and the grandfather in a dark suit and tie. The only other photograph among this set was a snapshot, really, black-and white and framed in a cheap silver snapshot frame, of two towheaded boys, wearing only shorts or perhaps bathing suits, standing side by side against the background of a busy pier and holding a swordfish lengthwise against their chests. The taller boy grinned and the smaller boy squinted into the camera, and looked as if he was trying to say something. Victor was astonished at how little the taller boy, his father, had changed in the thirty or so years since the picture was taken. Only his hair was different, in the photograph the boy's thick bangs swooped apart in a wide cowlick, whereas now Victor's father had only a fringe of close cropped blondish hair that reached from ear to ear around the back of his head, and just a sparse remnant of hair on top. The smaller boy, though not as recognizable, was obviously uncle Buzz; the pictured boy's expression of consternation had maintained itself, somehow, in the grown man's countenance.

There were several other snapshots, mostly in color, of infants and smaller children that Victor didn't recognize; these were mostly displayed, in their gift-shop plastic frames, on a plastic, faux driftwood shelf that hung on the wall to the left of the television. He was about to turn away from these when he realized that one of them was surely the picture of the baby his father's new wife had given birth to just weeks before Victor left the hospital, a baby girl, with an odd name that Victor had forgotten, but which he remembered disliking as soon as he heard it, an unusual name, but fashionable these days, a name that sounded more like a man's last name than a little girls name, he didn't want to remember it, but it came to him anyway; Madison.

Victor wondered if he would ever meet her. He had never met his father's new wife, whom he imagined to be, as the wedding pictures that were sent to him in the hospital indicated, a blonde, far younger than his father.

He stepped away from these shelves and looked at the wall above the couch. There was a painting there, or at least a print, of a familiar image, two small children, a boy and a girl, crossing a bridge, oblivious to the presence of a diaphanous, smiling angel hovering above them. Next to this there was an oval framed picture, which upon close inspection proved to be a very old photograph, of a little girl in a checked dress and what looked like saddle shoes, standing between a very wizened old woman in a shapeless flower-print dress and a glowering old man with a handlebar mustache and a watch chain looped across the vest of his black suit. Victor found he could not take his eyes off the image of the old man, he, more so than the little girl or the old woman, seemed to suggest another time, a way of life lost to the world. The old man looked out of the picture as if defending the very spirit of the past that his image represented, while the old woman and the little girl looked out with merry smiles. His image radiated disapproval as manifestly as the old woman's image radiated kindness and the little girl's reflected innocence. Victor wasn't sure how long he stood staring at that picture when the sound of footsteps behind him startled him. He turned to see his grandmother, in a ragged nightgown and strips of toilet paper clipped to her hairline, baring her bridgework at him.

"Morning, honey," she said. "Did you sleep good?"

Victor nodded.

"You're up mighty early. You hungry? I'll have some breakfast in a little bit. Do you like grits?"

He nodded. His mother, being from the north, never made grits, but they often had them for breakfast in the hospital, where he developed a taste for them. "Thank you," he remembered to say.

"It'll be a little while," his grandmother scratched a place on her nightgown just below her small, low slung breasts. "Just rest yourself some more, you worked hard last night. What have you been doing, looking around?"

"Yeah."

His grandmother smiled and pointed at the oval picture. "You know who that little girl is?"

Victor shook his head. "You?" he said.

Her smile drew itself in and turned upside down in the peculiar way it had. "Yes sir. Believe it or not, I was young once. That's me with my grandma and granddaddy. They had a big house on Harker's Island, and I used to stay there every summer. Granddaddy fished and was a part time Methodist preacher, and had nine children with my grandma and four with the one after her. He fathered a child at the age of seventy-one, can you beat that? That was my aunt Millicent, born when I was already thirteen. I'll have to take you to meet Millicent, she lives down east."

Victor looked at the old man in the picture with renewed curiosity. Ancient as time, yet he had not yet, when this image was captured, planted his last seed. "What was his name?" Victor asked.

"Carlos," his grandmother said, musingly, "Carlos Blattery. I always wondered, and never did ask him, or anybody, how come it was he had a Spanish name. The Blattery's as far as I know, come here from England. Maybe his mama just liked the sound of it. But that was his name, anyway. Not Charles, but Carlos. As mean as a snake, too, I never saw him smile for anything. But he provided for his family, that's for sure." With this she walked into the kitchen, but after a moment she came back. "You see how chipped the varnish is on that old frame? I'd take it down and put something else up there, but Shelby loves it so, I figure it don't hurt to leave it up there...."

"It's nice," said Victor. "It's probably worth some money."

His grandmother snorts. "Well... I don't know about that," a whistle that rapidly grew into an insistent shriek issued from the kitchen, where his grandmother had put on a teapot to boil. She went back in there to attend to it, and from the other room called out, "It's something to look at, anyway. Every picture tells a story, I reckon."

When breakfast was ready Victor's grandmother left the kitchen and rapped on Shelby's bedroom door and screeched for her to wake up, but she left her son alone. "He can't eat breakfast, and he can have his milkshakes anytime he wants them," she explained.

Shelby shuffled into the kitchen puffy eyed and yawning. She wore an enormous t-shirt that reached to her shins with a picture of a cartoon Tasmanian devil on the front of it. "Morning," she said to Victor, sounding as if she was speaking through a mouthful of glue. "Dang! I forgot you were here until just now!"

Victor was not used to eating breakfast, and left half the bowl of grits, though he finished the eggs and toast. Morning seemed to be a fairly relaxed time of day in the house, for a few minutes after the three of them were all finished eating, they lingered at the table, each with a refilled cup of coffee and a cigarette. Nobody said anything, but the silence was not awkward, and Victor unselfconsciously watched the play of cigarette smoke in the very bright morning sunlight that streamed in through the windows across from his seat at the table.

"I thought I'd show Victor around today, take him to the beach," said Shelby after awhile. "You put him to work before he even had a chance to get any culture."

"Just be back by quarter of three," said their grandmother.

"We'll need some money to take," says Shelby.

"What for? The beach don't cost anything!"

"We'll need lunch, won't we?"

"Then you better fix some. I'm not made of money."

"I can't drive yet," Shelby explained as she zipped the lid of the polyester cooler that held their food. "So we'll have to walk. You don't drive yet, either, do you?"

"No," Victor said, and he wondered just how much his cousin knew about his life. He assumed she must know, that his grandmother must have mentioned to her, over the years, that he had problems. And yet, he had to admit, she did not act as if she knew. Neither one of them did. It was as if, like Uncle Buzz's obviously uncontrollable alcoholism, the grandmother's guileless bigotry, and Shelby's mysterious, evil mother, Victor's hospitalization was just one of those things that happens in families.

"I took the road test in the spring, but I failed it," Shelby said. "I was supposed to practice some more with daddy, and take the test again on my birthday, but then daddy got worse. So it's on hold. My best friend has her own car, so I get around that way. You'll meet her pretty soon. She's a summer person, but we keep in touch when she's at home. She's from Raleigh, too. Her name's Dora."

Shelby handed Victor the little cooler, and shouldered her own enormous black tote bag, and they set out. Once outside the door, the heat of the sun smote them, but Shelby marched on as if in rebuke. Victor wondered if he would ever get used to the relentless, aggressive quality of this coastal sun; only a couple minutes out of the air-conditioning and the top of his head felt like it was being slowly eroded away by a laser beam. He had to work to keep up with Shelby's pace, which, despite her boxy stature and shape, was long and swift; she moved like a ship in a favorable wind, her long light skirt sometimes brushing the hot asphalt.

"It's about a forty-five minute walk," she said over her shoulder to him. "When we get to the highway, we go down that about half a mile, then we get to the bridge. Then we have to cross the bridge, and that takes about ten minutes. Then we'll be on the island, and it's about a twenty-minute walk from the bridge to where I like to go. If you need to stop, just let me know."

"I'm all right," Victor said, though he was already dizzy with the heat.

They did not talk much as they made the long, hot trek to the oceanfront. Victor found himself absorbed with the sights and sounds and smells along the way; the landscape was another world to him, for all that he had evidently been to the beach as a small child. There was a strip of sidewalk across the length of the bridge over the sound, and he stopped, for a moment, in the middle, and leaned over the railing to look down into the sound as the strong warm wind whipped his hair to one side. Shelby sensed that he wasn't right behind her and doubled back.

"Don't even think about diving," she said, "you'd break your neck. It looks deep, but it isn't really. And it's full of disgusting eels and jellyfish."

They walked on. When they came to the island, Shelby veered to the left, and they walked along the main drag, which was flanked on both sides with cheap motels, cheap but overpriced seafood and fast food restaurants, convenience stores, and dock houses. Shelby turned into one sandy parking lot and onto a wooden walkway that led over a set of dunes. They passed a shed that held changing rooms, and then Victor saw the ocean for the first time that he could remember. Inexplicably, the sight made his heart race. He shaded his eyes with one hand and looked out as far as he could to where the ocean and the sky merged into one hazy line. The crash and hiss of the surf was as rhythmic as a pulse. The sense Victor had that what confronted him had a life of its own was so powerful that he was compelled to speak. "Wow," he said, and as this expression seemed inadequate, he said it again. "Wow."

Shelby, in the meantime, trudged several yards ahead, and laid down a green bed sheet that she carried along in her black bag. Victor stood stock still at the foot of the dunes until the intensity of his encounter with the ocean passed through him. Once he situated himself next to Shelby on the bed sheet, his astonishment faded, but he could not dismiss his sense that the two of them, along with the dozens of other visitors to this particular stretch of beach, were there at the mysterious, innocent pleasure of the place itself.

"I like it here," Shelby said. "People don't come here because it's so close to the piers. They think the pier draws sharks. It does, but the sharks it draws are too small to hurt anybody. Besides, I don't go in the water anyway. Do you?"

"I've never been to a beach before," he said.

"Oh that's right," said Shelby. "Well, can you swim?"

He nodded.

"I can't," said Shelby.

This seemed incredible. "For real?"

Shelby reached into her big bag and pulled out a bottle of lotion, the contents of which she proceeded to languorously apply to her arms and face. "Me and daddy haven't always lived with Gum, you know," she said, "I lived with my mother until I was about four," Shelby gazed grimly at the horizon. "We never stayed in any one place for very long, so I never had a chance to learn a lot of things. I don't even really remember going to school very much until my mother left me with Gum. And by that time Granddaddy was dead and Gum had to start running the restaurant full-time, and she never had time to teach me to swim. So, even though I've always been around the water, I've never learned. Ironic, isn't it?"

Victor wasn't sure, exactly, what the word ironic meant. Shelby finished slathering her skin, drew up her knees, clasped her forearms around them and continued. "My mother didn't really *leave* me with Gum. She lost custody of me, then she kidnapped me, and then she brought me back here to live when it got too hot for her. Daddy divorced her, or she divorced Daddy, when I was about three. I can't even remember them ever being together. After that she started doing a lot of drugs, and I guess Daddy started to do a lot more drinking than he had before. He was still in the Coast Guard then, stationed in Charleston. My mother and me lived just about everywhere in the state, even Raleigh for a little while. She took me wherever whatever loser she was with took her. Eventually someone reported her for leaving me alone too much while she was out doing god knows what, so she left me with Gum. My mother's very beautiful," Shelby paused and looked out to sea. "She's Lumbee."

"Huh?"

"Lum-bee," Shelby rolled her eyes and enunciates. "Lumbee Indian. Haven't you ever heard of the Lumbee tribe?"

Victor shrugged. If he had, he couldn't remember. But that explained, then, his cousin's rose-copper coloring. Her mother was an Indian. Victor wondered what his grandmother thought of that.

Shelby sighed and spoke with the weary tone of one obliged to explain the obvious to an idiot. "We're the largest Indian tribe of east of the Mississippi. But no one knows anything about us, because we don't have federal recognition. Some people say we're the descendants of the Lost Colony, mixed with the Native Americans. That may be true, but there's also African blood in us. No one is really just one race, I don't care what anyone says. You can be racist against yourself, you know. You can deny who you are. But the fact is, we're a coat of many colors," Shelby looked at Victor as if she expected him to contradict her. Then her look changed, as if he had suddenly come into focus for her.

"Hey, you know, I've never even met *your* mother," she said. "I know that Gum likes her. I know they talk every now and then. What's your mother's name?"

Victor picked a handful of sand up from beside their bed sheet and let it sift through his fingers. "Veronica," he answered. "But she hates it. She won't let anybody call her that. She calls herself Ronnie."

41

"Veronica," Shelby said it musingly. "What a beautiful name. So European. I wonder why she doesn't like it...."

Victor shrugged. "She really hates it," he said. "What's your mother's name?"

"Tanya," Shelby said this as if the sound left a bad taste in her mouth. "Your mother's Italian?"

"I guess so. Her family name was Bassano. I think there's some French, too."

"Mediterranean," Shelby nodded approvingly. "Southern Europe is a mixture of all kinds of people, too. Like I said, no one's really any one thing. Certain people just want to think they are. Gum's like that," Shelby unclasped her knees and stretched her legs out in front of her. "Have you noticed that? That she's kind of racist?"

Victor nodded.

Shelby's lips, usually so full, compressed into a line that looked very much like their grandmother's habitual expression of grim forbearance. "It bugs her that I'm not white. It always has. She was brought up that way that people shouldn't mix, and she's never really gotten over it. I guess there was never any reason for her to try, until I came along. And she's tried, in her way. But I know it still bothers her. Some things you just can't change about yourself, even if you know you should," Shelby reached behind herself, untwisted the knot of hair at the nape of her neck, and let the sea breeze whip her thick, dark, rusty curls about her face. "It only bothers her, though, when she thinks about it. And she doesn't think about it, at least not nowadays, unless someone else does. That's how I can deal with her. Because deep down, it doesn't make any difference to her any more. It's just habit, that she says the things she does. She's a product of her environment. Just like the rest of us."

Victor looked down at his legs, long, thin, and pale, with fine dark hairs just beginning to coarsen near his ankles. With his dark eyes and hair, he favored his mother in looks, he had none of his father's sandy coloring and stocky build. His mother had mentioned to him once, long ago, that of all the people in the family, he most resembled her brother Anthony, who was evidently some years older than her, and who died in Vietnam, when she was just a little girl. Anthony was, in fact, Victor's middle name, and a name he liked much better than Victor, but when years ago he asked his parents if he could go by that name, his mother, though she said nothing, stiffened like a corpse and continued, as if he had said nothing, to call him by his first name, Victor.

While he remembered these things the wind that came in from off the water picked up, and the two cousins sat silent for awhile, listening to the sound of the breeze against their ears and the raucous cries of the seagulls and the crash of the waves and the squeals and shouts of the children running to and fro on the sand and splashing about on the water. The sense Victor had when they arrived, that the beach was as much of a participant in itself as the birds and the people inhabiting it returned to him with renewed strength. He had a sudden urge to walk out into the water, and he was about to stand when Shelby spoke again. "So, if your Mom is Italian, are you Catholic?"

Victor had a sudden image in his mind's eye of the tiny gold crucifix his mother habitually wore around her fat white neck. "I'm not anything," he said.

Shelby knocked him lightly on the shoulder with the back of her hand. It was the first time she touched him. "You know what I mean," she said. "If you were some kind of religion, that's what you would be, right? You get your religion from your mother. So, would you be Catholic?"

"I guess," said Victor. Though he could not specifically remember ever having been inside of a Church, he knew, in some vague way, that he had been, and that the Churches he had been inside were Catholic churches. He knew that his mother, for all that she had not attended a church service since long before her divorce, still considered herself a Catholic, and received newsletters and other mailings from at least three of the Roman Catholic Churches in the city. He also knew that he was baptized in a Catholic Church in New York, and that before they moved to North Carolina he was in classes being prepared for his first communion. He had, then, a very vague memory of those preparations, of being herded every week or so with other children into a brightly painted classroom, then herded back out again to present some piece of artwork to the adults congregated in a dark and fragrant sanctuary. All of this ended with his families move South, this and other, more meaningful but sketchy scenes of being one among a dozen or so children at large gatherings of what might have been his mother's extended family, of sleeping in the backseat of the car at night while his parents sat side by side in the front, driving home from somewhere, cocooned in a rare companionable silence. It was as if everything connected with his mother beyond her life with him and his father ended when they left New York, but she never, even after his father left, said anything about returning to it, or anything at all about her family up there, her friends, *or* her church. Victor asked her once, years ago, when his father was still living with them, why they had moved from New York, and she had said simply that there were better opportunities for his father in the south, and that she liked the warm weather.

But there was more to the move than this, and even as a child he'd sensed it. After the move, Victor saw less of his father, and watched more television than he'd ever been allowed to watch in New York. His mother had slowly and steadily put on weight until her once prominent cheekbones and chin became lost in the swollen roundness of an overweight face. Her dark hair, before always kept set, became stringy and streaked with gray, and her work as a nurse seemed to be constantly interrupted by some illness or injury. And his father would disappear for longer periods of time, during which his mother would only say he was on a business trip, until finally he was gone for good, leaving Victor with the present of a ten speed bicycle and the promise that they would spend every summer together at his new house in South Carolina, and that no matter what he was only a phone call away. "Your mom and me," his father had said, deadly serious for once, as he sat on the edge of Victor's bed the day he left, "can't agree any more about too many things. Sometimes, son..." Victor remembered that his father, at that point made a very characteristic gesture, something he often did when he was tired, of rubbing his entire face with the flat of his right hand, as if he were washing it, or wiping it clean of something that had been dashed into it, "...things just don't work out, and their ain't anything anyone can do but say to hell with it. I probably shouldn't be telling you this, son, but I don't know what else to tell you. All I want you to know, son, is that I love you, and I'll always be your pop. You got that?"

At that Victor had nodded, feeling nothing but bewilderment. His father's obvious distress seemed out of all proportion to what was happening. So he was leaving. It wasn't such a big deal. He was never around anyway.

Sitting on the beach beside his cousin, Victor involuntarily shuddered at the memory. Shelby reached into the enormous straw bag she'd brought along and handed him a small plastic bottle. "The suns getting to you, paleface," she said. "You better put this on."

Victor took the bottle from her and looked at the label. It was sunscreen, with a high SPF, and he squeezed a bit onto his hand and applied it to his face and forehead. He was too shy to take off his shirt, though it was only a tank top, in front of Shelby. She watched him bemusedly, and then reached in her bag for something else. "What were you thinking about?" she said.

Victor looks out to sea. "New York," he said.

"Do you miss it?"

"Not really. I don't remember it very well. We moved down here when I was about six."

"How come?"

"I don't know."

Shelby pulled a pack of cigarettes out of the bag, offered him one, then took one for herself. "Gum likes your mother," she said again.

"I know," Victor mumbled this around the cigarette in the corner of his mouth as he attempted, for the dozenth time, to light it with Shelby's clear green plastic Bic lighter. It was impossible to sustain a flame in the strong sea breeze. Shelby cupped her small hands expertly over his, and finally it got lit. "My mom likes her, too," said Victor. "I don't think my mom talks to anyone in her own family. But she talks to…" he hated to say that silly name, but he said it. "…Gum. Not all the time, but more than she talks to anyone back in New York."

Shelby turned to him, her eyes wide behind the enormous sunglasses she'd brought with her in her bag. "Why doesn't she talk to her family? I thought Italian families were close-knit and warm and loving!"

"Not hers, I guess," said Victor, smiling a little, though, for Shelby's stereotype stirred a memory of one or several large gatherings of his mother's extended family, in which food was served in the backyard of a row of houses, and dozens of other children were present, and his father and mother were absorbed into separate clusters of women and men. The memory was a pleasant one, and he remembered being presented to a very old woman, wizened and bound to a wheelchair and smelling of baby powder and urine, a figure so ancient that she seemed to be beyond speech or even thought, but who had seemed pleased with him and had babbled something in what he imagined now must have been Italian and stroked his head with fingers as rigid and fragile as a bird's claws. All the children there, he remembered, had been older than him, but they had included him in their games anyway. He remembered his mother seemed to be more relaxed than usual at such gatherings, letting the rowdier older children roughhouse in their way with him as if she could trust, somehow, that he would not get hurt. He tried to remember the other children's names or faces, but he couldn't, and when he tried to remember who, among the grown ups at the gathering, were his grandparents and aunts and uncles, there was no distinction among them. Only one woman's face stood out in his memory, a face younger than his mother's but strikingly similar, though more heavily made up, with long dark hair that reached nearly to her waist. "Her sister!" he said suddenly, "Debbie. She doesn't like her sister Debbie. That's why she doesn't talk to her family. She doesn't like her, or she had a big fight with her before we moved... Jesus..." Victor shook his head as if to clear it. "I don't know how I know that, but I do."

Now that he had called to mind the name and the face of this woman, who was once a part of his life, he remembered her with increasing clarity. She was a salesgirl at a department store in the city, he remembered, she always had Dentyne chewing gum in her mouth, and she was not married. He remembered that even as a little boy he had thought that his aunt Debbie was extraordinarily pretty, and affectionate, as well. His father, he remembered suddenly, with a distinct clutching sensation in his belly, had liked Debbie, too.

A feeling came over Victor like a dark cloud, and he stood up without looking at Shelby. "I'm going in the water," he said, and marched towards and into the waves that suddenly seemed to crash and hiss like a thousand red hot demons falling from heaven into the boiling cauldrons of hell.

Victor was unprepared for the chill of the water that met him; he stood for a long time at the very edge of the Atlantic Ocean while the shallowest of waves lapped about his ankles. The cries of seagulls just overhead seemed to accentuate the unearthliness of the moment as he hesitated, shivering, his arms wrapped around himself like a straightjacket. There were children in the distance, playing with abandon in water that looked as if it must be a hundred feet deep, but of course it could not be that much deeper than where he stood, even though it was so much further out. Victor eventually trudged forward, marveling at how quickly the cold sting of the salt water gave way to a pleasant coolness. Still, he hesitated to immerse himself totally. The murky greenish salt water had nothing in common with the clear, chlorinated pools he was used to; he could see nothing beneath the surface of the water except vague shadows. As he moved forward, however, the waves met him with greater force, until at last one swept him off his feet and laid him down; he fell back into the shallow water and emerged spluttering, completely wet from top to toe, with the curious sensation of having been, despite himself, utterly liberated. He turned and looked back toward Shelby, and for a moment he felt frantic, for he could not see her, with his salt stung eyes, amongst the dozens of reclining bodies on the beach. But then he spotted her, bent over a book that held her skirt to the ground between her upraised knees, it looked as if she was scribbling something in it. He turned back to the ocean and half hopped, half dove forward, and once again immersed himself in the cool, murky, and strangely invigorating waters. For what felt like hours he flung himself against and under and into the incoming waves, each of which seemed to carry its own individuality and its own particular reason for preventing him from moving too far out. When he had enough and finally made his way out of the water, trudging diagonally across the increasingly loose and burning sands to where Shelby sat hunched over on the green bed sheet, still scribbling, Victor had never felt so physically spent, and yet so very much alive. Shelby closed the clothbound notebook she had been scribbling or drawing something in, and squinted and smiled up at Victor as his shadow draped over her. "Did you have fun?"

"Yeah."

"Are you hungry?"

"Yeah."

Shelby reached into her straw bag and pulled out, in foil wrapped increments, their lunch. Victor wolfed down his own roast beef sandwich and was left to observe with what delicacy his cousin consumed hers, like a thoughtful bird over a hunk of bread, half of her sandwich, in fact, she threw to the gulls, who descended upon it with cries of joy. After the two humans had eaten and Shelby had gathered their trash into one compact ball of foil, Shelby suggested that they start the long walk back home to make sure they were ready for work on time. The walk back was indeed long; it seemed much longer than the walk from home, and by the time they arrived Victor felt as if his entire body was covered with an uncomfortable slime of sweat and salt. He lingered in the shower, fearing that the excessive use of water would be irritating to his grandmother, but he relished the strange sting of the water on his skin, which from exposure to the sun felt tight and raw and new, and not yet painful.

That evening at the restaurant was much as it had been the night before, except for the fact that this night, Victor had help gathering the bus pans in the form of Oliver, the Salvadoran prep cook, whose bright black eyes and snaggled teeth and short, strong body exuded an air of boundless energy and willingness to please. As none of the biker types that worked in the kitchen said much to Victor, he was grateful for Oliver's company and conversation, limited though it was by the barrier of language and by Oliver's predominant interests; he seemed to have conceived a passion for the blonde waitress named Kelli. "She is…" he said, nudging Victor, then rolled his brown eyes in a manner that somehow seemed incredibly lascivious.

Victor grinned and blushed, at the same time wondering at himself as he did so, for hadn't every other guy in the treatment center acted like this, hadn't most of the conversation between the residents there been about the physical attributes of the few females they saw every day? Why, outside of that place, did talk of sex seem so treacherous to him?

Oliver did not wait for any response, but slapped Victor on the back, giggling. "I make you… Nervous? I'm sorry. You saved? You go to church?"

"No," said Victor. "No church."

"No?" Oliver, for a brief moment, looked puzzled, but his agreeable smile did not falter. "I don't go to church here. But I am saved. I think, though, it's okay to say I like her…" and he placed his hands against his heart. "I don't bother her. She don't even know I like her. She don't like me. She has a boyfriend, anyway."

Victor shook his head and rinsed down a rack of dishes. He had no idea how old Oliver was, but in spite of his uninhibitedness he seemed not a little wise.

"Maybe you right," Oliver said after a moment, even though Victor had said nothing. "Maybe it's not good, to look too much, maybe it's a sin. *Pero*, I get lonesome, it's hard not to look. Maybe I need to go to church, get saved again, yeah?"

"I don't think that would help," said Victor.

"No?" Oliver, still smiling, looked at Victor as if he really believed that Victor could advise him.

"I don't know," shrugged Victor, "maybe."

The next day was Saturday, the day that Uncle Buzz was scheduled to move to the rehabilitation facility in Beaufort, just over a bridge and a few miles away. After nearly a week of sleeping in the living room, Victor had gotten used to it, and the prospect of another move, into Uncle Buzz's room, seemed at once welcome and jarring. Victor wasn't sure what exactly was wrong with Uncle Buzz, but whatever it was, Victor had never seen him wear anything except pajama bottoms and that same wine colored bathrobe. Uncle Buzz did very little besides sleep and watch television, and as his only form of nutrition was his supplemental milkshakes, he gave the impression that he never ate, but only drank; there always seemed to be a can in his hand. He did not seem to be suffering much, but he did not seem to be enjoying much either, he was like a shy ghost drifting through the house.

It was just before noon when a medical transport van arrived to take Uncle Buzz to his rehab. Why that van, which looked exactly like an ambulance was required, Victor didn't know, but evidently he was the only one surprised by its arrival in the driveway, as his grandmother, who was in the kitchen on the telephone with one of her many sisters and sisters-in-law came out into the living room, opened the front door, and said "Here they come..." as if they were not already there. "Honey," She called over her shoulder to Victor, "run tell Shelby. They're here to take her daddy over to the rehab."

Victor looked out at the huge vehicle, conspicuous even without its siren as it grumbled in the driveway. The driver and several other uniformed men climbed out and made their way to the front door as the grandmother opened it wide and waved them forward. "We're just about ready for ya'll," she called, as cheerily as if they were houseguests, "Come on in."

Victor slipped away and down the hall to Shelby's door, and tapped James Dean's jacket. He could hear eerie strains of music from inside, so he tapped again, a bit louder, and Shelby opened the door almost immediately. There was a yellow scarf tied around her head and the room was dark behind her.

"The ambulance is here," Victor said. "Gum wants you."

Shelby pursed her lips and nodded. "All right," she says. "Is Daddy all ready?"

"I don't know," he looked over his shoulder at the bare closed door to Uncle Buzz's room.

"Tell Gum I'll be there in a minute," Shelby said, and closed the door abruptly in Victor's face. Victor hesitated before Uncle Buzz's door, and then quickly moved away back down the hall, where he stood in the entryway to the living room and watched his grandmother herd the four transport attendants into the kitchen.

"I don't know why I can't just carry him over in the car…" the grandmother was saying. "But I know ya'll have your rules. As long as the insurance is going to pay their part of it, I ain't going to complain. Let me go make sure William's got everything he needs. Do ya'll want anything to drink?"

"No ma'am," said two of the transport attendants. One of them nodded at Victor, who nodded back.

"'Zat him?" one of the attendant's said.

"This is my grandson, Victor," said the grandmother, aghast. "William is my son. Does this boy look like he has cirrhosis, neuralgia, stomach ulcers and sugar? Victor, did you tell Shelby to get out here?"

Victor nodded.

"Well, what in the world is she doing?" the grandmother did not wait for an answer but made her way past Victor and down the hall, muttering.

Victor stood awkwardly in the kitchen with the attendants until his grandmother came back holding a large suitcase and a plastic shopping bag from Belk's, followed by Uncle Buzz, who, bereft of his usual can of Ensure, followed his mother wide eyed and with his mouth slightly open, the fingers of his right hand lightly grazing the wall as if he was caressing it. Shelby followed close behind her father, dressed for the day in her usual gypsy skirt and t-shirt, holding a large, thin book across her chest with one arm.

"You ready to roll, Mr. Flower's?" the oldest looking of the attendants said.

"Ready as I'll ever be," says Uncle Buzz in his slow, low, slightly tremulous voice. "How ya'll doing today?"

"Pretty fair," the senior attendant is the only one that answers. "You got everything you need?"

"Well, I could use about a million dollars and a brand new liver, but other than that I believe I'm all set."

"I hear you," said the senior attendant. "We'll let's get you situated. Ma'am…" he said to Gum. "You gonna ride with him?"

"Well, ya'll aren't gonna bring me home are you? I was just gonna follow in the car."

"All right then," the senior attendant jerked his head to signal his minions to go out to the van. Victor followed everyone else out and stood slightly apart as the attendants opened up the back of the vehicle, clambered inside to where a cot and a number of monitors waited for their next patient. They leaned out to guide Uncle Buzz inside and onto the cot, where he laid down at their firm instructions

The grandmother stepped up to the bumper of the ambulance. "Do you all want these bags back there, or should I take them in the car?"

"Take em in your car."

Gum turned and drew in her lips. Shelby climbed up into the ambulance and bent over her prostrate father. "I'll see you tomorrow, Daddy," she said, planting a kiss on his cheek. "Behave yourself."

Victor could not make out what Uncle Buzz said, but he heard Shelby's reply loud and clear. "I love you too, Daddy," she said. "See you tomorrow," she jumped out of the ambulance and came to stand beside Victor on the driveway. "Why don't you say goodbye?" she said to him, like a kindergarten teacher to a shy pupil.

Victor felt like a marionette, acting without will. He climbed up into the ambulance and bent over his uncle, and, not knowing what else to do, he held out his hand, which his uncle accepted and gave a weak, hot shake. "Take care, Uncle Buzz," said Victor. "I won't bother anything in your room."

The sick man looked up at Victor with suddenly shiny eyes. "You make yourself at home," he said. "You're welcome to anything I've got. I appreciate you're being here. I really do. I ain't surprised you're such a nice feller, your mama's a good woman. She deserves…"

"William…" the grandmother called up from the driveway. "These men have work to do, and you need to rest, now. Let's get to where were going, and you can talk to Victor on Sunday. Victor, you and Shelby go on inside. Thank you for helping," she gave Victor him a brief squeeze on his shoulder as he clambered out of the ambulance. "I'll be back in a couple hours," she said. "Shelby, don't you hole up in that room all day. Act like you have some manners, and pay some attention to your cousin."

Shelby tossed her hair in its yellow scarf and ignored her grandmother, but she grinned impishly at Victor as they went back inside. "Gum's convinced herself that I don't like you," she snickered. "She convinced herself of that before you even got here."

"Why?"

"She's just got it in her head," Shelby flopped down on the sofa like a man, lifting her sandaled feet onto the armrest, "that I'm a snob. I might as well be her own daughter for all the assumptions she makes about me. She sees everything I do in relation to her. Everything. If I took her too seriously, I'd go crazy."

When their grandmother came back home, later in the afternoon, she seemed to move within a mist of irritation and concealed distress so powerful that Victor found it unnerving to be in the same room with her. She would not sit, but instead stood in the kitchen, her flat and narrow backside resting without relaxation against the kitchen counter, and she smoked one menthol cigarette after another. It was Saturday and the restaurant had been open and run by Dottie since eleven in the morning for lunch customers, so the three Flowers had until five o'clock before they had to be there. Victor had hoped to go to the beach, but he did not want to take that long walk all by himself, and Shelby, when he asked if she wanted to go, simply and easily said that she did not. Victor spent most of the afternoon putting his stuff away into Uncle Buzz' room. As his stuff consisted merely of a duffel bag full of clothes and a few toiletries, this was quickly accomplished, but Victor stood for a long time in the middle of the room at the foot of the queen sized bed that had not yet been stripped of his uncle's linens, and looked around. Directly opposite the door a window with blinds raised and two nicotine colored curtains drawn looked out southeast over the front lawn to the house across the street. Right next to where Victor stood a tall brown dresser faced the foot of the bed; a large oval white lace doily set on top of this, and scattered upon that was an assortment of coins, a silver backed hairbrush, a butane lighter, an ashtray stolen from a pancake house, several books of matches with the logo of the family restaurant printed on the cover, a loose stack of frayed playing cards and the Timex wristwatch with a stretch wristband. Against the wall, on top of the dresser there was a row of athletic trophies, all of which were tiny statuettes of baseball players; their bases engraved with Uncle Buzz's name. Hung on the wall above all this there was a large framed print of a painting that depicted a storm tossed many-masted ship set within a sky roiling with clouds and a raging sea; it was, once Victor took a good look at it, an image of horrifying starkness. The prow of the ship was lifted out of the reach of the white-capped waves that seemed to be rising to grasp it and pull it down, and the sails, pregnant with wind, seemed painfully taut as they strained against the gusts. Dark, shadowy seabirds circled above the ship like vultures over carrion, and from the deepest, darkest clouds in the far background, jagged, sulfurous streaks of lightning descended. Nothing could be seen of any human presence aboard the ship; so dwarfed and obscured were the details of the vessel by the still tempest in which it is tossed. Nevertheless, the very countenance of the ship itself gave the impression of panic; the dark shadowed portion of the hull underneath the prow as it crested a foam capped wave was like a toothless, tongue-less abyss of a mouth gaping in a silent howl. Victor looked at this picture for a very long time; from the sinister formation of the circling seabirds to the lightning in the background to the lifting of the prow in the foreground; he gazed into it until an unpleasant tingling sensation in his foot made him glance down to see that he had been standing on his own foot. Shifting, he gazed again at this picture as one might gaze into a mirror. Victor guessed that for over forty years, the picture, the ship, the seabirds, the waves, had been arrested in that storm. Victor thought of his own bedroom at his mother's apartment, bare but for the scuffmarks where he had kicked the walls, or thrown things at them.

That night at the restaurant was the busiest since Victor had been working there, and even with Oliver's help, he had a hard time keeping up with the pace. The unexpected barrage of customers made all of the employees edgy, and at one point his grandmother came into the kitchen and informed him and Oliver, not without some harshness to her voice, that the bus pans at the wait station by her bar were all overflowing.

Oliver took the glasses and scurried agreeably out into the dining area, and Victor allowed himself a deep sigh. His grandmother had never, since he arrived, hidden her constitutional impatience, but she had also never directed it at him. Victor couldn't believe how bad it felt, to fall out, even for a moment, of the old lady's favor. He twisted his wet hands in his apron to dry them and loped out into the bar area of the restaurant to fetch as much of the mess as he could carry.

Making his circuit, he glanced over to the cash register near the entrance, where Shelby sat shaking her slippered foot underneath her skirt while she talked to another young girl who stood on the other side of the register. Victor could tell that the girl was not just some anonymous customer; Shelby was having a conversation, not just making small talk. Victor had not thought of Shelby having any relationships outside the family, but of course she would; she was not miserable like him. The girl would be one of her friends, for as out of place as Shelby, with her unabashed intelligence most likely was in this fairly small, tourist city, she undoubtedly had a few friends among the regular summer people. She would never be lonely if she could help it, he was sure. Before going back to the dish room, he allowed himself a good look at the girl Shelby was talking to, and he was surprised to feel a slight clutch in his belly as both girls turned their heads and looked not only in his direction, but directly at him. The other girl's eyes, even from a distance, were a very arresting pale blue, and even dressed as she was, like Shelby, in a loose top and a long skirt and sandals, Victor could discern a figure at once as willowy as Shelby's was stocky; her arms and neck were slender, her chest was full, her hair, cut bluntly at the line of her chin, was a deep, dark artificial red. As the two girls looked at him, the unknown girl's expression was arch, as if she'd caught him staring instead of the other way around. Then she either smiled or smirked, and she and Shelby turned their attention back to one another. He returned to the bright light and incessant noise of the dish room where Oliver was hard at work. After they got caught up he stepped alone outside into the back parking lot of the restaurant and smoked a cigarette and watched as pale stars appeared one by one in the slowly dimming summer sky.

As tired as he was after the restaurant closed and the money was counted and they got back to the house, it wasn't at all easy for him to go right to sleep in his uncle's room, in his uncle's bed. The rusty glow of the streetlights just along the front yard seeped in through the nicotine colored curtains and gave the night a sinister, burnished air, as if there was a conflagration outside the window. All of the coins on top of Uncle Buzz' dresser glowed in this light, as did the lineup of athletic trophies set up there against the wall. Uncle Buzz' bed was queen sized and hence far larger than any bed Victor had ever slept on before, and the odor of the linens, though they had been freshly laundered, was unfamiliar and vaguely unsettling, as if they retained some essence of the man for whom they were bought. Victor felt like an interloper, more so than when he'd been on the living room sofa. I won't be here long, he thought, lying in the eerie hellish darkness of the unfamiliar room, I won't change anything in here, he vowed to himself, to his uncle by proxy. I'll leave it just as you left it, so you won't even know I was here.

Victor closed his eyes and imagined that he was in Shelby's room, with daylight seeping past the fully drawn shades, the walls lavender and pink, the air heavy with incense and cigarette smoke. Hers was a room in which rest could come even without the aid of sleep, and Victor tried, with some success, to put himself there, if not in body, than in his imagination. Victor eventually slept, but not as well as he had on the living room sofa, and awakened terribly early the next morning to the sound of birds singing and Lily in the back yard, barking.

"Well," said the Gum, when Victor shuffled, still groggy into the kitchen where she stood over the sink with a cigarette in her hand, "You're up mighty early. I thought now that you have a whole room you might want to sleep in. Did you sleep all right? Sometimes, when the sun comes up, it gets too warm in there. William keeps a fan in the closet, I think, and that helps some. I'll pull it out after awhile."

"It's all right," said Victor. His voice was thick with the remnants of sleep. His grandmother was still in her night clothes, which consisted of a very tattered housedress, flannel slippers, and clips holding folded strips of toilet tissue to her sparse, stiff hair. "I heard the dog barking," he said. "I guess that's why I'm up so early."

"Oh, Lily," said the tired old lady, shaking her head. "That dog would let an armed robber crawl through the window in the middle of the night, but doesn't have sense enough to be quiet when some durn squirrel crawls on the fence. You'll get used to her."

The grandmother moved, her slippers slapping against the tiles of the kitchen floor, to the refrigerator and stood with her hand on against it. "You want some breakfast?" she said, and she did not try to hide the weariness in her voice.

Victor's heartbeat quickened. He was suddenly self conscious, standing before the old woman in the t-shirt and the basketball shorts he slept in. "I think I'll lay down for a while longer," he said. His grandmother's smile was grateful, and Victor returned to his uncle's room and opened the curtains and looked out over the lawn as the sleepy neighborhood slowly came to life. From now on he would stay put in the morning until his grandmother started making noise.

Later that morning Victor and Shelby went to the beach, and from the beach to work, as they did for the remainder of the week, and so a loose pattern was established. It wasn't long before it seemed as if Uncle Buzz had always been away, so seamlessly did his absent presence fit into the scheme of things. The grandmother spent a good part of most mornings at the rehabilitation center supervising her son's care, Shelby went along every weekend, and Victor went on Sundays. The rehab center was, to Victor, a surprisingly clean and rather cheerful place, set within a carefully landscaped yard near the general hospital, every room dominated by large, immaculate picture windows, wide corridors well banistered and decorated with motivational posters, and people of all ages, in various states of disrepair, ambled about alongside brisk nurses in pastel scrubs. The place seemed vaguely magical to Victor, and he wondered at Shelby's reluctance to spend much time there. One thing he noticed was that she seemed to have something against the nurses; she glared at them whenever they spoke of her as "Mr. Flower's little girl," and when Victor interrupted one of her harangues against them one day by suggesting that she become a nurse herself, she hit him on his shoulder, hard enough to hurt.

On the mornings that Victor stayed in the house alone while his Grandmother and Shelby were visiting Uncle Buzz he would idle away the time as he would at his mother's home, smoking cigarette after cigarette, visiting with Lily in the backyard, nosing through the books and magazines in the living room, wandering up and down the streets of the neighborhood, and occasionally, especially as the summer passed, he would throw himself flat on his stomach onto the bed in Uncle Buzz's room and imagine himself being seduced by that vague, compelling entity he'd glimpsed that night in the restaurant, the crimson haired friend of his cousin Shelby.

As a result of all the time that he and Shelby spent on the beach Victor's skin became almost as dark as his cousin's, but it was a darkness without depth, giving his appearance a mottled, uneven quality, since he was as pale as ever below the belt and above the knees of the cut offs he went swimming in. His hair grew so long that he had to constantly shake it out of his eyes, a gesture that was at once nervous and insouciant, and that he was totally unconscious of.

Shelby, for her part, never went in the water, but would only sprawl on the green bed sheet and read, or write in the notebook with the sturdy burlap cover embroidered with sunflowers that she brought along with her every day. Her reading material consisted mostly of astrology or self help books, with the occasional novel or biography, she interchanged the books she was reading frequently, and never seemed to finish any of them.

"How do you like it…" she asked him one afternoon, "…staying here all summer? There isn't much to do, is there… Most of the people who live here just work all summer. No one has much of a social life."

"What about your friend?" said Victor.

"What friend?"

Victor flushed beneath his tan. "The one you were talking to the other night. The one with the fake red hair."

Shelby tucked in her chin and peered over the scarlet rims of her enormous sunglasses at Victor. "You mean Dora," she said. "I told you about her. She's a summer person, the one that lives in Raleigh."

Although Victor had figured that out, he nodded as if it were news to him.

"I met her last year," Shelby looked out to sea. "And we've kept in touch. We have similar spiritual interests. She comes here every summer with her parents and stays in those fancy condos over on the rich side of the island. Her parents have a lot of money. But they're crazy. Do you want me to introduce you to her?"

Victor shook the hair out of his eyes, and shrugs.

"She's hot," said Shelby. "Don't you think?"

Victor shrugged again. "What's with her hair?"

Shelby laughed. "She changes it almost every week. She's like that. She likes to attract attention. Some people can get away with that. Dora is very dramatic. Dora isn't even her real name; her real name is Jennifer. She says Dora was given to her by her spirit guide," Shelby said this last as if it were perfectly normal. "That's not an easy thing to do, take on a new name. But she does what she wants. I told her you were from Raleigh. I think you'd like her."

"Why?" Victor looked out to sea. "Because she's crazy?"

"No! Because she's interesting."

"She sounds like a freak."

"Well, she's no more freak than I am," Shelby was quiet for a moment, then shifted her whole body on the sheet to face him. "Look," she said. "I promised Gum I wouldn't ask you, but if you don't want to talk about it, just tell me. I don't like to sidestep things. What were you locked up for?"

Victor drew up his knees and clasped his arms around them in an unconscious mirroring of Shelby. For the first time since he'd known her, he felt as if he had some obscure advantage. It was not an altogether comfortable feeling. He didn't know what to say. He could tell his cousin that he was put in the hospital primarily because

61

he wouldn't bathe, but he didn't really want her to know about *that*. He could rattle off his list of diagnoses, but that wasn't what she was really asking. What she wanted to know, he knew, was what it took to be really considered unacceptable. The simple answer was that it takes the desire to be repulsive to others and comforting to ones' self. But --it was more than that, but-- the more was impossible to articulate. It was a kind of surrender, but to what he could not say, and at any rate it was the kind of thing that was different for everyone. He thought of Steve, of likening himself to Steve again. He could tell Shelby that he'd been busted for possession and had stolen hundreds of dollars from his mother, which was what sent Steve to that place. But deep down he knew that Shelby would not think much of Steve. Suddenly he remembered one of his fellow patients, a boy by the name of John who was on the ward only for a few weeks before being sent to another facility, a tall, rather spacey towheaded young man of about seventeen who had become permanently addled from sniffing paint fumes. Victor smiled as he recalled how John would sit peacefully in the dayroom for hours on end, jiggling his leg and staring blankly into space like a great blonde bunny in a hutch.

"I wouldn't go to school," Victor felt a strange release as he entered without intention into the truth. "You wouldn't believe how crazy it makes people if you really refuse to go to school. Especially when you're only sixteen. It's like you've turned into a criminal," as he said these things, Victor realized for the first time how true they were. Refusing to go to school at that age and refusing to bathe were not the same thing. When he would not go willingly to school, he crossed the line from being troubled to being trouble. Not just to his mother, but to the world, it seemed.

"Why wouldn't you go?" Shelby said.

"I just didn't want to."

"You have to have an education," Shelby said reasonably. "In order to contribute to society."

"No you don't," he said, with an adamancy that seemed to come from nowhere into his voice. He remembered again how John, his brain dissolved by fumes, somehow maintained, for the short time he was on the ward, peace among the rest of them. It had been impossible, in John's silent, mindless, agreeable presence, to behave with too much aggression. It was as if there had a newborn baby on the ward, that overgrown bunny innocence was so contagious. Simply being there had been John's contribution to their society. Victor did not try to explain that to Shelby, he merely looked at her, and did not look away.

"Maybe you're right," Shelby shrugged. "But I'm going to get my Ph.D."

"In what?" Asks Victor.

"Psychology," Shelby sounded almost apologetic. "I'm going to be a shrink," she said then, as if in the face of a challenge. "They aren't all bad, you know."

"Oh, I know," said Victor.

When Victor woke up the next morning, he sensed an absence in the house. He rose, shit, showered and shaved, and wandered into the kitchen to find that the coffee pot was on and half full. He peeked through the living room blinds to find that his grandmothers' sedan was not in the driveway. He looked at the clock above the television. It wasn't quite nine o'clock. Where could she be? Victor wondered if something had happened over the night to Uncle Buzz. He opened the front door and stepped out on to the concrete stoop that served as a front porch. The morning sun had even this early turned the sky a blinding white. He gazed across the street at the ranch house opposite theirs, and shuddered at the thought of his Uncle dead and his grandmother and Shelby weeping and wailing and himself in their midst, with no way to escape. "For God's sake, don't die…" he muttered under his breath.

When he let himself back into the cool of the house, at that very moment Shelby emerged, like a drowsy owl, from her dim and smoky lair. They came together in the kitchen where she poured herself a cup of coffee and liberally lightened it with milk and sugar.

"I think Gum is gone somewhere," said Victor. He straddled the back of one the cushioned aluminum chairs that were placed at the cardinal points around the round kitchen table and watched as his cousin blew on the surface of her coffee.

"Church," said Shelby between blows. "It's Sunday."

So it was. Sunday, that most depressing of days, that day that did nothing so well as to accentuate the loneliness of the alone, had snuck up on Victor, for the first time ever. "I didn't know she went to church," he said. "She didn't go last week, did she?"

Shelby sipped and grimaced, then smacked her lips. "She goes every once in awhile. It all depends on her mood. If she's got something on her mind, she'll go. Or sometimes if she's in a good mood, she'll go. I bet it's a little of both, this time. We've had a good week at the restaurant. But she's probably worried about daddy."

Shelby spoke as if her father was nothing to worry about. She took a long swallow of coffee and leaned back into her seat, as relaxed as if she were drinking ambrosia. "I'll tell you what, though, as Christian as she thinks she is, she never comes back from church without something to complain about. Either the service was too long or it was too short, or someone didn't take their baby out when it started screaming, or someone was wearing blue jeans, or the building was too hot, or the parking lot hasn't been paved yet, or the choir sucked. She's been like that for as long as I can remember, but she's never stopped going to church completely. I stopped going when I turned thirteen. Actually, when I got my period… that's when I stopped going. I just knew that I shouldn't go anymore, that it would only piss me off. Daddy used to go with Gum every once in awhile, but he has another Church he belongs to, right off the highway heading back towards Havelock. The preacher there is his Sponsor."

Victor wasn't sure what she meant by sponsor, but he nodded anyway.

Shelby rested her elbows on the table and her chin in her hands. "I'm not crazy about Daddy's church. It's very conservative- they speak in tongues, and all that kind of shit... but it's better than First Baptist, where Gum goes, where she used to drag me. I was the youngest person in the choir there before I quit going. Didn't you ever have to go to church? I always had to go, even when I was living with my mother. She'd party on Saturday and sing in the choir on Sunday," Shelby rolled her eyes. "At least *she* went because it made her feel good. It did do that. Gum just goes because she thinks she's supposed to. She doesn't get a single thing out of it that I can tell."

Victor thought of his own mother. Being divorced, and Italian, and Catholic, and from the Northeast, she no longer felt welcome at any Catholic Church, but she still wore her tiny gold crucifix, she still occasionally mumbled grace before meals and then crossed herself, totally unselfconsciously, as if there was nothing at all strange about this behavior. Did she get anything out of this sense of herself as a Catholic? Victor knew, somehow, that her parents had been upset with her, at least at first, for marrying Victor's father, a non-Catholic, so obviously her Catholicness had not stood in the way of her doing what she wanted. And yet she would not dream of going to church now that she was divorced. He wondered what, if anything, his father believed.

"Have you been baptized?" Shelby asked.

Victor nodded.

"When you were a baby?"

"Yeah."

Shelby shook her head. "That's so cruel. At least the Baptists don't do that. They leave it to you to submit to the pressure, and I guess that's at least giving you a fighting chance. I think baptizing infants is as bad as circumcising them."

65

Victor blushed.

Shelby went on. "I got baptized when I was eleven. I know now that I shouldn't have, but everybody else was doing it. Now that I look back I can see how it inhibited me. I really felt like I'd made a decision for Christ. It took me years to realize I could make a decision for myself. That's when I got into the Old Religion. I had to dance naked under a new moon for three months straight to counteract the influence of that half-assed baptism but in the end it was worth it. I don't cramp so bad now when I'm on my period, and I'm more confident. Nothing's irrevocable. But you have to really want to change. Do you believe in God?"

It occurred to Victor that he had never before been asked this question. "Umm..." he hesitated.

Shelby answered the question as readily as if she'd asked it of herself. "I do," she said. "But that doesn't mean I can't believe in other things, too."

Victor suddenly had the strange sensation that he was shrinking. He stood up, as if to assert to himself that he was not, in fact, all of a sudden smaller than his cousin. "Where are you going?" she said, easily.

Victor had nothing in mind, but when he opened his mouth he heard himself say, "I have to call my mom."

Shelby nodded sympathetically and took her cup of coffee and went to her room as if to give him privacy.

Victor dialed the wrong number twice before finally getting through to his mother.

"Victor!" she exclaimed. "It's about time I heard from you! How are things, hon?" Victor felt a surprising, unbidden stab of homesickness at the sound of her voice.

"So how do you like the beach?" his mother went on. "What do you think of your grandmother? Is she there? It's good to hear from you, baby!"

Victor shuffled out onto the front stoop with the cordless phone receiver. "Just Shelby's here. She says Gum... our grandmother's gone to Church. Uncle Buzz has already gone to the nursing home..."

"I know," his mother said. "I feel so bad for your gramma. *And* Buzz. *And* poor little Shelby. So how are you and Shelby getting along? Do you like her? She must be sixteen by now, isn't she? I know she's not quite a year younger than you are..."

"She's sixteen," he said.

"Well, what do you think of her?"

He shrugged, though she cannot see. "She's okay."

His mother laughed. "It's really good to hear from you, hon. I've talked to your grandmother a couple of times, and she says that you've been a big help. Not just at the restaurant, but at the house, keeping Shelby company, and being so patient while Buzz was still in his room. Listen, how is he? How does he look to you?"

"He...." the image appeared in Victor's minds eye of his uncle, gripping his can of Ensure, his tattered crimson bathrobe gaping open above the belt to reveal a pale and hairy and bony chest. "He looks pretty sick," he said in a low voice. "He can't eat."

With an almost audible click, like a cap on a pen, his mother's professional nurse's demeanor came to the fore of her voice. "Is he on any supplements?"

"Yeah."

"Is he sleeping a lot?"

"He was when he was here. I don't know about now. I guess he's getting better."

"Cirrhosis doesn't get better, babe. But they can slow it down. Is he jaundiced?"

"Huh?"

"Yellow. His skin and the whites of his eyes. Have you noticed..."

"No," the concrete stoop, even through the thick cloth of Victor's cut offs was hot to the touch. "Mom, is he going to die?"

His mother sighed, "Sooner or later. Yeah. There just isn't a whole lot they can do with a damaged liver. Sometimes they'll arrange a transplant with cirrhosis patients, but your uncle isn't eligible, because he was such a heavy boozer at one time. A body can only take so much abuse before goes to pieces, baby. You're Uncle did a lot of hard drinking for a lot of years before he finally started trying to get himself together. And by then, the damage was done, and it was too late. It's got to be hard on poor little Shelby, especially with that Mother of hers. Listen hon, tell me what you think of Shelby. Is she nice?"

"She's different."

"Well, with what she's been through..."

"I don't mean..." as usual there seemed to be a word that he could not find for what he wanted to say. "She's just smart," he said. "She's very smart. She reads a lot and she..." Victor grinned, imagining the expression on his mother's face if he told her that his cousin danced naked under the new moon when she had her period. "...She's just different. But she's all right."

"I can't even remember the last time I saw her," Victor's mother said. "She wasn't even out of diapers. She was the cutest, chubbiest little thing, with the biggest green eyes, just like a little calf. Is she still cute?"

There is a long pause. "Well, she's still chubby," Victor said, then instantly cringed. He was never sure how his mother would take any reference to weight. Still, she had asked.

His mother sniffed. "Well, her mother was very attractive," Victor noticed for the first time how nasal and hard her voice sounded when she was displeased, how Long Island it became. "For what that's worth. Does Shelby talk about her much?"

Victor decided to say no.

There was a long pause and Victor pulled a weed out of the crack between the stoop and the first slab of the sidewalk that led away from it. "Have you heard from your father?" his mother said, and her voice was still brittle, though not so much as the moment before.

"No."

"You can always call him, you know. He... I know he'd like to hear from you."

There was nothing to say to this, so Victor said nothing.

His mother cleared her throat. "Well, I'm glad you're having a good time. I thought you might enjoy yourself down there. Do you like the beach?"

His response was automatic, and stronger than he would have liked. "Yes."

"Really!" his mother sounded pleased. "I never liked it much. Do you go with Shelby?"

"Yeah."

"Be careful in the water. You don't go out too far, do you?"

"No."

"Well, this is running up your grandmother's bill," his mother said after an awkward, silent moment. "Tell her I'll send her some money next week. Do you need anything?"

"No."

"You sure?" his mother seemed reluctant, all of a sudden to end the call.

"I've made three hundred dollars, mom."

"Already?" she sounded genuinely surprised. "Don't blow that money Victor. Send it to me and I'll put it in an account."

"I'll keep it," he said. "I'm not going to blow it."

"All right, Victor," she sighed. "I'll let you go. Tell your grandmother to call me. I'll talk to you later in the week, okay?"

"All right."

"Be good. I love you."

"All right," he repeated.

"Goodbye, son."

"Bye," Victor pressed the button to hang up and put the phone as far away from himself as he could reach, and looked at the weed in his left hand that he had, without thinking, pulled up by the roots and ground within his fist until it was nothing but a dark, stringy pulp and a green stain in the center of his palm.

Sunday nights at the restaurant tended to be slow, and Victor was pleasantly bored as he idled away his time in the dish room, listening without appreciation to the strains of deadhead music that issued from the stereo in the kitchen. Oliver was absent again. This allowed him to linger about the dining area when he made his rounds to gather the bus pans. At one point while he was at the bar fetching for himself a Styrofoam cup of soda, he noticed Shelby's friend standing at the cash register, talking with not a little animation to Shelby. The two girls sensed his attention almost immediately, and after exchanging a brief look with her friend, Shelby beckoned him over. Despite the calm that his afternoon with Lily left him with, at the prospect of actually speaking to Shelby's friend Victor became immediately paralyzed. At once he was conscious of his appearance, the sheen of sweat on his face, his slightly crooked teeth, the tattered ball cap on his head, his damp and food stained dingy white apron he wore. As always after a few hours of work, he smelt of sweat, fish, bleach, and grease, an odor which to him had become pleasant but which he knew better than to expect others to appreciate. He shook his head, but Shelby only magnified her beckoning gesture, sweeping her whole arm in a kind of inverted arc, like a siren attempting to guide a ship to crash upon hidden rocks.

Rather than risk the real possibility that she might call his name out across the dining room, Victor had no choice but to go over. He set his bus pan on the edge of the bar and trudged over to the register.

"What is it?"

Shelby snorted. "I didn't mean to *bother* you. But I told you I wanted you to meet my friend Dora. Dora, this is Victor. Victor this is Dora. I forgot if I told you, Victor, but Dora's from Raleigh, too."

Victor's hair was underneath his cap, so he couldn't toss it out of his eyes. Her gaze at him was as direct and uninhibited as that of a cat, or a little child. He nodded curtly and turned back to Shelby, who heaved an exaggerated sigh.

"Aren't you two going to speak? God, what idiots...." said Shelby. "Victor, Dora drives. She has a car, a convertible. We're going to Swansboro tomorrow to see a friend of ours. Do you want to go with us?"

"What's Swansboro?"

"A town about an hour from here. Across from the other end of the island. Here..." Shelby took one of the large, folded, laminated menus, on the back panel of which there was a tourist bureau map of the Outer Banks of North Carolina and pointed to a black dot on the edge of the southern mainland. "That's Swansboro. It's all historically preserved and pretty, I think you'll like it. Come with us. We'll be back in time for work. And you can meet another cousin of ours, Troy. He works at a store me and Dora have to go to."

Victor looked from the map to Shelby. "Our cousin?"

"Well, he's our third or fourth cousin, or something like that. You want to come?"

Victor spoke to Dora for the first time. Somehow, now it was easier. "You don't mind?"

One side of Dora's mouth lifted into what looked like a smirk but might have been a smile. "Not at all," her voice, like Shelby's, was low for a young girl, and her words were clipped, as though she was affecting a foreign accent.

"She'll be over at about eleven tomorrow morning, so be ready," Shelby fanned her face with the menu and shifted on her stool, which indicated effectively to Victor that he was dismissed. "We'll get lunch there, so bring a little money. Ask Gum to give you some out of what she owes you for the week."

Victor blushed to hear his grandmother referred to by that ridiculous infantile name in front of this girl who was a stranger to him. "It was nice to meet you," he mumbled.

His awkwardness seemed to amuse the girl. She smiled at him and then laughed, quite without restraint. What a bitch, he thought, and he trudged back to the dishroom, where, without Oliver to keep him company he became careless and dropped a knife into the disposal, making a horrible racket that brought his grandmother running.

When Dora pulled into the driveway in her rather rusty, but vintage and clearly expensive old Mustang Convertible the next morning at well past eleven o'clock, Victor was sitting on the foot of Uncle Buzz's bed fresh from the shower, trying with all his might not to feel impatient as the minutes past eleven crept by. He had spent a restless night in and out of outlandish fantasies regarding Dora, in which she was at once submissive and elusive, he slid from these into dreams that were disjointed yet shared a common mood of unfulfilled desire. Despite all this he woke refreshed, as if the strains of the night had in some mysterious way rested him

He stayed put, behind the closed door of Uncle Buzz's room as the front doorbell rang and Shelby's sandals slapped hurriedly down the hall to answer it. The sandals slapped back down the hall, followed by a lighter patter, as the two girls went back into Shelby's room. Interminable minutes passed, and then there was a rustle of activity, then finally a tap on his door. Victor rose from his tense seated position on the foot of Uncle Buzz's bed, took a deep breath, and opened the door. "We're ready to go," Shelby said, as her friend smiled or smirked at him over Shelby's shoulder. "Are you coming or not?"

They parked in front of a store on the main street of the town, where Victor wandered bored and restless amongst displays of books, candles, crystals, oils, and odd appliances while Shelby and Dora visited with the store's proprietor, a chubby, effeminate, almost middle aged man whom Shelby introduced to Victor as their cousin Troy. Troy took Victor's hand in his own two delicate, warm, and soft palms and pressed it. The older man was dressed in a black turtleneck shirt and his hair was so thick and dark and impeccably styled and such a contrast to his pink skin and pale brown eyebrows that Victor suspected it was actually a toupee. Each of his fingers bore some ornate ring, and about him was a faint odor of the same incense that Shelby used.

The girls chatted with this cousin, and Victor, with nothing to say, poked around the store, flipping through book after book without any interest. Finally, he settled upon one in particular, a magazine sized paperback called *Curse into Blessing*, which turned out to be about the monthly cycle of women as a spiritual journey. Without even realizing it he became engrossed, and he blushed furiously when his cousin Shelby appeared, as if out of nowhere, to smack him on the shoulder and told him that they were ready to go. He returned the book, cover face down, to its spot on the shelf and followed her back to the front of the store, where the cousin Troy handed him a small, smooth black stone and a business card and told him to come back anytime. An ugly inner voice shouted "Faggot!" as Victor shyly accepted the stone, and he ducked his head with as much shame as if he'd been unable to restrain some spiritual fart. Back in Dora's car, Shelby remarked that Troy was psychic, which made Victor feel even worse about those things that went on in his untrustworthy, unattractive mind.

When Dora dropped Victor and Shelby back at the house in Morehead City, their Grandmother had already returned from the rehab facility. She met them at the door and ushered them in, closing the door firmly as if to accentuate that Dora, who had already pulled out of the driveway anyway, was not to be invited in.

"What's wrong?" Shelby said.

"Your daddy's back in Intensive Care over at Carteret General," the grandmother said. "His sugar got too low, and he had a seizure. They say his liver enzymes are all too high… Lord, I don't know. They told me he's in stable condition, but they don't want to move him to a floor yet, before they know what happened. They think it might be the new liver medicine…"

"It *is* their toxic medicine," Shelby sat down on the sofa and scowled.

Their grandmother took off her glasses and rubbed the bridge of her nose. "That kind of talk ain't gonna help anything. Good medicine or bad, whatever it is, he's sick as he can be. I *knew* he wouldn't do as well away from home. I'm not gonna let them put him back in that nursing home. I don't care how fancy it is. I can look after him better here, seems to me…" the grandmother clenched her gnarled little fists at her side, then took a deep breath and went into the kitchen.

"Where have ya'll been all day?" his grandmother called from the kitchen. "We went to Swansboro, like I told you!" said Shelby. She swung her feet off the floor onto the coffee table.

"Don't put your feet on the table," the grandmother said from the kitchen. "Did you take Victor to see the old Governor's mansion?"

Shelby sighed. "No!" she called. "We went to the bookstore."

"The bookstore! You can go to the bookstore here! Why didn't you show Victor the Governors Mansion? That's what you go to Swansboro for."

"I wanted to take him to Troy's bookstore."

"Who?"

"Troy! Troy Sykes. You know. That lived in San Francisco, and had that place in New Bern, and has the metaphysical bookstore. He was at Aunt Patsy's funeral…"

"I don't know who in blazes you're talking about…." there was a pause. "Oh. The fruit." the grandmother came to the kitchen door and shook her head. "Shelby. Of all our people around here, why would you take Victor out to someone like that? What's the matter with you?"

Shelby did not answer, but pursed her lips and looked sidelong at Victor, who swallowed hard. No matter what he might say, he would alienate one or the other of these women. He lifted his right leg slightly and stepped hard on his own left foot. He looked down at it, and his hair fell forward to form a fringe about his face. He searched his mind like a cluttered drawer for something to change the subject to.

He looked up and could not avoid seeing his grandmother's pursed, self-righteous, and somehow adorable face. "Oh, don't be like that, Gum," he said, calling his grandmother for the first time by Shelby's embarrassing name for her.

The old woman tsk'd. "Whale," she said. She retreated into the kitchen, resigned to the relaxed morality of the youth. Shelby swung her feet onto the coffee table again, her upper body vibrating with silent laughter.

"She'll never change," said Shelby with the weary pride of a mother in an indomitable child.

That night they all went to work at the restaurant as usual, as if Uncle Buzz's turn for the worse was nothing to lose business over. Shelby sat on her stool at the register and read her book and chatted with her customers; and Victor found that he hardly thought of his uncle at all. Oliver was there, and together he and Victor comprised a dishwashing team of such speed and efficiency that they were able, despite Gum's obvious irritation, to spend a great of time standing at the cashier's station in their dirty, damp aprons, talking to Shelby. Oliver was mildly but persistently flirtatious with Shelby, which, to Victor's astonishment seemed to fluster her; her only response to his salacious compliments was to giggle and tell him to shut up. Victor was relieved when Oliver finally went too far by snaking his arm around Shelby's waist; for then she jerked away and hit him on the shoulder with the spine of her book, just as she would have hit Victor or anybody else; lightly, but meaning business.

The next day Victor woke up, face down as usual, drooling onto Uncle Buzz's pillow, and, just as if he was back at home with his mother, he felt like he would rather die than get out of bed. He guessed, by the intensity of the sunlight streaming underneath the dingy shades, that he had slept later than usual, and he moaned into the pillow, anticipating that any moment his grandmother would come knocking on his door, and if he didn't answer she would become at first concerned, then frantic, then she would let herself in, find him still in bed; she would then coax, then nag, then become alarmed; then she'd call his mother who would say that this is how he gets, and apologize, and he would get sent back to her in Raleigh to live with his mother and die. Just get up, he told himself, just get going, but there was another voice within him, a voice that was strong and familiar and as close to him as any other, and that always said the same thing… What's the point? Who cares?

He lay there with his body still as a corpse while his mind writhed and fretted like a man in a straitjacket. Inevitably, a tap on his door came, and his muscles tensed. "Victor?" his grandmother's voice was tentative through the door, tentative and timid; unlike her. "Victor, honey?" she whispered. "You still sleeping? It's past ten o' clock…"

Inevitably, the door opened a crack and she peeked in. A moment passed during which Victor heard the sound of a bird warbling on the sill of his window, then the door shut again with a click. There was then the sound of footsteps leading up to the door, and Victor could tell from the heavy slapping sound of sandals that it was Shelby. "What's going on?" she said, in a voice of normal volume.

"Shhh…" the grandmother said. "He's still sleeping. I reckon he's worn out."

The left half of his face still mashed into the pillow, Victor's right eye opened, and he was instantly awake. It had never occurred to him, all those times before when he'd been unable to get out of bed, that he might just need more rest.

After awhile he heard his grandmother's car pull out of the driveway, and then a few minutes later the doorbell rang. Up and down the hall Shelby's sandals slapped, and Victor could discern by the lowered voices and occasional laughter that Dora had come over. He effortlessly rolled out of bed, dashed into the bathroom, and in a few minutes he was standing at the door to Shelby's room with his knuckles a half inch from knocking. Then he decided he needed a cigarette first. He went out into the front lawn and smoked one, then returned to knock on Shelby's door. There was a silence inside, then some movement, then Shelby opened the door a crack. "Yes," she said.

"I'm bored," he said, spontaneously and with truth.

Shelby opened the door another inch. Behind her Dora was lying on her stomach across the foot of the bed, the calves of her legs held up in the air and crossed at the ankles. She was wearing, of all things, black lacy stockings.

Shelby opened the door a bit more, but continued to stand in the opening. "Have you been sleeping all this time?"

"No," said Victor, and then he said something strange, something he had not planned on saying, and could not remember ever hearing anybody say, though once he has said it, it sounded familiar. "I was just resting my bones."

Shelby laughed, a merry, surprised laugh. "You sound just like Daddy!" she said. Victor was sure he had never heard his Uncle say anything like that, but he smiled and shrugged. Shelby opened the door all the way and stepped aside to let him in her room.

Dora had brought a baggie of marijuana, and as soon as Victor stepped in and settled himself in his usual place against the closet door, she showed it to him. "We were about to smoke a bowl," she said. "Do you want some?"

Victor looked at Shelby with surprise. He would not have thought, with her ambition to be a shrink, and her contempt for her crack smoking mother, that she would smoke marijuana. But then again, she was that type that always makes a distinction between weed and other illegal drugs.

"No thanks," he said. Shelby gave him a sympathetic look. He'd forgotten he'd told her about the treatment center.

The two girls lit their pipe and passed it, and when the thick, ropy smell reached him, he was tempted, but it passed. Victor had only smoked once before, with a friendly kid in the neighborhood who he'd sometimes played video games with shortly before he dropped out of school. The kid's name was Dillis, and the marijuana had been so powerful that Victor's first 'high' had been instantaneous, intense, and utterly beyond his expectations. His senses, particularly his perception of color and light, had become so hypersensitive that he was convinced he was losing his mind. Sitting in Dillis' basement, Victor became paralyzed with fear and disorientation, and though Dillis seemed to have understood and in fact expertly and gently talked him down, Victor could never bring himself to go back to Dillis' house. He'd indicated to Dillis before they smoked that he was a pro. Dillis had been his first chance at having a friend, and he'd blown it. When Shelby held the pipe with its glowing, fuming, crackling bowl out toward him he agonized for a split second, then shook his head.

"Oh, right," Shelby said, "Sorry. I wasn't thinking. It doesn't bother you, does it, if we smoke in front of you?"

Victor shrugged and let his hair fall over his eyes. "Why should it?"

From he seat against the headboard of Shelby's bed Dora gazed upon him. "You must be a Christian," she said, with not a little sourness.

Shelby, exhaling marijuana smoke, shook her head. "Be nice, Dora."

Dora was unperturbed. She smiled languorously. "Just asking," she said.

Victor felt warmed by Shelby's protection. "It's all right," he said, "I don't care." He looked at Dora with a mixture of generosity and contempt. "I just got out of rehab," he said.

Dora looked skeptical. "Really?" she said. "Where were you?"

Victor named his treatment center.

"Really?" said Dora. She was impressed. "Just for smoking pot?"

"And some other things," said Victor like a jaded jet setter describing his travels. "It sucked."

Dora lit a regular cigarette and placed one of Shelby's ashtrays on the pillow beside her, then curled herself on the bed, her head propped up on one arm. It was a sultry pose, and in the darkness Victor blinked and gulped. "What other things?" she said.

Victor was silent. As if sensing his unease, Shelby passed the pipe to Dora, who took it and drew from it, holding the smoke in her ample chest, never taking her inscrutable catlike gaze off of Victor. Suddenly it all seemed absurd. How serious they were about this stuff! It was somehow liberating to stand by, sober, and watch other people get high. It was like watching cult members prostrate themselves before some self styled deity. He laughed merrily.

Dora's catty gaze faltered and she looked at Shelby. "I guess we should stop," she said.

Victor stood. "It's okay," he said. "I've got some stuff to do, anyway," and with that he left Shelby's room to the girls and went into his own, or Uncle Buzz's room, lay down on the bed, and let him mind teem with visions of Dora's legs in their black lace stockings.

Victor watched television in the front room until his grandmother came home. Exuding weariness and self-sacrifice, she repaired to the kitchen to put on supper. Victor offered to help.

"Well, if you want to!" she said. She handed him the salad fork that she had been poking and prodding three sputtering pork patties with. "Just turn these over when they get good and brown around the edges. I'm gonna sit right here and have me a cigarette."

And with that she went over to Victor's seat at the kitchen table, turned it to face the stove, and stretched out her legs as if to get her tiny feet in their bedroom slippers as far away from the rest of her as possible.

"Oh, me," she sighed after her first drag. Victor glanced away from the stove to see her exhale two streams of smoke from her nostrils like an elderly little dragon. "If it isn't one thing it's another. I can't believe they let William get like this. You'd think they were trying to kill him. Sometimes I wonder if any of these doctors know what they're doing. And not one American doctor in the bunch. I don't think I've seen one American doctor in that whole hospital! I'm telling you, it's something these days."

Victor bit his lip and poked a pork chop.

The old lady, wreathed in smoke, lowered her voice as if they were under surveillance. "I believe one of them's from I-rack," she shook her head in disapproval. "Now what kind of training can they get over there? With all that mess going on? But you have to do the best you can with what you've got, I guess," she stubbed out her cigarette after a few minutes of companionable silence and watched as Victor poked at the pork chops. "You ought to flip those over now," she said. Victor flipped them with some difficulty, spattering his wrist with a few tiny droplets of grease, which stung rather pleasantly. His grandmother made no move to take her place at the stove, and Victor was happy to stand there for as long as she would let him.

The kitchen smelled strongly of steam and grease and pork meat, and the temperature in there was stifling. The heavy afternoon sun beamed a deep light through the windows over the sink and the dinner table. After a moment the old lady asked Victor if he knew how old she was. He shook his head.

"I'm gonna be seventy-four years old come December," she said. "Born the day after Christmas in 1931. You'd never know it to look at me, would you?" she said, smiling her seamed upside down smile at him.

Victor shook his head again, although he would have guessed anywhere from sixty-five to eighty.

"I sure feel it, though," she continued, "I feel every single day. A woman shouldn't have to work like a dog all the way into her seventies the way I do just to get by, but that's the way things are these days," she sighed again. "I draw your granddaddy's social security and my own check, but it still ain't enough to make the house payment, pay for Williams' doctor bills, keep Shelby in some decent clothes- not that she ever wears anything decent, she just gets everything from the

Goodwill like some charity case. I can't tell you what a big help you've been. Not just up at the restaurant, but with Shelby. It's been good for her, having you around, someone who's got a little more sense then these friends of hers. That Dora …" the old woman's voice lowered to a whisper and Victor could scarcely hear her over the sizzle of the meat. "…That purple hair… and the crazy way she looks at you… like she's on drugs or something… I don't understand why Shelby has to take up with such sad sacks all the time. You should see some of the boys she's brought over. Look more like girls to me, with their earrings all over their face and their hair. Young people don't want to look nice any more, like there's something wrong with being cute…."

On and on she went, babbling like a brook as the pork chops sizzled and slowly darkened, and it was all one to Victor, it was as if all the sounds in the room worked together to form a symphony of hominess. He didn't even like pork chops, but he would eat these, having cooked them. "They're done, honey," his grandmother stood and peered over his shoulder. "Set them on that plate with the paper towel," she said.

He stood by idly, one foot on top of the other, until his grandmother suggested, with the air of a mother directing a small child, that he set the table and then go get Shelby. Then, before he could move, she stopped everything and put a frail hand to his sunburnt arm "Look here," she whispered conspiratorially. "I'm serious about that Dora. I think she's trouble. You've been around her some. Do you think she's good for Shelby?" her grip on his arm became a bit firmer. "Shelby's so close with her daddy. I'm just afraid…" her mouth pursed. "I just can't keep my eye on her every minute. You know what I mean? I just hope she's got good friends. Not junkies."

"Dora's a good friend," he said, reassuringly, "She's not a junkie."

Thursday of that week was the fourth of July, and the restaurant closed early that night while a fireworks display was performed over the sound for the entertainment and diversion of all citizens and tourists in the area.

Gum closed up the restaurant at eight o'clock that evening and dismissed the barflies by telling them there was plenty of beer to be bought at the grocery store just down the highway. The waitresses and the surly kitchen help all went on their way leaving Oliver and Victor and Shelby and their grandmother to walk the half-mile from the restaurant to the banks of the sound and the foot of the bridge that spanned it. There the entire population of the county seemed to congregate, standing in clumps or sprawled out on towels or beach chairs. There were also people lining either railing of the bridge. They drifted to a spot just large enough for Shelby to lay out her bed sheet and collapse upon it while Victor and Oliver their Grandmother stood looking at the people around them. To their left a large Mexican family seemed to have camped for the night with a number of Styrofoam coolers, beach chairs, and a portable stereo spewing some accordion music. Gum peered sidelong at this family with unveiled disapproval until one of the children, a chubby dark haired little girl barely old enough to walk, beguiled her by opening and closing her little fist in greeting. "Well, ain't she cute..." Gum said to Oliver. "Tell her hey for me, Oliver..."

Victor squatted down beside Shelby and looked across the water at the gaudy lights of the hotels and restaurants and surf shops on the island that obliterated any glimpse of the ocean beyond. These lights danced on the slightly troubled dark waters of the sound as the dusk slowly deepened and the barge from which the fireworks were to be launched made its slow approach underneath the bridge to where the distance between the island and the mainland was at its greatest, near the inlet. Clearly the bridge was the place to be to get the best view of the show, and Victor leaned over to his cousin and suggested that they go there.

Shelby rolled her eyes. "Why? It's already crowded," she says. "That's where all the dingbatters… the tourists go. I need to be where I can sit. You can go up there if you want to. We'll be here."

Victor sighed. Oliver was already introducing himself to their Mexican neighbors, so Victor didn't ask him to come along, but loped away without another word. With innumerable masses about him and the slowly emerging stars above him he felt suddenly anonymous and he shook his hair into his face and gazed through it with surreptitious interest at people in the crowd until he was noticed a couple holding hands at the foot of the bridge, a tall, lean shirtless blonde surfer boy with tattoos covering both arms and a girl with a flowing skirt, high heeled sandals, and blood red hair.

She spotted him before he could look away. She beckoned him over. The fellow with the tattoos with whom she was holding hands looked at him as one might look at an approaching panhandler.

"Hi, Victor," she said. "What are you doing here? You're not by yourself, are you?"

"No," he said. "Shelby and Gum…. our grandmother are back there."

Dora disengaged her hand from the tattooed fellow and turned to him. "This is Victor, my friend Shelby's cousin, from out of town. I told you about Shelby. The one who lives here year round?"

"Yeah," the young man's lifted his chin in greeting at Victor. "'Sup."

Victor shoved his hands into his pockets and tossed his hair. Dora linked her hand with the surfer's again. "This is Dave," she said to Victor. "He has a place right above my stepfather's condominium. You know where I'm staying?"

Victor shook his head.

Dora pointed across the sound to the eastern end of the long barrier island. "Down there by the old Civil War fort. There's a bunch of condominiums. That's where I stay in the summer. So does Dave."

Victor nodded. He stole glance at Dave, who despite having only a bathing suit and sandals on, despite his windblown, sun streaked matted curly hair, the tattoos on his arms and chest, and sedated aspect gave the impression, as did Dora, of coming from money. His body had a slim, suntanned beauty, though his square jawed, small-featured face was like a mask. He wore his near nakedness as if even the shorts covering his genitals and buttocks could be shed without shame. In his own mindless way, he was as fascinating to Victor as Dora. Victor lowered his head and stared at a discarded candy bar wrapper on the ground between them.

"So what are you doing by yourself?" said Dora. She was smiling, but not smirking, and seemed altogether like a different person, as if her haughtiness had personified itself in the form of her mute companion, leaving her free to be friendly. "Just looking around?" she prompted.

"I was going to go up on the bridge," Victor mumbled. "Shelby wanted to stay down there," he stepped backward, tried to think of some excuse to turn around, to get away from the lovely couple. Dora turned herself toward him even leaned a bit forward as if Dave was nothing more than a prop. "We were just up there," she said. "It's too loud. I couldn't deal with it," she smiled. "Tell Shelby I'll call her tomorrow."

"Okay."

Though his closed expression and languid stance did not alter, somehow the silent surfer exuded impatience. Dora gave him a quick look. "Dave's looking for some friends," she said. "We have to go. Have fun on the bridge. Maybe I'll see you tomorrow," before the words were out of her mouth she was led away. She laughed. Victor was left to wend his way through a string of mindless revelers to the middle of the bridge.

He squeezed himself into a barely open place in the midst of all the shouting and carrying on and leaned over the rail. The dark water underneath, glittering with the shattered reflection of a thousand lights drew his gaze and held it as securely as a planet holds a moon. He couldn't tune out the merriment that surrounded him like a swarm of flies around a turd, and he seethed in contempt and envy as he dangled his arms over the wide steel railing. People with their warm, damp, thoughtless flesh moved about in their loose clusters jostling him and pressing him even harder against the guardrail, but he made no attempt to shift into a more comfortable position. He was exactly where he somehow felt compelled to be ever since arriving with Gum and Shelby at this frivolous celebration; alone at the top of the bridge, leaning precarious yet protected over the sound's still water.

It was an eerie place to be as the night became progressively darker. The afternoon had been overcast, and so the coming of the night seemed more than usually gradual, with clouds and the lights from the buildings on both sides reflected in the sound. The night was different here than where he lived anyway, thought Victor, there was something in the nearness of the ocean that gave the impression that, no matter how dark it might be, sunrise was just over the horizon if one could only see past it.

But now, more so than at any other time, the night seemed held at bay by a riot of unnatural light. All around Victor there was a collective break in the omnipresent chatter and a low murmur as the initial fireworks were set off. The crowd turned as one to look to the east where the barge was but Victor stayed where he was and stared instead at the flickering water of the sound, oblivious to the show overhead. The prospect of the plunge was still strong. Victor felt compelled to imagine the impact and the aftermath of his own sudden dive, the consternation he would create if he would only hoist himself a bit off his feet and climb onto this sturdy railing and toss himself into this water that was only deceptively deep, to find, if not death, then at the very least an end to life of mere inertia. If he jumped, he would at least be moving.

A series of explosions overhead drew his attention away from himself and he turned to the east to see a rainbow of colors erupt and disappear into the night leaving only ephemeral trails of smoke in the night sky. The crowd cheered as if they won some kind of victory, and Victor felt a thousand years old. He bent over the guardrail and spit into the water, as if to join at least something of himself to its treacherous, seductive expanse. With that he pulled the remainder of himself together and the bridge to find his place with his grandmother and Oliver and Shelby.

There came a tapping against his bedroom door as soft and insistent as the ticking of a watch. It was a few moments before Victor was awake enough to drag himself out of bed and over to the door. He opened it a crack to see his grandmother standing outside, still dressed in her threadbare flowered cotton nightdress, open toed flannel slippers, and a band of toilet tissue pinned about her hairdo.

"Gum!" he said. "What's going on?"

"I hate to get you up..." she stepped into the room. "The hospital called," her voice was apologetic but urgent. "William had a bad night. He's just not getting any better, and honey, it don't look good. I'm..." she looked past him to the bed. "I'm going to need your help with Shelby."

Victor stomach rolled. His grandmother was a tiny woman; he noticed that the top of her head barely reached to his collarbone. She was holding the front of her housedress together with one tiny, gnarled hand. "Okay," he said.

"Thank you, son," she blinked rapidly. "I haven't woke her, I thought I'd get some breakfast on first. And I didn't want you to get took by surprise if she... gets upset. I don't think she will, but..." Gum inclined her head in the direction of Shelby's room. "She don't never take nothing quietly. She's gonna have plenty to say, believe you me," the old lady reached for his hand and squeezed it, then dropped it. "You come on out to the kitchen when you're ready, I'm gonna fry some eggs."

Victor got showered and dressed quickly, feeling nothing of his usual early morning torpor. He went into the kitchen where his grandmother had prepared him a mug of coffee. The mug was plastic and a faded red, with the words 'Triple-S Pier, Atlantic Beach North Carolina' in faded black script around it. She set a sugar bowl on the placemat in the center of the table and sat on the edge of the seat beside him. "Well," she began, "William's kidneys have shut down. This is what they were afraid might happen, and now they're asking *me* what to do about it. I thought *they* were supposed to be the doctors…" Gum broke off and her mouth formed a seamed line and her eyes filled. She took a deep breath and looked at Victor and the tears were absorbed back into her self. "So, what it comes down to is, I have to be right there in case there's anything needs to be decided. I'm gonna have to put Dottie in charge of things at the restaurant… at least for a couple of days. I hate to do it to her, but sometimes you just have to do things you hate to do. In the meantime, I'd like for you to help me with Shelby, just stay close. It's gonna mean your gonna lose some work at the restaurant. I know you counted on the money so I'll do the best I can to pay you for your time, but it's not going to be the same as if you were actually working, cause it's gonna be coming out of my own pocket…"

Here Victor broke in. "Don't worry about that… I've saved a lot of money already."

His grandmother covered his wrist with her tiny gnarled hand. "No, honey. I'm gonna do right by you. You didn't come here to sit around a hospital, this ain't how it was supposed to be. But we've got to do the best we can. Now, if you think it'd be better for you to go on home to your momma, I'll understand…" the old lady released his wrist. "I'd probably do the same thing if I was in your shoes. But

Lord knows you're welcome to stay…" her pale blue eyes filled with tears again.

"I don't want to go home," he said bluntly.

His grandmother clutched his wrist again. "Bless your heart. Thank you honey. That means a lot to me, and I know it'll be a blessing for Shelby. I tell you what, she may have a smart mouth on her, but I can tell she enjoys having you. I have to admit, I was a little worried when I told your mama you could come stay, because Shelby is so strong minded, and I don't know how much you know about your daddy and her daddy, but they never have got along," she shook her head.

"They haven't?"

"Now don't get me wrong…" the old lady put a hand up. "I'm not saying they don't love each other. They're brothers. I know you don't have any brothers or sisters, so you don't really know how it can be, but believe me, you can love someone and hate them at the same time. It ain't nothing unusual. With Eddie and William, it was the two of them against the world outside the house and the two of them against each other inside. I reckon that's just how boys are. Always got to be the big dog. Eddie liked to devil William from the day we brought him home from the hospital. First thing he did was tell him he was ugly. But let anyone else say something against his baby brother and Eddie was a raging bull. Defended him like he was his own baby…" Gum settled back into her chair with a distant, faint smile on her face until the coffeepot on the kitchen counter began to gurgle. "Listen to me… I didn't mean to talk your ear off. Listen, I'm gonna get Shelby up now, I reckon. I just wanted to let you know first, so you can be prepared if…" her eyes welled up again. "If Shelby's upset."

But instead of getting up like she said, Gum continued to sit at the dinner table with her hands held loosely around her coffee mug, her head shaking, or rather trembling slightly in negation as her mind drew inward and her eyes looked down into the coffee in her mug, giving the impression that she was watching some far away figure retreat even further.

"I'll go get her up," he said, and his grandmother smiled up at him gratefully.

When he knocked on Shelby's door, she opened it to peer out with a cross expression meant for Gum, a scowl which softened but did not entirely disappear upon beholding Victor. "Whazzup?" she said fuzzily, her right hand on her hip and her left hand palpating like some feeding lamprey within the tangle of her curls.

"Gum's making breakfast," he said. "She told me to get you up. We all have to go to the hospital."

Shelby's hand froze in her hair and her eyes, which had been squinting at him nearsightedly, widened. "What's happened?"

"Something with his kidneys."

"His kidneys!" Shelby opened her bedroom door wide and stepped out, forcing Victor to retreat towards the kitchen. "Have they failed?"

"I don't know," Victor lied.

Shelby closed her eyes for a moment, then turned away, toward her room. "Tell Gum I'm coming," she said, and shut herself back into her bedroom.

Victor returned to the kitchen to find his grandmother still sitting at the table where he left her. "She's coming," he said, and the old lady nodded. When Shelby appeared she was dressed in her usual outfit of t-shirt and skirt and sandals, and her brown face was damp and shiny from having been hurriedly washed. "What's going on with Daddy?" she demanded.

"His kidneys have shut down," Gum sighed. "So he's back in intensive care."

"What are they gonna do?" Shelby did not come to the table where her grandmother and Victor were sitting, but backed up against the oven, clutching the counter on either side with white knuckled hands.

"They want to wait and see."

Shelby growled. "Wait for what? See what?"

Gum shrugged. "I don't know, Shelby. They're the doctors. Not us."

"Is he conscious?" Shelby glared at her grandmother as if she was aiming a gun at the old woman.

"He's in and out," Gum said, "He's real sleepy. From all the medicine."

"It's the medicine that's done this," Shelby spoke through tightened lips.

Gum shrugged and said nothing.

"Well, are they going to do anything?"

Gum stood up slowly, her head still slowly shaking. "Of course they are, Shelby. Of course they are. My Lord. They're going to do everything they can," she approached the oven and Shelby moved over. "Just go sit down, Shelby. Let me fix some breakfast, and then we've got to get to the hospital."

Shelby's chin puckered and then relaxed as her grandmother, without looking at her, gently pushed her toward they table and away from herself. Never had Victor seen his grandmother look so much like what she was, a tired old lady, and never before had he seen Shelby look so much like a motherless young girl. "Just let me handle this, Shelby," the old lady said, firm but so quietly that Victor could barely make her words out. "I've gone down this road before, and you haven't. This ain't the first time your daddy's been in trouble."

Victor could see Shelby's throat constrict as she swallowed. He had no idea what his grandmother was talking about, but he could see that Shelby was chastened by some bitter memory. He watched as his cousin came to the table and sat down opposite him. When she looked into his eyes it was like he wanted, at one and the same time, to embrace her and to run far away.

91

"Well …" she said to him, sounding very much like their grandmother. "I bet *you* can't wait to get back home."

I am home, Victor thought, but he could not say it. He blushed and shrugged, and inexplicably remembered Dora smiling at him at the foot of the bridge. "I can wait," he said, defensively, and Shelby smiled.

Although all three of them went to the hospital, only Gum actually was permitted to see Uncle Buzz in the ICU; and even she was only allowed in for a few minutes at a time every two hours. Much of the day was spent in the crowded waiting room, flipping over and over through the same dated magazines, watching other families, some of whom were camped out with blankets and pillows, or staring at the muted television bolted high in the corner of the room.

At one point, towards the middle of the afternoon, Shelby decided she was starving, so Victor tagged along after her to the cafeteria on the ground floor of the hospital. They were sharing a paper bowl of soggy nachos slathered in incandescently orange melted cheese when Victor screwed up sufficient courage to mumble to Shelby that he was sorry that her dad was so sick.

Shelby held up a dripping nacho and regarded it before putting it back into the bowl. The cafeteria was empty except for a couple of housekeepers sullenly carpet sweeping the dining area.

"Daddy's always been sick," Shelby said. "He's had diabetes for as long as I can remember. It's hard for me to imagine that he was ever in the military, but he was. I guess his problems didn't start until he started to drink really heavily, and that was when I was living with my mother, and he was out God knows where. Me and Daddy came to live with Gum at about the same time, but we didn't come together, did you know that? Daddy doesn't have legal custody of me, Gum does. Isn't that twisted?"

"Who came first?" said Victor.

Shelby's brow furrowed. "You know, I'm not really sure," she leaned back in her seat and looked up at the ceiling fans whirring noiselessly overhead. "I think it was me, but I was so young... I was only four. Daddy left the coast guard after my mother left him, and then he went all over the place, but he never stayed anywhere for long. He stayed in YMCA's and Salvation Army's all over the south, I know that, and I know that he was arrested a few times too, for fighting, and public drunkenness, and that kind of thing," Shelby leaned forward. "He wasn't a bum. It's not like it sounds. He was just wild and out of control. It was hard on him, when my mother left him. He really loved her," Shelby rolled her eyes. "He still does, for some reason."

Victor was more curious than ever about this almost universally reviled figure, Shelby's mother, whom everybody, especially Shelby, despite her pride in her mother's Indian heritage, loved to hate, but he didn't want to ask and upset her. He reached for a nacho.

Shelby leaned back her seat and crossed her arms underneath her small breasts "So, basically Daddy ended up back here because he didn't have anywhere else to go. He couldn't go back into the service, and he'd lost every other job he ever had because of his drinking, so he moved back in with Gum and since our grandfather was dead by then he took over the kitchen at the restaurant. And he's done pretty well ever since then, but for a few years there, he kept drinking. It wasn't until he got really sick with the diabetes that he stopped completely. Before that he'd go on binges, but he never got ugly, I've never seen him get violent or anything. He would just get silly sometimes, and sometimes he'd get sad and start crying about my mother, or about how rotten he is as a father and how he never made anything of himself. And it's not like he drank all the time, either, there would be months, maybe even a year now and then, when he didn't touch a drop and he went to AA meetings. He still goes, when he can. That's where most of his friends are, people he met in meetings. He's not bad," Shelby said again. "He's got a disease. And…" she caught Victor's eye. "It's a disease that runs in the family. Granddaddy was a problem drinker, too, did you know that?"

Victor shook his head.

"And *his* father was a moonshiner back during prohibition. He was in prison for almost ten years in Charleston. So it's not like you can necessarily help yourself when it comes to things like that. Sometimes…" Shelby's wide little jaw, so reminiscent of her father and of their grandmother, asserted itself. "Sometimes you're cursed from the womb."

There was a silence, and then she smiled cheerfully as if they were not in the cafeteria of a hospital where her father would surely die. "You don't know much about our family, do you?"

Victor shook his head. It had never seemed important to know about what came before him.

"You'll learn," she said, and it was as if she were a jealous witch in a fairy tale laying a curse upon a long awaited prince.

Back in the ICU waiting room, their grandmother sat chatting in confidential tones with a lady whose fast asleep and snoring husband was seated on the other side of her with the bald crown of his head resting against the wall. As soon as Victor and Shelby walked in their grandmother's entire demeanor changed from one of relaxed amiability to indignation. "I was this close to having you two paged on the system!" she said. "What on earth have you two been up to! Does it take that long to get something to eat and come back to where you're supposed to be?!" without waiting for an answer or an explanation, she turned back to the lady with whom she'd been chatting. "I swear to Jesus, you can't turn your back for one minute!"

The woman nodded at Gum and winked at Victor and Shelby. She was a heavyset woman, well powdered and coiffed, about the same age as Gum, and she seemed as content as if she was on a cruise ship rather than an intensive care unit waiting room. "These are your grandbabies?" she said. Her eyes lingered on Shelby for a split second longer than on Victor and she winked again. "Well, they are just as handsome as they can be. Don't look a thing alike, though. Isn't that something..."

Shelby nudged Victor.

Gum cleared her throat. "Shelby is Williams' daughter. His only. Victor is my oldest's, Eddie's son, by his first marriage."

Victor felt his stomach tighten. He'd never heard it put before, so plainly, that he was no longer his father's only child.

"Oh, so they're *cousins*," the woman, who was wearing a baby blue sweatshirt embossed with a stitched slogan in ornate script that proclaimed, 'Angels are Everywhere!' sounded relieved. Beside her, her sleeping husband made a snorting, choking sound, opened his eyes, smacked his lips, crossed his legs in their rose-colored slacks, and then closed his eyes again. "And they both live with you? My goodness. What a blessing. Especially right now."

"Victor lives in Raleigh," said Gum with an enigmatic glance in his direction. "He's here for the summer. I don't know what we're going to do without him when he leaves."

"Oh my. Raleigh," the lady said, as if Raleigh were on another planet.

"Well," Gum put the magazine was resting on her lap onto the end table beside her and leaned forward. "Let me get these kids home before they wander off again. I'll see ya'll later on tonight if you're still here."

95

"We'll be here," the lady said. "Unless they move mama up to a floor tonight, which I know they won't do. She was fighting like a tiger when she came up out of surgery. They had to restrain her *and* sedate her. I don't know what got into her, she didn't act ugly at all last year after her hip replacement…"

"Bless her heart…" Gum said, only half listening. "Shelby, come get this bag for me," she indicated a plastic courtesy bag full of some of Uncle Buzz's garments. "I got to take these home and wash them. Victor…" she beckoned him forward and held out her arm as if she was about to pass out and was expecting him to catch her. He rushed over and she whispered near his ear in a voice that was not as confidential as it was apologetic. "I called your daddy. He said to tell you to call him soon. He said…" she lowered her voice even further. "He said he's glad you're here with us. Real glad you're here with us. I told him I was, too."

Victor had the sensation that her arm across his shoulder, as light as it was, had the hidden capacity to bear down until he crashed through the tiled floor into some dank and limitless labyrinthine foundation underneath. Just when he was starting to feel at home, here comes his father to make a joke of everything.

Later that evening, after they got home, Victor and Shelby were in her room smoking cigarettes and watching, but not listening to, an entertainment news show on the small television set atop her dresser. It seemed to Victor as if it had been a long time since he spent any time in Shelby's room, and he luxuriated quietly in it like a cat on the warm hood of a parked car. He was grateful to be free, for Shelby's room to be free, of Dora's alluring, disturbing presence. From his usual seat on the floor against the closet door he looked surreptitiously at his cousin. She had her journal out, but she was only chewing on the end of her pen, not writing; the paisley clothbound notebook wasn't even open. She was staring glassily at the television as if hypnotized, and by this Victor could tell that she was thinking about her father. It was her policy, usually, to criticize whatever the television might be showing lest it be mistaken that she was really watching for pleasure.

"Daddy might die this time," she said during a commercial.

Victor held his breath.

"If Gum called your dad, then it's serious. It's more serious than it's ever been before. She doesn't call your dad about anything. They don't get along."

Victor hoped she'd say more, but he was silent.

Shelby herself was silent for awhile, sucking the cap of her pen, then she closed her journal and rolled over on her back to gaze at the ceiling. "I've always known Daddy wouldn't live to be very old. He has too many health problems. And I don't think death is the end. I *know* death isn't the end," Shelby's voice was low and ruminative, and her expression, from what Victor could see of it, was calm. "But I'm not ready," she said. "I don't think I'm supposed to be," she rolled over again, this time onto her side, so that she was facing the headboard of her bed, and away from Victor. But she continued to speak in the same low, speculative tone, as if she was writing in her journal.

Victor made a low, noncommittal humming noise, hardly loud enough for even himself to hear. Shelby kept talking. "Daddy has a good life. Even if some people think he's wasted it because he has a drinking problem and because he's never really been able to make it on his own, that doesn't mean he doesn't have a good life. He's kind to everyone, and he likes working at the restaurant, and he loves Gum and me. Lots of people who've been through what he's been through haven't come out so well. He's not bitter, he's not resentful, he takes life day by day, and he never bothers anybody. He's got a good life, and that's what I don't understand about this whole thing," she turned over and faced Victor, and even though she seemed to be looking into his eyes he knew she was addressing something far beyond him. "Why should he have to miss out on the future? It doesn't make sense to me."

Shelby rolled over on her back again to stare at the ceiling. "I'm glad you're here," she said, and Victor, though he knew that she was talking to him now, didn't know what to say. He asked her, after a while, for a cigarette.

Gum told them the next morning that Uncle Buzz was to be moved from Intensive Care to a private room up on the fifth and top floor of the hospital. "They can do as much for him in his own room as they can do for him in the ICU," she said. "As long as I'm there to keep an eye on them. He did pretty well last night, so I don't reckon ya'll need to go to the hospital today if you don't want to."

Shelby raised an eyebrow. They were all in the kitchen, sharing a breakfast of coffee and instant grits. "Is he conscious?" she said, with a glance at her grandmother that was an attempt to be formidable.

"I can't imagine he could be, with all that they're giving him. But I didn't ask, Shelby."

"How can you not ask if he's conscious, for Pete's sake?"

Gum stood up, took her mug to the sink, and then returned to stand over Shelby with her pale, veiny speckled arms crossed hard against her chest. "Well, maybe because I know a little bit more about what's going on than you do. What are you jumping all over me for?"

Shelby twisted in her seat to glare up at the old woman. "Why are you getting so upset?"

"Why are you getting so snippy?" Gum fired back.

"I'm not getting snippy. I'm just saying… If you know so much about what's going on, why don't you tell me? What is it you aren't telling me, Gum?"

Throughout this exchange, Victor stared into his reflection in his coffee.

Gum walked over to the sink, ran a bit of water, then turned to face Shelby. "Honey, I'm telling you everything I know. Your daddy's kidneys have shut down. That's serious. He might have to go on dialysis."

"He *will* have to go on dialysis," Shelby said. "I know that much, at least. Unless he...." she broke off.

Gum walked back over to stand behind Shelby's chair. "Nobody's said anything about him dying, Shelby. I swear to you. But he's real, real sick."

"Why did you call Victor's father, then?"

Gum said nothing for a moment. Then, "Well, I had to let Eddie know what's going on, Shelby, It's his only brother, for Pity's sake!"

"Is Uncle Eddie coming here, then?" Shelby's tone was sullen.

Gum's voice was tight. "He might," she said. "If your daddy gets any sicker, he will," she paused, "He's got a lot going on right now, a new baby..."

Shelby and Victor exchanged a glance across the table.

Gum heaved a sigh like a woman who has just baked a cake only to watch it fall. "Look here..." she said to Shelby. "Why don't you just stay home today with your cousin. I want him to stick around home in case Eddie calls here, and there really ain't no need for you to sit around in the hospital all day anyway. Your daddy's stable; and I'm pretty sure they're keeping him under sedation until they can either get his kidneys working or get him on a machine, and they aren't gonna let you in to see him anyway. You might as well just stay home. I'll call you if I need to, and you can have your friend Dora carry you over to the hospital, can't you, if anything happens?"

"Yeah," Shelby said sulkily. "I'll call her in a minute to make sure."

"Then y'all just stay here," said Gum, with undisguised relief. "Just don't go anywhere- like I say, Eddie might call here first looking for me. And I know he wants to talk to Victor anyway."

Victor felt his lips purse in a manner identical to that of his grandmother and his cousin whenever they were suppressing some curse or complaint. At the same time that he dreaded the prospect of talking to his father, some delighted part of himself marveled at how in such a short time around these two women he had absorbed some of their ways.

The grandmother wandered off to her room to make herself ready and Shelby leaned over to nudge Victor. "I've just had an awesome idea," she whispered. "I'll get Dora to work up a ceremony…" she clasped her hands and rubbed them together like an imp. "For Daddy. We'll have a healing ritual, to set him free…" she glanced over each shoulder and lowered her voice, as if she was afraid some hidden presence might be listening, "…from any negative influences. To release his strength."

She spread out her arms in a hieratic gesture that made her look ludicrous in that she was wearing her dingy tattered nightshirt with the image of the Tasmanian Devil glowering and slobbering in a friendly fashion upon it. "We'll need to use Daddy's room, if you don't mind."

Victor nodded.

"Good," Shelby's arms dropped and she scratched a spot underneath her small breasts, her nails caressing the tip of the Tasmanian Devil's drooling tongue. "Just don't say anything to Gum," Shelby took her coffee cup to the sink, "She'd kill me."

By the time Gum left for the hospital it was almost noon. Shelby left Victor to himself, locking herself in her room to concoct her ceremony, he guessed. He wandered out into the back yard with the intention of taking Lily for a walk around the neighborhood, but the old dog was in a lazy mood and would only offer him her belly to rub.

When Victor tired of indulging her she rose, gave him a reproachful look, shook herself, and trundled off to the shade of her doghouse.

Forgetting that he was supposed to stay close in case his father called, Victor headed down the street toward the bridge. There had been a brief but intense thunderstorm late the night before, so the air wasn't as heavy as usual, and the strong sun seemed to burnish, rather than broil the skin of his face and limbs. His skin had darkened over the summer on account of the time he'd spent at the beach. On first glance, he was almost as dark as Shelby, but it was of course a darkness without depth that would end with the summer.

He slipped off his t-shirt, as if in a gesture of trust toward a sun that was for once intimate and gentle today. He admired the vivid blue of the sky and the bright green of the lawns he passed them, and his mind was free of all thoughts of death, or other such difficulties, when suddenly, turning in his direction off of a street ahead that led into the development from off the highway, he saw a white convertible driven by a pale woman in dark glasses and hair the color of blood.

It was Dora. She stopped when she recognized him and honked, and Victor paled and crossed his arms across his bare chest like a woman. His t-shirt was slung over his shoulder and he clambered into it as frantically as if he had been caught completely naked. Dora pulled her car up and looked across the passenger seat at him. Her amused expression and her dark glasses made her seem older, almost grown up.

"Out getting some sun?" she shifted the car into park and peered out over the black rims of her black lenses.

"No," said Victor. "I'm just... walking."

"Walking where?"

"Nowhere."

Dora reached to her dashboard and turned down the radio. "I'm on my way to your house," she said. "Do you want a lift?"

Victor looked with no little lust at the burgundy vinyl interior of Dora's vintage Mustang convertible. It really was a beautiful car.

"I'm supposed to stay away, I think," he said.

"From what?"

"You know. Whatever you and Shelby are going to do."

"The ceremony?" Dora looked over her sunglasses at him again. Her eyebrows, he noticed, were plucked into a thin arch.

"It's not a big deal," she said, "Did Shelby tell you you had to stay out of the way?"

"No…"

"Then don't. Maybe you can help."

The last thing Victor wanted was to be a part of a healing ritual, but he got into the car. Once he was in he fastened his seat belt, then blushed when he noticed that Dora hadn't bothered with hers. She was wearing, aside from her sunglasses, a loose white dress belted with a scarf. Holding back her hair was a white scarf wrapped so thickly around her head that it looked as if she was wearing a turban. "Do you want to ride around for a little while?" she asked with a knowing smile, as if she'd read his mind.

Without waiting for an answer, she turned into the nearest driveway, and turned around and headed back out towards the highway. At stoplight after stoplight heads in closed cars turned to admire the Mustang, and Victor coolly ignored them as if he were accustomed to such luxury and envy. At the edge of town Dora made a U-turn and headed back towards the neighborhood. Once they turned into the subdivision, she slowed the car almost to a stop, looked over her sunglasses at Victor and said, "I hope he's not going to die."

Victor knew she meant Uncle Buzz. "Me too," he said, "But it doesn't look good."

Dora brought her car to a complete stop and put it into park. She sighed and took off her dark glasses, and looked at her reflection in one of the lenses. "Shit," she said, "That sucks. I like him," She put her glasses in her lap. "You know what?"

"What?"

102

"My father's dead," she said. "and he'd still be alive if it wasn't for me. I have to live with that every day. I don't know why I'm telling you this," she smiled. "I guess I just trust you."

Unconsciously, Victor reached for the car door handle.

Dora looked at him. Her blue eyes, underneath her plucked eyebrows, were clear and dry. "He died in a car crash. Two summers ago. He lived up near DC, in Alexandria, and he was coming down, because I'd called and upset him, and he was easy to upset, he had a lot of issues. He was a big shot Episcopal priest at a really rich church. I just had a big fight with my mother, because she was getting serious with my stepfather, and I hated him. I knew that if I got my dad worried enough he'd step in, so I called him, and I made it all sound a lot worse than it was. Nobody's sure exactly what happened, but he went off the road somewhere around the state line. My mom and my stepfather didn't even know he was coming. If they had, they would have stopped him . . . or tried at least. He'd still be alive today."

Dora put on her dark glasses again. Victor felt stunned. It was the saddest story he'd ever heard, and yet Dora spoke with flat detachment. If what she was telling him was true, and Victor had a sinking feeling that it was, then Dora was bearing, perhaps, the heaviest burden that a person could bear in the world- a feeling of responsibility for the death of not just another person, but of a significant person, a loved one. It was a burden the weight of which Victor could not even imagine- he only had his own timid shortcomings to bear. He wondered, suddenly, what it must be like for his mother to raise on her own such a miserable son as he had proven to be. He thought, with a contrition as painful as it was fleeting, of all of the meals that his mother had cooked over the past year that he had been too depressed, or simply too spiteful to eat. He had never thanked her for a single thing.

"So there you go," Dora said. "I don't know why I'm telling you all this," she repeated, "I haven't even told Shelby... I mean, I've told her that my dad died... but not... not that I killed him," she said this last with a note of challenge.

"You didn't kill him," he couldn't bear not to deny it. "You didn't *want* him to die."

"It doesn't matter," she said. "If it wasn't for me he'd still be alive." Dora started her car and began to drive toward Gum's house. "I'm not his only child," she went on. "He had a baby boy with his second wife. I guess he's not a baby anymore. I don't know. I've never seen him… my own brother. They didn't take him to the funeral. One of these days, I guess I'll have to meet him. He'll be curious, don't you think… when he grows up… about what happened to his father?"

"Yeah."

"I bet he'll hate me. I would."

Victor turned in his seat and did what he never before in his life had ever been able to do for another human being. He placed his hand on Dora's flesh- on her soft, pale, round shoulder, and immediately took it away, to give her comfort.

By the time their grandmother got home later that afternoon the ritual that Victor had refused to watch was long over, and Dora had long since left, but Uncle Buzz's room and the area of the hall just outside still smelt strongly of burnt incense and sage. Victor and Shelby waited for their grandmother to sniff suspiciously and accuse one or the other of them, most likely Shelby, of smoking marijuana, but if the old lady smelled anything at all, she didn't let on. She grumbled her way into her room and took awhile changing her clothes, then knocked on Shelby's door and told her to order a pizza or something; she didn't feel like cooking.

They ate their pizza in front of the television, which Shelby had tuned to a program chiefly consisting of rap music videos and inane commentary, all of which was unspeakably lewd but which Gum was obviously too preoccupied to object to or even notice. However, it wasn't until there was a relatively placid commercial break that she said, not looking at Shelby, but at the television screen, "They moved your daddy today."

Shelby reaches for the remote and turned down the volume. "Is he any better?"

Gum hesitated before answering. "Yes."

Shelby put down her plate. "So his kidneys are working?"

There was another pause before Gum said. "No."

The old lady and the young woman looked at one another for a long, long moment. It was Shelby who broke the silence. "So that's all they're going to do? Stick him in a room to…"

"There's nothing else they can do, Shelby."

"What about dialysis?"

Gum shook her head. "That's not going to help his liver. Only thing that will is a transplant, and that ain't going to happen. They're going to keep him comfortable, and…"

"…and let him die," Shelby stood up, her fists clenched by her sides, then sat down again and put one set of knuckles to her teeth. "Motherfucking shit," she said through them.

Gum's lips compressed. "Shelby," she said sternly. "It's not time to give up hope. There's always God. Miracles do happen."

Shelby turned to Victor, who was sitting on the couch on the other side of her, and gave him an outraged, imploring look, as if rally him to her cause. But when she turned back to her grandmother, she said nothing, but wrapped her arms around the old lady. Victor gulped.

Gum patted her granddaughter's back with her freckled, veiny old hand and the two of them clung together, rocking slightly.

"Oh, me," said Gum, "I don't know what were going to do," she detached herself from Shelby and smoothed the girl's unsmoothable hair in a gesture that was at once intimate and distancing. "Don't give up, sugar," she said. "He ain't gone yet."

"I know," Shelby whispered.

"I just can't believe…" Gum stood up and held her arms out, palms up. "That it's God's will for a mother to have to bury her child. It's against nature."

With that she went into the kitchen, and Victor suddenly remembered an image from his Catholic childhood, a picture that he must have seen in church or Sunday school; a picture of a statue of a woman who must have been the Virgin Mary cradling in her lap a skinny, naked, and lifeless adult male body. Beside him Shelby, having reassumed her usual stubborn composure, rose from the couch and groaned and announced that on top of everything else, she'd just started her period.

There was a brief clatter of dishes and Gum appeared at the opening in the wall that divided the kitchen from the living room. "Shelby!" she half whispered, half screeched. "Good Lord! Keep that to yourself!"

There was still the faint odor of burning sage in Uncle Buzz's room when Victor retired for the night, and it was this, perhaps, that kept him from being able to go to sleep. Not for the first time he wished that there was a television in Uncle Buzz's room like there was in Shelby's. After half an hour of staring helplessly into the dark, he turned on the lamp on the bedside table and rolled himself out of bed and began to pace around. In the weeks since he'd been sleeping in there, he had kept his clothes and things in his duffel bag that stayed unzipped just beside the closet door, he had never opened that closet, because it never occurred to him there might be anything interesting inside. He never lost the feeling that, although the room was in some sense his, in a more permanent sense it belonged to Uncle Buzz.

He got out of bed and walked over to the bureau and pulled out the top drawer. Inside it there was nothing more interesting than a collection of rolled white socks and neatly folded underwear. Noting that his uncle wore boxer shorts, he closed the drawer and opened the one underneath, where there was more underwear and a set of men's pajamas never taken out of the package. In the drawer underneath that a number of cardigan sweaters were neatly folded, and in the fourth and bottom drawer, he found an assortment of things, a leather belt missing a buckle, a couple of worn out billfolds, a tin can empty except for some residue of snuff, a cordless electric shaver that looked much used and little cleaned, and a carton of Camel cigarettes. Victor, after dismissing a twinge of conscience, helped himself to the carton of cigarettes. It would be a welcome change from the menthol cigarettes that Shelby provided, and after all, if he didn't smoke them no one would. "Thanks, Uncle Buzz," he said under his breath.

Next he tiptoed over to the closet and opened it, gingerly and with his teeth gritted lest it squeak and reveal to the women, who might, after all still be awake, that he was awake and exploring. The closet was tiny and impeccably ordered, indubitably by Gum; about a half a dozen pairs of shoes were lined like soldiers on the floor. Sets of pants, then jackets, then button down shirts hung from the bar, and on a shelf above this there sat a baseball mitt, a baseball cap with fishing lures pinned to it, and what looked like a tackle box. Victor reached for this box and opened it only to find the inevitable collection of more lures and packages of hooks and line. He replaced this and turned his attention to the jackets. These were mostly sport coats, but Victor found, fingering the sleeves in turn, that one was leather. He lifted this one out, again gritting his teeth, and examined it. It was a motorcycle jacket with a blood red quilted lining that faded to pink alongside the seams. It was an unexpectedly heavy garment, and Victors arm got tired holding it up. He put it on. It was far too wide in the shoulders, and he felt dwarfed and foolish, but after he took it off he held it by the collar at arms length, its unzipped front towards him, and regarded it with mysterious longing. He could imagine Uncle Buzz wearing this jacket no more easily than he could imagine himself being seen in it, and yet its unobtrusive presence within Gums carefully ordered closet suggested hidden romance. Victor closed the closet door like a person closing a book having finished reading a particularly sweet but impossible story.

He crawled back into bed, but immediately remembered that underneath it lay yet further unexplored territory. Tumbling out of bed and lying on his side, he reached into the jumbled darkness between the box spring and the floor, and pulled out the first thing his hand encountered, an empty wooden 81/2 x 11" picture frame. He set this behind his back and reached underneath the bed again. This time his hand brushed against fabric, and he pulled out a crumpled fatigue jacket that smelt unpleasantly of mold and tobacco. With a grimace, he shoved it back underneath and reached in again. Propped up and splayed amongst all the junk underneath the bed were at least three long wooden slats that his hand inevitably knocked loose, and the resulting clatter seemed as loud as gunfire. He grit his teeth and waited for his heart to stop racing before he reached underneath again. This time he came up with noting but a manila envelope filled with what looked like tax forms. With a tsk of distaste he shoved it back where it came from and sat up. Aside from the cigarettes and perhaps the leather jacket, there had really been nothing worth finding. And yet even now, there seemed to be something beyond himself driving him to search through what his uncle was leaving behind.

Victor lifted up the mattress from the box spring. Sure enough there was something hidden there, scattered upon the surface of the box spring were about a half a dozen thick magazines. Holding up the mattress with one hand, Victor reached with the other hand for the nearest slick magazine, and the image on the cover, of a young woman bent over the hood of a black limousine wearing only the stringiest of thongs and a pair of spike heeled, open toed shoes, once again caused his heart to race. The pictures inside the magazine were exponentially more graphic, far more straightforwardly designed to arouse and inflame than any pornographic pictures he had ever seen before, and he flipped through the pages and scanned each picture as if searching for one that would, upon his discovery, come to life, in all of its lewd availability, and gratify his longing in a way that no mere image ever could. When he had looked at every picture in each magazine, even the tiny pictures in the ads, he stacked the magazines neatly with shaking hands and placed them at the bottom of his own duffel bag, then put the duffel bag under the bed. For the first time in his life, Victor felt sure that he was doing a decent thing. It would be terrible, he realized, if Shelby or Gum came across those magazines after it was all over with. That night Victor slept well and deeply, without any dreams.

Uncle Buzz, Victor thought, looked pretty good for someone who was supposed to be dying. Victor had expected to see wires and tubes and monitors and such, but there wasn't even an IV. Uncle Buzz lay in his bed as still as a bone, and breathed in and out at a slow but steady pace. His eyes were open, but just a slit, and to Victor he seemed enviably relaxed.

It had been decided before they went to bed last night that all three of them would spend the day at the hospital now that Uncle Buzz was in a private room. Though the idea of drawing near to someone dying made Victor uneasy, it seemed a less depressing prospect than spending an entire day all by himself nothing to do, really, but poke around his grandmother's house, play with the dog, and inevitably return to Uncle Buzz's porno magazines, and wait for his father to call.

When they arrived in Uncle Buzz's room, Shelby tromped to the bedside, her sandals slapping the hard floor, and hollered at her father as if he was simply taking a catnap. "Daddy!" she called. "How are you feeling?"

The only response from the figure on the bed was a slight lift in of one of his eyelids, which Shelby interpreted as a welcoming response.

"I brought you a get well card!" she practically shouted, "It's got Woodstock on it. I'm gonna put it right here on your table so you can see!" she reached into her purse and pulled out the card she bought in the lobby gift shop, removed it from its envelope, held it for a split second in front of her fathers face, then propped it open on his bedside table. Gum gave Victor a wary look and approached the bed to stand beside Shelby.

"William?" the old lady spoke about as loud as her granddaughter, but without Shelby's determined joviality. "Mama's here. Can you hear me?"

There was no response at all from the man on the bed, though to Victor it seemed as if in the few moments since they arrived, his Uncle had become less relaxed.

"Did you have a good night? Did they look in on you?" Gum's gnarled fingers clenched around the strap of her handbag. Still there was no response from the dying man. Gum turned to Shelby. "I'm going to buzz for the nurse and see what's going on," she leaned over and pressed an orange button on the armrest of Uncle Buzz's bed.

While they were waiting, they claimed seats; Gum took a small portable plastic chair like the ones you find in conference rooms, which she pulled over to the hallway side of the bed. Shelby sunk into the recliner that was set just beside the bed on the window side of the room, and Victor leaned against the wall opposite the bed, just under the television. Neither of the women seemed to notice that there was nowhere for him to sit, and for this lack of consideration, he found himself obscurely grateful. For the first time since arriving in the town, he felt invisible, and pleasantly so.

Soon a nurse, or some hospital functionary who looked like a nurse, in loud floral scrubs, arrived, clipboard in hand, and greeted the grandmother. "Hey, Mrs. Flowers," the nurse, who was plump, white, and densely freckled, said. "He's been real quiet all morning.

110

Who's this…" she smiled across the room at Shelby, who looked away. She didn't seem to notice Victor at all.

"That's Williams' daughter, Shelby," Gum said hurriedly, dispensing with small talk. "Has Dr. Patel been in since last night?"

"I don't believe he has," the nurse's manner became haughty. "He should be in later today. I checked Mr. Flower's just before you got here, and every thing looks good, pressures 132 over 70, temps good, he looks comfortable…."

"When's the last time he got his morphine?" Gum peered at the dime sized face of her watch.

The nurse glanced at her clipboard. "Say's six-thirty. He's so quiet, and his breathings good, I wouldn't give him any more right now. I'd wait until this afternoon, at least…"

Victor pressed his back against the wall upon which he leaned, as unobtrusive as a shadow, and looked with renewed interest at Uncle Buzz. Was he aware of anything at all, with all the morphine in him? Was he as relaxed as he looked? Did it take away fear as well as pain? Was he afraid?

Suddenly Victor wanted a cigarette, badly.

Gum reached for Uncle Buzz's hand, which lay heavy and limp on his belly. "When's the last time he was turned?" she said.

"Six-thirty," the nurse's lips compressed.

"It's about time again, isn't it?" Gum stroked Uncle Buzz's forehead.

"I'll send an aid in," the nurse turned on her heel and her rapid, furious footsteps faded down the corridor.

Gum pulled the crisp white sheets up to Uncle Buzz's collarbone and patted his hand. "I swear," she said, to him perhaps, or to herself. "If you want something done right, you've got to do it yourself."

Shelby removed her glasses for a moment, and her eyes appeared an almost unnatural, intense, concentrated green as she looked at her grandmother. "Why don't we take him home, then? They aren't doing anything here we couldn't do with…" she broke off.

111

"It's not time for that," Gum said. Against the wall, Victor was puzzled. Then it dawned on him. Despite the inevitability of death, Gum was not prepared to give up hope. To take home her son at this point, to call in hospice, would be to admit that there was nothing left to be done. Even though Uncle Buzz was no longer being fed, and hydrated only enough to keep him comfortable as opposed to alive, the fact that he was in a hospital bed meant that, despite what the consent forms said, the invitation to death can at any point be withdrawn, and the effort to prolong the life of a dying man resumed. It was this last hope that Shelby was challenging her grandmother to forego. But Gum was not giving up, and Victor could see that Shelby was relieved.

It was a long, long day at the hospital. Shelby having laid claim to the recliner, didn't seem to want to leave it, while Victor, chairless but too restless to go to the trouble of going down to the nurse's station, as Gum suggested, and ask them to find him a chair, stood by the windowsill and watched his uncle's chest rise and fall with slow and steady breathing. For the first time he noticed that Uncle Buzz's arms and bony chest were punctuated with several tattoos, so blurred and faded by time that they looked more like bruises than designs.

There was not much conversation after the first hour or so, instead, they all watched television. Talk show after talk show aired, absorbing their attention with calculated inanity. It was following lunch that Uncle Buzz seemed to become somewhat more animate, if not exactly alert; his eyes opened from time to time and seemed to be taking in some invisible scene on the ceiling. Every once in a while he groaned or sighed, or moved one of his limbs spastically. This caused Gum and Shelby no end of concern, and even Victor felt each motion of the dying man's body with the intensity of an earthquake. With every motion Gum reached over to her son and called his name, and asked him if he was in pain, but there was never any response from him other than a lapse back into stillness. But it was not until Uncle Buzz moanings became nearly articulate that Gum buzzed the nurse to administer more morphine. By the time she arrived the dying man was clearly, if weakly, whispering the word "No..." and the grooves in his face were deepened by either pain or anxiety or both.

It was following this that Shelby, without a word either to Victor or their grandmother, lifted herself out of the recliner with a sudden sticky tearing sound as the bare flesh of her arms and calves detached from the vinyl upholstery. It was clear from her silence that she wanted to be alone, so Victor did not follow her, but assumed her seat beside the bed until she got back. From there he could see that Uncle Buzz's tattoos consisted of a crucifix on his wasted left pectoral, the lower part of which was obscured by the hospital gown, a skull and crossbones on the pale, hairless flesh of his left inner forearm, and the name Tanya, in what was once ornate, flowing script, spanning his right bicep and forming a legend for the very blurry image of what appeared to be a mermaid. To his astonishment, tears filled Victor's eyes at the sight of this, and he had to stare with all his strength at the raucous scene on the television until there was no danger of the tears falling. In the chair on the other side of the bed his grandmother drifted in and out of sleep, so Victor muted the television and watched a silent parade of meaningless images. As the only one in the room who was conscious, Victor felt at once abandoned and responsible, like a prophet of old, a shepherd of his people. When Gum woke up as her pocketbook slipped off her lap and spilled its contents onto the floor, she looked around for Shelby, and, on finding her still gone, sighed deeply. "What are we gonna do with Shelby..." Gum said to Victor, and her tone was that of an adult to another adult, plaintive yet undemanding, more an appeal for understanding than advice. Victor picked his grandmothers pocketbook and its spilled contents off the floor and handed it to her.

"I'll go look for her," he said, and as he said this, he had a mental image of his cousin, perched on the curb of the walkway leading up to the hospital lobby, so clear and familiar that it was almost like ESP, and he would believe it was if he had the inclination to believe such things. "I'll bet she's outside smoking..." he said to his grandmother, and sure enough, she was.

Shelby had the habit, which Victor would imitate if he could ever remember to, of smoking almost an entire cigarette without using her fingers, but simply holding it in the corner of her mouth. This gave her normally rather square, gap-toothed face a squinty pugilistic expression that she seemed wholly oblivious to. If she spoke while smoking in this manner, her voice was that of a lady pirate, tight lipped, throaty and growling, and when she removed the cigarette every few moments to flick the ash, her countenance changed so completely that it was as if she has removed a mask. Victor wondered where she picked up such a remarkable habit.

When he joined her on the curb, she gave him only the most cursory of glances and continued to puff away on her cigarette, the fingers of both her hands interlaced and clenched together in the dip of her skirt between her knees. He told her that Gum had fallen asleep.

"She hasn't been sleeping at night," Shelby growled. "She hasn't for days. She's gonna make herself sick."

Victor was alarmed. If Gum hadn't been sleeping, she'd probably heard him snooping around the night before. "Have *you* been sleeping?" he asked Shelby.

"I can always sleep," she growled. Flicking her ash, she looked at him. "What about you?"

"Oh, yeah," he said. Shelby smiled, or perhaps smirked, replaced her cigarette, and placed each hand upon a knee as if she was about to stand up and leave. Behind them, a steady stream of humanity entered and exit through the revolving door of the hospital lobby. Victor felt a sudden dread of the prospect of going back up to Uncle Buzz's room. "I never noticed," he said, "that Uncle Buzz had tattoos."

"He was in the service," Shelby said tersely. "What do you expect? Probably half the men his age who live in this town have tattoos. It's a part of the culture."

Victor felt something relax in his soul. Despite the scowl and the growl, Shelby was still 100% Shelby, who loved to talk of culture as if it explained everything.

"These days," she went on, around her cigarette, "every dumb-ass kid with permissive parents or any college idiot with a little bit of money has some kind of tattoo, but it wasn't like that in daddy's day. Even granddaddy had a couple of tattoos... I don't remember what they looked like. Gum, I'm sure, remembers. At least I hope she does. I don't know if Uncle Eddie has any or not..."

As always, it took Victor a second to remember that his father was Uncle Eddie. He emitted a harsh, barking facsimile of a laugh, "No."

Shelby stubbed out her cigarette and looks at him. "I guess that's not surprising," she says. "They're like oil and water, my dad and your dad. Being in the Coast Guard was just about all they had in common. Besides having the same parents. I wonder if your dad will even come to the —" she left the word funeral unspoken.

"I don't know."

Shelby's tense smile faded into a softer expression. "It's not a big deal," she said.

The silence that ensued between them, punctuated as it was by the rush of cars on the roads somewhere in the distance and the jumble of voices and footsteps as people bled in and out of the hospital building, was comfortable. Victor was seized by a sudden melancholy that was sweet in comparison to his more familiar depression. It was, he realized the anticipation of homesickness. He would miss this place beyond imagining when he had to leave it.

115

Shelby interrupted his melancholy with a deep sigh. Victor looked at her questioningly.

"I want to go home," she said. "I want to go to my room and crawl into bed and do nothing but watch TV and listen to my music. I can't stand hospitals. I wish Gum would just let them bring daddy home. That would be better, I think. Don't you?"

There was nothing for Victor to do but nod, to agree with her, since, after all, the matter was out of his hands.

"She won't do it, though," Shelby said this matter-of-factly, without any discernible bitterness. "She's going to leave him here and stay right by him if it kills her. She just can't stand the thought of –" she broke off and it seemed to Victor that her gaze was following the ascent of a lark from the interior of the pine woods in the distance into the open summer sky. When the lark reached the distance at which it gradually became invisible, she continued as if there had been no pause, "him leaving."

That afternoon was long and quiet. All together, they alternately watched Uncle Buzz and the television as the hours passed, the tedium mitigated only by the arrival of various hospital functionaries as they went about the business of attending to Uncle Buzz, who throughout their ministrations remained silent and oblivious. At one point a timid, balding, bespectacled young man in a dark suit came by and introduced himself as the chaplain, and asked them if he could visit with them for awhile. After an awkward moment, Gum dismissed him with the lie that they were expecting a visit from their own pastor and the little chaplain nodded and smiled with professional sensitivity and left, clearly relieved. When the five o'clock news came on, Gum stirred and said that she needed some fresh air.

"Are we all going to stay the night?" said Shelby, who was fanning herself ineffectually with the perforated insert from the magazine on her lap.

Gum rubbed her forearms as if they were cold. "I am," she said. "I'll take ya'll back to the house and leave you some money for the pizza boy, and then come on back here. He's been so quiet I just don't want to leave him. I just…" She shook her head vigorously, shrugged, and hefted the strap of her purse onto her shoulder, "I just think someone ought to be here."

"I'll stay," Shelby said as she crumpled her makeshift fan into a wad in her fist.

"No, honey," said Gum, "you go on home and relax. I'll call you if anything happens. And Rhoda told me she'll bring you here if you call her and Ed." Rhoda, Victor remembered, was his grandmother's neighbor just down the street, a heavy, fiftyish woman with a Long Island accent.

"That's stupid, Gum," Shelby grunted and the footrest of the recliner went in and she was propelled into an upright sitting position. "I'm staying too. If you think you should stay, then I think I should stay."

"Shelby…" Gum closed her eyes behind her slightly tinted bifocal lenses, and there was a kind of concentrated repose about her countenance as if she was searching patiently for the right words. Victor had never seen his grandmother look so thoughtful. "Shelby, I don't think there's any need. If I did, honey, I'd tell you. I just feel like I ought to stay tonight, have some time with your daddy. Honey, I've been through this before…" Gum opened her eyes and looked cautiously at her granddaughter, "…and quiet days most the time turn into restless nights. That's all. I just don't want your daddy to be by himself tonight. All right?"

"Then let me stay," said Shelby. "*You* go home and get some rest. Let me stay here with Daddy. You know I'll be all right."

"Shelby, if I went home, I wouldn't *get* any rest. You know that."

117

Shelby took this in, and seemed to assent. Then, with lightening swiftness, her expression became as resolute as that of an Easter Island statue. "I'm gonna stay," she decreed.

Gum turned her own countenance to the ceiling, or rather to the heavens beyond. "Lord," she said hopelessly. She looked to Victor, as if for reinforcement. "Looks like you're gonna be all by yourself tonight, since your cousin wants to be hardheaded. I'll take you on back to the house whenever you're ready."

Victor's long body was stiff from sitting in the inhospitable hospital chair by the window. He stretched out his legs and unthinkingly cracked his knuckles. His grandmother winced. "I can walk back," he said.

Gum bristled. "You can not!" she cried. "It's more than two miles! In this heat! Boy, you're crazy!"

She said this last completely without guile, and Victor's heart warmed. "Maybe. I really want to walk. I've been sitting around all day."

"Well," the old lady sat back down in her chair, as if overcome by this fresh and unexpected display of willfulness from another quarter, "I'd be more than happy to drive you." But her heart was not in the struggle with Victor as it had been in the struggle with Shelby. Before long she wrote Rhoda's phone number on a receipt she pulled out of her pocketbook. She then announced a second time that she needed some fresh air, meaning a cigarette, and she left Victor and Shelby alone with Uncle Buzz.

Sure enough, as soon as the old woman was gone, there came signs of life from the figure on the bed. The legs moved in a slow, halting motion underneath the crisp bed sheets, a hand lifted slightly, the mouth and eyes opened for a moment, then closed again. Shelby scrambled to her feet and leaned over her father.

"What is it, Daddy? Do you need anything?"

The rheumy, pale blue eyes opened again then just as soon closed with a decided air, as if he had opened them just to confirm that there was nothing worth seeing. Earlier the dying man had been turned on his side to face the window, and in the afternoon sunlight jaundiced the pallor of his face made his countenance seem as bright and translucent as the moon. The delicate blue veins across his temples pulsed in a simple steady rhythm. He inhaled and moaned, and the sound was like that which Victor made when he dragged himself out of bed each morning. Shelby, clearly alarmed, looked at Victor with wide open, fierce eyes.

"He's in pain," she said. She reached for the call button that rested beside her father's pillow and rang for the nurse. Although there was no further sign of distress from the man on the bed, after a minute passed Shelby pressed the call button again hard and insistent.

A mangled voice of a woman, came over the intercom, "Can I help you?"

"Mr. Flowers is having pain," shouted Shelby. "It's time for his morphine."

"Be right there," the voice said, after a pause.

It seemed like an eternity before the nurse arrived with the medicine cup and swab with which they administered Uncle Buzz's morphine directly onto his gums. She was a large, not fat, but a robust looking woman with thick, reddish hair held in one single swaying braid, and constellations of freckles on her face. She was younger than most of the other nurses and there was something about her that suggested that she was infinitely more intelligent. She eased Uncle Buzz's mouth open by gently pressing a spot just above the hinge of his jawbone. In small motions that seemed as orchestrated and effortless as a dance, she swabbed his gums. When this was done she stood up, and Victor could see that she was taller than him and far broader, particularly in the shoulders and hips. She nodded at Shelby.

"That should make him feel better," she said. "Was he getting restless?"

Shelby seemed daunted by the woman's unexpectedly masterful presence. "A little," she said. "He was groaning."

119

The nurse looks at the chart she brought in. She made a note in it, then flipped over a few pages. "You're Shelby?" she said, "His daughter?"

Shelby nodded.

The nurse smiled, revealing large, square, slightly yellowed teeth. "I'm Jackie." She held out her hand, which Shelby took. "I've been looking after your dad most evenings since he's been on the floor. Your grandmother's told me all about you. And this must be…" she turned to Victor, holding out her hand, "Victor."

Victor nodded. The nurse's gaze was as direct as a pointing finger. Her grip on his hand was firm and sure and did not linger. She turned back to Shelby. "How are you doing?" she said, and it is clear she was not just making conversation, but that she expected an honest answer.

"Fine." Shelby's voice was clipped.

The nurse stuck her pen in the breast pocket of her scrubs. She looked down at Uncle Buzz. His mouth was open and his breathing was very slow, but deep, like that of a sleeping baby. "He's resting now," she said.

The nurse moved toward the door, and Shelby's shoulders, held tensely in a position higher than normal as her delicate brown hands griped the handrail of her father's bed, lowered with relief. "Thank you," Shelby said, grudgingly, to the nurse.

"You're welcome," the nurse said. When she turned and walked out the door Shelby raised her right hand from the handrail and held up her middle finger at the woman's swaying braid. The gesture was so unexpected and hostile that Victor forgot himself and leapt out of his chair to his cousin's side and put his hand on her back. "What's wrong?" he said, his voice high with shock.

Underneath his hand, the muscles of Shelby's back were as hard as ice. She stayed still beneath his touch, and when she spoke her voice was strangled with tears. Then she turned to him, and incredibly, his arms were around her, comforting her, as her soft, damp face pressed like a child's against his bony chest. "What's wrong?" he whispered, "What's wrong?"

Against his chest her head shook as if in negation, and her voice was muffled, but he could understand her and her words, spoken against his flesh, vibrated and resounded in the very tissue of his heart. "I hate this!" she moaned.

Almost as soon as she'd lost control, Shelby regained it; she pulled away, smiled weakly, apologized and lifted her shirttail unabashedly up off of her plump midriff to wipe her face. By the time Gum got back from her 'fresh air' break Shelby was back in the recliner and seemed less embarrassed than relieved by her outburst, but Victor felt like some foundational part of himself had been jostled completely out of alignment with the rest of him. He did not have the wherewithal argue with his grandmother when she foisted a twenty-dollar bill upon him with the instruction to pick something up for himself along the way and to buy himself a bottle of water in the lobby to carry along on the walk. He thanked her and slumped out of the room.

It wasn't as hot out of doors as he'd expected. The long walk put all thoughts of his family on reserve; he breathed in the sharp salty air as he loped down the highway. By the time he got to the house, his clothes and hair were as damp as if he'd crawled out of the sound.

He stood for a good while in the cool darkness of the living room, simply savoring the delicious chill of the central air as it raised gooseflesh on his suntanned skin. After a while he stripped off his shirt and scratched his chest and belly, taking advantage of the rare privacy of the dark and empty house. He was hardly ever in this house alone. It was different than being alone at his mother's where he was so often and so completely alone that it didn't even feel like home at all.

When the telephone that rested on the kitchen counter rang he nearly jumped out of his skin. He dropped his shirt on the floor and ran into the sunlit kitchen to pick it up. "Hello?" he said, his voice high and breathless with surprise.

121

"Shelby?" The voice on the other end was female, and familiar, but he couldn't place it.

"She isn't here," he said lowering his voice far beneath his natural pitch.

"Is this Victor?" The voice on the other end betrayed amusement. Of course it was Dora. Victor was suddenly aware of how cold the sweat on his skin and clothes had become.

"Shelby's at the hospital," he said with studied seriousness, rebuking Dora's light tone. "She's going to stay the night."

"Oh, my god. Is everything okay?"

"I guess so," he said in a softer tone. "You know... they're just keeping him drugged."

"Do you think," Dora was either whispering, or the charge of her cellular phone was fading; Victor could barely hear her, "do you think maybe... tonight?"

Victor, alone in the kitchen, shrugged. "I don't know. He looks all right to me."

There was a long pause. The kitchen telephone was cordless so Victor walked back into the living room and stood beside the sofa, too nervous to sit. He could hear a blur of noise from the other end and he guessed that Dora was in her convertible, driving somewhere. She said something that he couldn't understand.

"What?" he shouted.

"I said, I need to talk to Shelby!" The tenuous connection crackled and faded. "I guess it'll have to wait."

"I guess so," Victor enunciated. As poor as the connection was, he didn't want the call to end... not yet.

Dora, however, seemed ready to hang up. "Well," she shouted over the sound of traffic, wind, and interference, "if you talk to her, tell her I called. Tell her to call me when she feels like it."

Victor nodded. Then suddenly Dora's voice came through loud, clear and intimate. "I feel so bad. Poor Mr. Flowers. He's such a nice guy. Do you think he's suffering?"

There was no answer to this. Victor floundered in silence for a moment, and then said, "They're giving him morphine."

"Oh."

"He's mostly sleeping."

"That's good, I guess."

Dora's dead father became horribly present as they avoided making reference to him. The interference from Dora's end became as constant and intrusive as hellfire. "I'll tell Shelby you called," Victor hollered above it.

"What?" shouted Dora.

"I said, I'll tell Shelby you called."

Dora's voice was as distant as the horizon, "I can't hear a word you're saying."

Victor's fists clenched. "I hate these fucking phones," he said, mostly to himself.

"It's a bad connection," Dora continued. Clearly, she had not heard him. There was a rustle of activity and then a brief moment of clarity through which he could hear her vehicle accelerating. "Look," she said, "can you hear me now?"

"Yes."

"I've been hanging out with some friends in Beaufort," she said. "I just crossed over the bridge. Are you there alone?"

"Yeah." The hair on Victor's arms stood up.

"Maybe I'll drop by for a second," she said. There was a distinct, measured coolness in her voice. "This phone is about dead. I need to recharge it. Is that okay?"

"Sure," Victor said. He picked his discarded shirt up off the floor and held it against his chest.

"Cool," she said. Her voice was beginning to fade again. "I'll be there in a minute."

"Wait —" He said, because he knew he would need more than a minute to make himself presentable, but the connection was gone. For a moment he stood holding the phone, as immobilized as a fox run to ground, and then he dashed to the bathroom where, without even pausing to cut on the light, he showered, applied deodorant. He then streaked across the hall to Uncle Buzz's room to put on a fresh shirt and jeans and went back to the living room to wait for almost a half an hour for Dora's Mustang to pull into the driveway.

Victor opened the door before she was even out of the driver's seat. He stood half in and half out of the house, watching as she made her way toward him, holding her old fashioned black patent leather clasp pocketbook and a brown shopping bag in one hand. She was wearing a loose-fitting dress covered in a pattern of multicolored modish circles. For once she wore no makeup, and Victor could see the pale sandy brown roots of her flaming red hair as she drew closer. Her appearance had none of its usual forbidding polish, and it occurred to Victor with a twinge of disappointment that, without all the effort she usually took to be noticed, she was really rather ordinary looking.

His disappointment was forgotten, however, when she gave him one of her bold, direct looks, and then smiled at him with her crooked, mischievous smirk. Without makeup on he could see that there were pale, almost invisible freckles across her nose, cheeks, and on her upper arms as well, exposed as they were by the short sleeves of her dress. She nudged past him into the house, bringing along her usual air of scented oil and deodorant and set her bags onto the coffee table. The paper grocery bag settled with a heavy *thunk*, and Victor wondered what was in it.

"I stopped by the store and picked up something for you," she said, smiling at him as she relaxed onto the sofa. "I thought you might get bored being here by yourself all night. It's in that bag there."

With all the blinds drawn, the room was so dim that Victor had to turn on the lamp on the end table just beside Dora in order to see the label of the bottle that he lifted out of the grocery bag. Even then he couldn't read it, as the whole thing was in a foreign language that he thought might be Spanish, but he could tell at least, that this was a bottle of wine and not one from a corner store. Dora, or somebody, must have spent some money on this stuff.

"Mogen David," Dora said. Her face, beside the lamp with its battered shade that had yellowed through the years like old paper, is golden light and shadowed, and her blue eyes sparkled. "The blood of Christ. They use it for Communion wine in Catholic churches."

Victor puts the bottle on the table. "Thanks," he says. "How did you get it?"

"A friend bought it for me," she said mysteriously. At the mention of this friend, Victor could only imagine the tattooed surfer from the fourth of July, even though he couldn't have been old enough to buy a bottle of wine. He picked the bottle up again and peered at the label without comprehension.

"Do you drink?" Dora said.

He looked at her, "I have." And he had, although years ago as a child. His partaking consisted of sipping the foam off of the head of his father's weekend beers. He remembered enjoying the taste, as one sometimes enjoys a sensation that is more unpleasant than pleasant, like peeling off a scab. But he had never, as they say, gotten drunk, though he always knew that it was just a matter of time.

"I thought so," said Dora, "since you're Italian."

Victor laughed. Why his cousin and her friend insisted on thinking of him as an Italian when he himself never did would never cease to puzzle him, but if it made him seem less uninteresting to them, he wouldn't complain. "All I need now," he said, "is spaghetti."

Dora smiled. "All *we* need," she said, "are a couple of glasses." She put her elbow on the armrest of the sofa, drew her legs up underneath her skirt, and rested her temple against her fingertips. Her gaze was steady upon him.

"I'll get them," he said. He went into the kitchen and returned with two plastic stadium cups, both sporting faded illustrations of racing cars and statistics on them. Dora laughed and accepted one of them. "You know how to open a bottle of wine?" she said.

"No," he said. In the instant that it took for her to take the cheap plastic cup from him, something changed. There was no disputing now that Dora was fully in control of the situation, and that he had no choice but to follow her lead. In such a situation, truth is best. "You'll have to do it," he said.

She reached for the bag and pulled out a corkscrew and opened the bottle with a practiced air. "Sit down," she said, patting the cushion beside her on the sofa. Terribly conscious of how his underarms were sweating, despite the chill of the dark room, Victor walked around the coffee table and sat beside her, as stiff as a corpse. She handed him his cup half full of the warm, dark wine. It really did look like blood, but without blood's thickness. He lifted it to his mouth, but she held up her hand. "Wait."

He looked at her over the edge of the cup.

"We have to toast," she said. She touched the rim of her cup to the side of his. "To Shelby," she whispered.

To do something in Shelby's name without Shelby's knowledge, especially while Uncle Buzz was dying seemed improper to Victor, but he was so spellbound that he did not resist. He drank. He was at first repulsed by the taste of the wine and the warmth of it. It had an odd flavor reminiscent of fresh dirt, and at the same time there was sharp and sweet taste within it. It was first unpleasant, then not quite pleasant, then interesting. After holding the first sip on his tongue for a while, he swallowed and felt the wet warmth course into his body; then he took a second, fuller sip. In a short time, he drained the cup. He experienced a very satisfying, slow heat in his cheeks and in the deepest pit of his stomach. He felt as if his eyes were shining like coins. He looked at Dora and grinned.

"More?" she said.

He nodded and she lifted the bottle and filled his cup with just a bit less than before. She sipped her own wine delicately, looking at him over the plastic rim of her cup, and he wondered what she was thinking. For a split second, he felt a stab of fear that he had somehow made himself ridiculous, but the next swallow of wine dissolved this last resistance and he abandoned himself to the sweet taste and the warmth. When his cup was empty he reached for the bottle himself, but Dora put out her hand to stop him, closing her fingers around his wrist.

"Wait."

Despite the wine, Victor's mouth went dry as a bone and his heart began to thud in his chest. The sound of his pulse in his ears was so overwhelming that it was like a helicopter descending on him from directly overhead. Dora's grip on his wrist loosened, and her fingers, cool as a breeze from the sea, interlaced with his.

She leaned toward him, placing her other hand on his denim covered knee. The alcohol flared and glowed in his belly like some internal sun. Dora lifted one eyebrow and made a small humming sound. "Your lips are as red as mine," she said. "It's beautiful."

He opened his mouth to speak, but suddenly her own mouth was against his, and her tongue, cool and sweet from the wine, was flickering against his teeth. Though his flesh was paralyzed by the novelty of the situation, he felt something within him retreat, as if in terror of the obliterating intimacy of this contact, leaving him numb, and with only the voice of some deep, detached inward observer left to tell him what to do. With his free hand he reached for Dora's breast, and upon encountering its surprising softness, some feeling returned. Grinning against his mouth, Dora shifted her whole body towards him then pulled back to look at him, one purple painted fingernail between her teeth. Her usually straight red-brown hair was rumpled, and he lifted his hand to stroke it.

She tossed her head. "I should go," she said and she pulled away, but he caught her by the wrist, as she caught him, and he did not release her.

He was still on the sofa, his face buried in his hands when the roar of her Mustang's motor and the screech of its tires as she backed out of the driveway and tore off down the street signaled her furious departure. He told himself that it had been a dream, a nightmare of unsurpassed and sinister vividness, conjured up by his deepest fears to alert him to their hidden but powerful existence. True to the most desperate cliché, he pinched himself savagely, on the inside of his thigh, but there was no change, no awakening. It was no dream.

He took in a breath and released it, a long, shuddering sigh. Despite the fact that he knew he could not escape what he had done, a fresh defense arose against it. He decided he must have been imagining things. Stuff like this only happened in the movies, real people like himself did not do such things, did not lose control in such humiliating ways. But it was no good. He had thought, once, that people like him did not get sent away to psychiatric facilities, but the truth was that they did. The things that happen to you, and the things you do, are equal in horror and absurdity to anything that you could ever dream or imagine.

Finally, as the sun set outside, gradually dimming the light that came in through the kitchen doorway, he told himself that at least he did not rape her, that it wasn't rape. And, because technically this was true, he was able to lift his head and gaze without seeing the last pearly vestiges of daylight fading to dusk in the kitchen doorway. It wasn't rape because he hadn't entered her, it wasn't rape because he hadn't even got his clothes off, or hers off of her, it wasn't rape because, in the end, she had no trouble flailing and kicking him off of her, it wasn't rape because he lost control the very instant he managed to press his relentless body's full-length against her struggling body, it wasn't rape because of any restraint on his part, but because of his lack of restraint. It was an act at once brutal and pathetic, and the worst part of it was the nagging feeling that would not go away no matter how wrong he knew he was to feel it, that Dora was the one to blame for what he'd done.

Just the sound of her name in his mind was enough to make him moan with shame. He stood and the cold dampness against his thigh made his stomach turn. His impulse was to go to the bathroom and take off his clothes and take a shower, but it seemed pointless now to even try to wash the reminder away. He could shower all he wanted, but he would never be clean again.

He stood in the middle of the living room where he spent his first week or so in Morehead City. The conditioned air, the shadows of pictures on the wall, the blank eye of the television, the still, heavy curtains on the windows- all the furnishings of this room had come to feel, in many ways, like a part of his soul. He had become fond, over the weeks, of their novel familiarity, so evocative of his grandmother's guileless bourgeois sensibility. He felt like he had desecrated the innocence of this place. Despite his better judgment, he clenched his teeth and fists and gave himself over to a shudder of rage at Dora for having brought to pass this worst of all possible things. He would kill himself, if he thought for one moment that she would not take pleasure in her triumph over him. Then he remembered how her father died, and suddenly he sank to his knees. He really couldn't kill himself, now, for that would be to magnify the injury he now accepted that he had visited upon Dora, who in the end was far more helpless and lost than he. Come what may, he was going to have to live with what he'd done. With nothing left inside to comfort him in his total defeat, he went outside and to the backyard in search of Lily.

Lily obliged him by trotting up to him and wagging her tail when he let himself in through the fence into the backyard. After having her belly rubbed her interest was diverted by an itch in the area of her abdomen just before where her tail began, and, bending her snout to her groin she gnawed at this spot unselfconsciously and with determination. Thus ignored, Victor left Lily to that undignified exercise as the fireflies shone their uncanny, short-lived lights in the deepening dusk.

Back in the living room, he saw the open bottle of wine and the two garish stadium cups still sitting on the coffee table. Before he could stop to feel or think anything, he picked up the cups, took them to the kitchen sink, squirted liquid detergent into each of them, filled them with warm water, scrubbed them with the sponge that sat behind the faucet, rinsed them, dried them, and put them away. It was a routine so ingrained from his work at the restaurant that he could do it without thinking about how the cups got dirty in the first place. He went back into the living room for the wine bottle and brought it to the sink with every intention of emptying it down the drain. It was a great big bottle, barely tapped from what he and Dora drank, and it was still heavy with the dark red wine inside. Victor held the bottle by the neck up to the light that glowed on the ceiling, and he could not help but appreciate the bloody, haunting beauty of that deep red color. More so than the earthy taste of the stuff, that rich scarlet color cried out, it seemed, not to be poured down the drain, not to be wasted, especially when there was so little else now for him to take pleasure in now that even sex had failed to free him from who he was. The bottle that held that color, and the memory of the warmth inside him as it went down, stayed his hand. He set the bottle in the sink, his arm tired from just a few seconds of holding it up to the overhead light. Dora had taken the cork, still impaled upon the corkscrew when she left; she'd shoved it, along with her cigarettes, lighter, and cell phone into her purse.

She had not left in such a hurry that she hadn't stopped to gather her things together. She had pressed her knee against his crotch and pushed him off of her after that as easily as if he'd been an overfriendly puppy. After the initial struggle, she was not panicked, or even frightened, it seemed to him, only mad. She'd pushed him off her and screeched that he was an idiot. Not a rapist, not an animal, not even a pervert, not a bastard, or an asshole even, but just an idiot. She had reacted, in the end, as if what he had done had been no more than a nuisance; he might as well have spilled the wine on her dress. And yet, she had left. She had driven away screeching her tires like someone being chased. She'd made the most of it and the least of him in the end, and yet he could not help but see that this was only the beginning for her, that what he had done would only further her advent into a perilous world where she would continually be weakened by her delusion that she was in control of some uncontrollable forces. But what could he do for her now? He'd said over and over to her after she'd pushed him off her and stood up panting until she'd told him to just shut the fuck up, that he was sorry. All that was left for him to do, that he could see, was to clean himself up, take the rest of the wine to the room he shared with Uncle Buzz's things, and drink from it until he was able to sleep.

That he did, and though he had not half finished the bottle before he found that he was seeing double, he was able to crawl into Uncle Buzz's bed with the feeling that he had accomplished a mission. Sleep came almost immediately, bringing strange, unremembered dreams, and he woke up early the next morning with an erection, a painfully full bladder, a dull headache, and a mouth that felt and tasted like he had spent the night eating ashes. Dragging himself into the bathroom, he urinated endlessly, which relieved him a little, and afterward, he squinted into the mirror. His face was as pale and mealy looking as the meat of a baked potato, and the inside edges of his lips were rimmed with a dry black crust from the red wine. The memory of Dora returned, and he watched himself cringe. His face was an awful sight, and he looked down into the slate-colored porcelain sink, filmy with the residue of countless spits of toothpaste. He brushed his teeth and wet his face, and afterward, except for a headache, felt much the same as he felt any other morning upon just waking up, achy and without energy. It was hard to believe anything devastating had occurred the night before. The sun was up; he could tell from the brightness outside of Uncle Buzz's blinds that the sky would be blue, and that the birds were singing merrily. On the floor at the foot of Uncle Buzz's bed, the bottle was still heavy with wine. He carried it into the bathroom and emptied it into the toilet without the slightest hesitation. He rinsed the bottle under the bathtub faucet, dried it and stowed it under Uncle Buzz's bed. He went to the kitchen where the morning sunlight blazed in through the south and east windows and asserted itself like a spirited guest. Victor gulped glass after glass of water like a man who has just crawled in from a desert. Then something within him revolted and he vomited a tiny bit of sour water into the kitchen sink. He then giggled. Suddenly he felt quite giddy. It was as if the cold, bracing water, which felt so good going down in a totally different way than the wine, had him drunk all over again. He got so lightheaded he had to sit down, so he went to the kitchen table and sat for a long time. As long as he didn't see that sofa, he felt okay.

Gum and Shelby drove up sometime later, while Victor was in the sloppy process of sweeping coffee grounds off the floor that he had spilled after making himself a pot. They came into the kitchen looking at once exhausted, restless, and clearly sick of one another's company.

"How is Uncle Buzz?" Victor asked leaning on the broom.

"Quiet now," said Gum. "He had a long night, though. Agitated. They couldn't keep his throat clear. I had to keep suctioning him."

"*We* had to keep suctioning him," said Shelby.

"It was a hard night," said Gum, "and I'm worn out. I need a few good hours in my own bed before we go back, or I'm going to get sick myself. And Shelby, the same thing. I want us all to be ready to go on back to the hospital by three, even you honey." Gum looked over at Victor as he dumped the coffee grounds in the trash and propped the broom back in its corner. "You're Daddy's on his way." Gum looked mildly triumphant. "He's gonna be here around three, he says."

Victor had a vision of himself picking the broom back up and running through the house with it, knocking over lamps and chairs and stabbing it through windowpanes.

"Your daddy, and Martha, and the little boy, and the baby." Gum's voice was bright with forced cheer. "They'll be here around three. I'll finally get to meet my third grandbaby. Madison. I wonder where in the world they got that name, for a little girl."

Across from Victor, Shelby snorted.

Victor tried and managed to think of something neutral to say. "Where are they going to stay?" he asked his grandmother. *Not here!* He pleaded silently.

"At the Ramada on the beach," Gum smiled. "Your daddy used to play baseball with the night manager there, and he got off season rates. Ain't that nice? 'Cause they may be here a good while, depending on how things go." This last statement, made off the cuff, seemed to cast a pall over her, and her eyes blinked several times, her mouth set into that familiar pursed line. His father would not be on his way now unless there was a good chance that Uncle Buzz would be dead and buried before he had to spend too much money at the Ramada Inn.

"I haven't met Martha yet, either, or the little boy," Gum said. "'Course I've spoke to her on the phone, several times. She seems real sweet. Have you talked to her any, honey?"

"No," said Victor.

"Well, she seems real sweet." Gum brushed the front of her blouse in a nervous motion and stood up. "Well, I'm gonna lie down. Shelby, you need to do the same."

"You think so?" said Shelby.

"Smart mouth," said Gum mildly, and walked out of the room.

Left alone, Shelby and Victor regarded one another across the kitchen table. "That old lady's about to drive me crazy." Shelby said removing her glasses and rubbing her face with one hand. "She wouldn't shut up all night. She called your father four times and bitched at him until he promised he'd drop everything and come today. I don't know why she insisted he get here so soon; Daddy's vital signs are still good." Shelby replaced her glasses and looked at Victor. "It's more for her than for Daddy. She's getting edgy. She wants your father to come up here and take over, make some decisions."

Victor was silent for a long moment. "He won't," he said finally.

Shelby nodded. "I know," she said. "Gum knows it too. But she's got to try, you know…"

Victor nodded. The prospect of his father's family's arrival loomed before him like a wall of infinite dimensions, unsurpassable, insurmountable. All he could do was stand helpless and still before it, and wait.

Across from him, Shelby yawned unselfconsciously like Lily, scratched her head, and sighed. "So what did you do last night?" she said wearily.

"Nothing," said Victor.

Once his grandmother and Shelby went to their rooms, Victor decided that he could use more sleep. He still felt the effects of last nights' wine; the dull pain in his head, though weakened, was still there. He awakened after a couple of hours feeling much better, and by the time Shelby and the old woman were ready to head back to the hospital, he was eager to get away from his own company. It was hard to believe that his father was actually coming, much less his wife and kids. The prospect of seeing his father was like the prospect of rain on a clear day, it just didn't seem real or possible until it actually happened.

They got lunch at Burger King and Gum ordered a cup of ice for Uncle Buzz. When they got to the hospital room, Victor could see right away that his Uncle was different than the day before. While he was not exactly conscious, he was more responsive. His half open eyes looked at his mother and daughter when they spoke to him, but he did not answer or even seem to realize that it was him to whom they were speaking. From time to time his fingers picked restlessly at the sheets that covered him up to his collarbone, and his breathing, while regular, didn't have the depth that it had the day before. For all of that, he seemed comfortable enough. Shelby and Gum, having grown accustomed over the night before with this more alive and yet somehow less present Uncle Buzz, did not seem the least bit disturbed or concerned by what, to Victor, was his ghastly half-lidded stare or his scuttling, crab-like sheet-picking fingers. "Hey, Uncle Buzz," he said before taking his seat right by the window, and Uncle Buzz answered him, or appeared to, by closing his eyes and becoming still for a moment.

Gum held a large ice chip to her son's lips to moisten them, and this seemed to please the dying man, for he closed his eyes as she did so, as if he was receiving a kiss. Shelby, standing on the other side of the bed just in front of Victor, lay her hand on her father's forehead, then his shoulder, and then she sighed and crawled into the recliner, turning on the TV. This, like the bright sunshine and the blue sky outside the huge window did nothing to dispel the fragile, solemn mood in the room. Victor felt like an outsider.

He turned to look out the window. It was cheering, at least, to be able to look down upon the city, at the cars and people moving about seven stories below, to look far off into the distance to see the water of the sound glittering under the sun. Beyond this the hotels on the island stood overlooking the ocean like totems, and the sparkling sea, vast and timeless, led his gaze to an indistinct horizon, where the blue of the sky and the glare of the sun on the waters surface blended into an ever present, ever receding seam of light. On the television a studio audience screamed with laughter in response to some celebrity's quip, and Victor turned from the window as if awakened from a dream and he saw that his grandmother had taken off her glasses and was holding a Kleenex to her eyes. Uncle Buzz, his eyes still half open, and his face turned to the window, was making a low, harsh, repetitive noise with the roof of his mouth that could have been snoring.

After just a few minutes of the mindless chatter of the television and the empty discomfiting sound of Uncle Buzz's breathing, Victor looked at the clock to learn that it was approaching 2pm. Another hour at least, until his father and the others were due to arrive. He tried to imagine what he would say, what he would do, what was expected of him. It has been, he had to think… at least two years now, since he last saw his father and over… six months, yes, since Christmastime since he talked to him. His father had called him on Christmas Day last year, just a few weeks after coming home to his mother's from the treatment center, it was a tense and joyless day. He had slept until well past noon that day, his mother had first attempted to wake him with an attempt at joviality, saying that Santa had come, then she had rapped on his door and demanded that he get out of bed, come out to the living room, and look at the new shirts she'd bought him.

For his own part he had not gotten his mother or anybody anything. He'd had no money. His father had called late in the

136

afternoon, and his mother, who had answered the phone, had spoken with him briefly and tersely, then held the phone out to Victor, who was watching television, and insisted that he speak. His father wished him a Merry Christmas, and told him that his gift was on the way. "I know you're glad to be out of that place!" His father had said heartily, as if Victor had just been let out of school for the summer. He remembered hearing his father's voice fading in and out, the sound of traffic in the background, which told him that his father was on his mobile phone, perhaps having thought it either necessary or diplomatic to remove himself from his new home, newly pregnant wife, and new stepchild in order to make the obligatory call to his old fat first wife and his maladjusted first child on Christmas Day. "How are you doing, son?" his father had said after a long silence during which Victor flipped through the channels of the TV.

"I don't have any money." Victor had said. "I couldn't get anybody anything."

His father had said that he had sent him some money. "It's not much," he said, "but it should help you out until you get a job."

Getting a job had not occurred to Victor at that point. He hadn't even returned to school yet, and the days since his discharge were filled with a dreadful but hypnotic rhythm of restless sleep, television, and silent meals with his mother, a life of such bottomless emptiness that it seemed eternal, like hell. It didn't seem possible that a job, or even school, would do much to alter the dark boredom of the days. He held dearly and stubbornly to his gloom out of an inchoate sense that any attempt to change things would only deepen the ghostliness he felt. His father's talk of work was the irrelevant cant of a man on another planet. He'd got up and handed the phone to his mother. That had been the last time he'd spoken to his father.

Victor stole a glance at Shelby, who appeared, with her legs tucked under her skirt and her eyes closed, to be meditating. He hoped that she wasn't, for it seemed like an immodest thing to do in the presence of someone dying, particularly someone you love. Uncle Buzz was still snoring, his eyes half open, slivers of yellow eyeball glimmering and shifting in his pale face. Gum had her hand in Uncle Buzz's hand and seemed to be deep in some reverie. Everyone, thought Victor, was in their own little world.

Victor and Shelby were at their usual smoking place in front of the hospital lobby when Victor's father arrived with his new family. It was Shelby who recognized him first; he was dashing the perspiration from his pale pink forehead as he swaggered in his familiar, bowlegged gait up the walkway from the parking lot holding a baby carrier in his left fist. A thin, but broad shouldered and large breasted blonde woman followed right behind him, holding the hand of a little dark haired boy who seemed reluctant to approach the hospital building. Shelby, stubbing out the cherry of her cigarette, squinted and pointed towards this unremarkable group and nudged Victor with her elbow. "Isn't that him?" she said, and Victor had to stare for a moment before he could be certain enough to say so. "Yeah," he said, and turned his face away, toward the moat of bark and shrubbery that bordered the hospital building.

As the little family drew closer, it became clear that Victor's father had no idea that the two teenagers sitting on the curb in front of the lobby were his niece and his own son. Preoccupied, perhaps, with the heat and the weight of the baby in its carryall, he passed them, oblivious of Shelby's scrutiny, and came to a stop before the revolving doors, shifting the carryall to his right hand and waiting for the blonde woman and the little boy to catch up to him. The little boy tugged at the woman's hand and looked up at her in that wordless appeal that young children use when they want to be carried. The woman shook her head, dropped his hand, and reached for the baby carrier.

The little boy, undaunted, tugged at Victor's father's belt, and Victor's father, as if by reflex, stooped down and scooped him up.

Watching all this, Victor felt only a kind of impersonal amazement that his father could be so close to him without recognizing him. It was only upon taking in the familiar details of his father's appearance, the loafers, the khaki pants, the salmon colored knit shirt, the thick blonde hairs on the pale pink skin of his forearms, that he felt he had to make his presence known. "Dad," he called.

His father turned and his eyes cast about for a moment until they lit on Victor's face. "Vic!" he said, shortening Victor's name in the way he shortened everybody's name, and as spontaneously as he'd picked the little boy up, he bent and set him down with a movement so swift and sure that the little boy, taken off guard, released his hold automatically. "Jesus Christ!" the man said walking over, reaching up, and grabbing Victor by the shoulders. "Look how tall you've got! When the hell you gonna stop growing, boy!"

Instinctively, Victor twisted away from his father's touch, but his father, undaunted, grabbed him back and enveloped him in a swift, backslapping embrace. This done, he held Victor at arms length again and beamed up into the boy's narrow, expressionless face. "It's been too long!" his father cried, as if calling to someone half a block away. "I barely even recognized my own son! Martha!" Victor's father released his son abruptly and turned to his wife, "Over here! This is Victor, I didn't even recognize him, he's got so dadburn big! Now how about that!"

With both the baby and the little boy in hand, his father's wife stepped forward, a tired, timid smile on her carefully made up face. She looked at least twenty years younger than her husband, closer to Victor's age in fact, and she had the frazzled air of a first-year elementary school teacher, totally swamped by the demands of an unmanageable and almost totally uncivilized set of charges. "It's so good to meet you," she said, in a tone more apologetic than anything else. "Eddie has told me so much about you."

139

Victor could only nod in reply. He looked down at the little boy, who's tiny hand was totally engulfed in his mother's, and who was staring unabashedly up at him as if he was deciding whether or not to be frightened. Returning the stare, Victor tried to remember what the kid's name was. The little boy scowled and stepped back and to the side to peer at Victor from behind his mother's rear.

"That's Jason," his father's wife smiled, "and this is Madison." She lifted her forearm to bring up the carrier and Victor bent slightly to look at the sleeping infant. To him, she looked like any other small baby, fat, bald, and without personality. Only from the soft pink and yellow of her blanket was her gender discernable. This, then, was his half-sister, the new addition to his family, the sister with whom his mother had no part. Looking down at her as she slept the magisterial sleep of the healthy, well cared for infant, he felt a definite stab of resentment. Madison, he thought, such an ugly name for a girl. And she was an ugly, snotty looking baby. In her round, pink, imperturbable face there was something of his father, though Victor could not put his finger on what exactly it was. At any rate, he could only nod in acknowledgement of her as he stepped back and looked over his shoulder for Shelby, who, thank God, was still standing right behind him. At that moment his father noticed Shelby. "Don't tell me," he said, "that this is little Shelby. God almighty, last time I saw you you weren't any bigger than Jason here. How are you doing, sugar? Remember you're Uncle Eddie?"

Victor watched as Shelby, a fresh cigarette dangling from the corner of her mouth, regarded his father. "I sure do," she said dryly in her pirate drawl, holding out her small copper-rose hand for his father to shake. "Nice to see you, Uncle Eddie."

Victor's father hesitated before taking Shelby's hand, but he took it. Victor regarded his cousin with curiosity, then it registered that she had held out her hand not so much to be polite as to politely ward off an embrace. She doesn't like him, Victor realized. Looking back at his father he saw a familiar wariness in his expression, a kind of vague, anxious, placatory smile that Victor thought only his mother could call forth. Looking back at Shelby, Victor found his sympathy careening towards his father. If looks could kill, he thought, Shelby would be killing him. And yet her expression was not hostile, it was simply bright and straight and penetrating, like a flaming sword. Shelby withdrew her hand after a brief shake, and continued to peer at her uncle as a scientist might peer at a germ under a microscope

"Well!" said Victor's father after a moment, during which his wife, with children in hand, drew up beside him as if his discomfort had drawn her like a magnet. Again Victor felt a stab of resentment. "Well, here we all are!" His father reached over and draped his arm casually across his wife's shoulder. "Let's go find Mama and Buzzy!" he said. He led them through the revolving doors and through the lobby. He hummed and jingled the contents of his pants pockets jauntily, and nodded and smiled at the other passengers as they crammed into the elevator. He hurried with no sign of reluctance into the room where his brother lay dying and where his mother, perhaps sensing his arrival, was waiting with open arms and a barrage of anxious reprimands.

For the first few minutes it was as if no one else was in the room, so taken was Gum with her latest granddaughter. After squeezing her son, greeting Martha and waggling her old fingers at the little boy Jason, she asked Martha if she could hold the baby and then commenced to coo, goggle, and murmur over the infant with such absorption that everyone else in the room, except, of course, for Uncle Buzz, laughed at her.

"Ain't you a pretty little princess!" the old woman babbled, holding the grizzling infant upright. "Yes you are! Ain't you precious. Ain't you a precious angel from heaven above! Yes, you are!"

"Would you look at that," said Victor's father, beaming. Gum had taken the baby over to her chair at the side of the bed, he walked over and stood above them. "Well, Mama," he said, "should we keep her?"

Gum clicked her tongue and held the baby to her narrow chest. "Don't you pay no attention to that silly daddy of yours." She planted a kiss on the side of the baby's exposed head. "He's just a silly old daddy, ain't he? Victor, honey," she looked around the room for her grandson, "Will you go tell the nurse that we need to find a couple more chairs?"

Victor left and returned dragging two stacked plastic chairs from the nurses' lounge, unstacked them, and pushed one towards his father and one towards Martha, who thanked him in her quiet drawl and sat down, hoisting the little boy Jason up onto her lap. Shelby, ensconced in her recliner, watched them all with her arms crossed against her chest and Victor crossed the room to take his own seat in the chair against the windowsill. In the silence that followed, Gum began to cry, removing her spectacles, shaking her head, and dabbing at her eyes with a tissue from her pocketbook.

"It's so good to have everyone together," she said in a quavering voice. "It's been too long. Too long. I wish it didn't have to be at a time like this."

Victor and Shelby looked at one another. Gum handed the baby to Victor's father and scooted her chair up even closer to Uncle Buzz's bedside.

"William?" she called, "Honey, Eddie's here. He's brought Martha and her little boy and the new baby. Baby Madison. And she's just as pretty as she can be, isn't she, with her great big blue eyes." She leaned toward Victor's father. "Go on and talk to him, Eddie. He can hear us."

Victor's father handed the baby back to his mother and cast a glance at his wife before leaning over to place his hand on the bed sheet just beside his brother's left arm. "Buzzy?" he said, with the self-conscious tone of a man forced to speak to an inanimate object.

142

There was no movement from the figure on the bed. This lack of response seemed to hearten Victor's father, who drew up closer to the bed, and placed his hand on the short sleeve of his brother's hospital gown. "Buzzy?" he said again, a bit louder. "It's Eddie. Good to see you, bubba. It's been too long. You're looking good, though."

There was a soft scrabbling noise from the recliner, and they all turned to look as Shelby hoisted herself out of it. She walked outside without a word or a glance at anyone and when she was gone Gum put her hand on Victor's father's arm and said, in a very soft voice, "She's having a hard time."

Victor's father only smiled. He squeezed Uncle Buzz's shoulder. "Little Shelby is all grown up. I know you're proud of her. She doesn't look a thing like her mama…"

"Eddie," Gum's whisper was a warning. Victor's father glanced at her, shrugged. "Well, she doesn't. Shelby looks like she does good in school. I wonder where she gets it from…"

"Eddie," Gum's whisper became merely an expression of exasperation. She cuddled the baby, who squirmed in her arms.

The little boy Jason, fidgety in his mother's lap, twisted himself free and crawled up onto Shelby's recliner where he lay his small body sideways and belly down in the seat, his bare legs and sandaled feet dangling over the side of the armrest. From this situation he twisted his head around and peered over the other armrest to scrutinize Victor.

"The kids are getting cranky," Martha smiled nervously at everyone in the room in turn, even Uncle Buzz. "I should get to the hotel and get us checked in. Honey?"

Victor's father looked up at her blankly. He reached in his pocket, and handed her a set of keys. "I'll call you around five." He spoke as if to a servant. Martha reached for the baby, and Gum stood up and handed her over. The little boy was still staring at Victor over the armrest of the recliner, his little fingers gripping the upholstery as tightly as if he was hoisting himself over the edge of a cliff.

"Come on, Jason," his mother said, tiredly. "We're going back to the hotel room. Say bye-bye to Victor and Mrs. Flowers."

Jason did not stir, but continued to stare at Victor, only his eyes and forehead and curled little fingertips visible over the top of the armrest.

"Looks like he's found him a friend," said Gum

When Victor's father returned from walking his wife and children out to their vehicle, the nurse was in the room taking uncle Buzz's vitals, turning him, and suctioning him. Victor's father stood in the doorway.

The nurse left and Victor's father took the chair at the foot of the bed that his wife had been sitting in. He wiped his face with his hand. "Lord, Mama," he said, "I just can't believe this is going on…" He looked at Uncle Buzz and shuddered.

"Eddie," Gum said softly, scolding, "William knows you're here." She gave him a look full of gentle warning, that nothing should pass his lips that would not be fit for the dying man to hear; there could be no mention of death.

Victor's father shrugged. "Is he in a, you know… coma?" He lowered his voice, "Like Daddy was?"

"No," Gum said. "He's on morphine. It keeps him comfortable, and he just sleeps." Now her voice lowered to a whisper, "Nothing but morphine. No fluids, nothing."

Victor's father grimaced. "Why?"

"Liver shut down. Kidneys shut down. His belly won't move. Nothing that goes in can come out. It would just rot in him. But it was still hard to tell them not to feed him, not to give him any fluids. A mother shouldn't have to make a decision like that."

Victor's father closed his eyes. "I know, Mama," he sighs. "I shoulda come sooner."

Gum lips drew in and seamed, and her expression became that of Benjamin Franklin on the $100 bill. "Well," she said, after a moment. "It *has* been up and down lately. Hard to know what's going to happen from one minute to the next. And you've got a brand new baby to worry about." She paused. "And Victor's been here. He's been such a good help, Eddie. You've got a good boy there. You sure do."

All eyes turned to Victor, who was rigid in his chair by the window. He blushed. Her praise, as usual, made him feel like a charlatan.

His father beamed upon him. "I still can't believe how tall you've got," he said. "When are you gonna cut that hair?"

"Never." Victor knew it would only be a matter of time before his father said something about his hair. His father hated long hair on men. "I can't understand," Victor remembered his father saying several times over the years, "why a man would want to look like a woman from behind."

Victor decided that his father deserved to be left alone with Gum.

"I'm going to look for Shelby." He rose. "She's been gone awhile."

"All right, honey," said his grandmother. "Ya'll don't sit outside smoking all afternoon, though. It'll be time to figure out what we're going to do about supper before long."

As he passed behind his father, his father craned his neck around and winked at him, as if they shared some jolly secret camaraderie in opposition to his grandmother. Victor ignored this, and abandoned his father to the old woman.

Expecting to find Shelby outside, Victor stepped out of the elevator into the lobby to see her talking on one of the payphones just to the right of the revolving door. She did not see him until he

145

was next to her, and when she did, she waved him away with a scowl. At first he was frozen with horror, certain that it was Dora to whom she was talking, and certain that Dora had told her everything. But as Shelby rolled her eyes and continued to wave him away, he realized that to some degree at least, he was still safe; for if Shelby knew, he was sure, she would not be shooing him off like he was some pesky little brother, but rather she would be piercing him with the same pantocratic glare she had turned on his father.

He went out to the curb and waited for her, for she kept the cigarettes in her big bag. While he waited he saw a pair of male Siamese twins, joined at the base of the spine but possessing separate sets of legs, making their way with a scuttling, crablike coordination, one facing ahead and one behind, out of a large white van in the parking lot, up one side of the round driveway, through the revolving doors, and into the lobby. They seemed to be in their late teens; both had crew cut red hair and wore identical red t-shirts with collegiate lettering. It wasn't until they were out of sight that it struck Victor that he had seen something that was not only interesting, but rare.

Shelby came through the revolving doors just as the conjoined twins disappeared through them. She sat down beside him at a slightly larger distance than usual. "Did you just see the Willis twins go in?" she said. "Those red haired Siamese twins? Matthew and Mark are their names. I wonder what they're doing here?"

"You know them?" said Victor.

"Sure," She said. "They're Willis's. That means we're related, somehow. On Gum's side, actually. I think Gum's mother was a Willis. Anyway, everyone around here knows them. They're famous. They've were on Oprah." Shelby lit a cigarette, handed one to Victor.

Victor lit up. "Who were you talking to on the phone?" he said, with careful nonchalance.

"Nunya," Shelby said, the cigarette clamped in the corner of her mouth.

"What?"

Shelby removed the cigarette. "None of your business. Nunya. Haven't you ever heard that before?"

"No."

"Well, you've heard it now." She smiled. "How's your dad doing up there? I saw him take his wife and the precious angels out and send them on their way."

Victor shrugged. The degree to which he was bothered by the fact that Shelby wouldn't tell him who she was taking to on the pay phone surprised him. He scowled. "He's so full of shit," Victor said.

Shelby did not disagree. She took a deep drag on her cigarette. "You know; they haven't spoken in years. Not since we were little," she said, exhaling. "They don't like each other at all."

Victor looked at her.

She nodded sagely. "My dad and your dad. They're like Cain and Abel. Daddy never said anything about it, but it's always been obvious. He would never talk to your dad on the phone. Never."

"Why?"

"I don't know." Shelby turned up her face to catch a breeze, and once again Victor noticed, as her eyes squinted and her full lips narrowed, how subtly but unmistakably she resembled their grandmother. "But I'm sure it has something to do with my mother." She mentioned this as dispassionately as she had mentioned that she and Victor were somehow related to the Siamese twins, as if as there was nothing unusual about the fact that two brothers in their family should be joined at the base of the spine, there was nothing unusual in the fact that two brothers could be separated completely by a woman.

"What do you think happened?" he said.

"What do you think?" Shelby gave him a sidelong glance.

Victor deepened his pensive scowl and remembered, with a terrible clarity, the first time he ever noticed any discord between his mother and father. It must have been back in New York, he figured, because he'd been very young and in this memory his mother was thin and sharply dressed and lively; whereas by the time he was in kindergarten she had gotten fat and was more often than not laboring under some physical complaint. At any rate, she had been a different woman on this long ago day. They were at some sort of fair or amusement park, his parents and he, and Victor was being treated with something like a snow cone that his mother was holding while wiping his face and hands as he ate. They were seated on a bench in front of a vendor, and his father, who seemed the same now as then (so little had he changed from his relationship with Victor's mother), had been watching the crowd pass and chattering about this and that while Victor and his mother, absorbed in the snow cone and the mess it made, half-listened. Even then, the times that his father was around were few and far between; he might even have still been in the military then, and so his father's presence gave the outing the air of a holiday. Victor knew that his father liked to make people laugh, and at one point he turned his attention from the snow cone his mother was feeding him to his father's running commentary, and it was at this point that his father referred to some woman passing by as a fox. Victor knew what foxes were, he had seen them in picture books and on television, they were clever looking creatures like dogs that lived in the woods and who had long, pointy noses and big grins and they were generally tricky or mean. To describe a woman as such an animal struck Victor as absurdly funny and yet somehow apt, and he began giggling uncontrollably, wriggling away from his mother's touch as she tried to wipe his hands and face clean. And a change had come over his mother at that moment that seemed to Victor as if his pretty, gentle, attentive, patient mommy had somehow gone away, leaving the stiff, cold, and angry other mother in her place. Her grip had tightened on his sticky hand while her other hand tossed the half eaten snow cone into the wastebasket beside them and then gripped his face hard by the chin and turned his face toward her. She'd wiped his mouth hard and efficiently with the napkin, then afterward, she'd balled up the sticky napkin in her hand and threw it in his father's face. His father must have thought she was being playful, for he laughed, but Victor's mother had stood up then and, still clutching Victor by the wrist, dragged him off the bench. "What's the matter, Ronnie?" his father had called out, bewildered, and with that the memory faded into a general sense of unease. He shivered as if touched by a cold wind. Sitting on the curb next to his cousin, he felt terribly alone. It was like remembering the moment that he'd grabbed Dora's wrists as she pulled away; both memories made him feel as if there is no such thing as love, only a terrible, violent need that brings people together only to tear them apart. And yet, when he looked at his cousin Shelby, he had the profound sense that nothing would ever come between the two of *them* at least, that despite everything, the bad feeling between their fathers, their short time together, their conflicting tastes, despite even Victor's assault of Dora, he and Shelby were, beyond the fact that they were cousins, friends. It was as if they were born for one another for the purpose of getting through life, linked invisibly but as surely as Matthew and Mark Willis were linked by a connection of flesh and blood. Some people were just meant to be together, Victor realized for the first time in his life.

When they got back upstairs, the door to Uncle Buzz's room was closed, and Gum and Victor's father were standing in the hallway. "What's going on?!" Shelby squawked.

"Hush!" Gum scowled. "They're giving him a bath, for God's sake. And it's about time, too. I swear it's been three days."

Shelby put her hands on her hips. "Did they check his blood pressure?"

"It's a little lower," the grandmother said. "That's all."

The four of them stood in the hall, awkward and exposed and uncomfortable with one another until the door opened and out came an orderly and a nurse's aid. Gum stalked over to the bed. "His face is as red as a beet. Look at that. Why do they have to be so rough?"

Uncle Buzz did appear unsettled; his eyes were wide open and stared at nothing. But he was unquestionably clean, his face and hands shining with lotion, his sparse hair damp, the sheets tucked crisp and tight around his still body. "William," Gum whispered, "Mama's so sorry."

Victor's father walked over to the bedside to stand next to his mother. "They woke him up," he whispered. "His eyes are open."

"I can see that," said Gum. "You better believe I'm going to call Dr. Patel about this."

Shelby crossed over to the other side of the bed. "You all right, Daddy?" she said.

Uncle Buzz turned his face slightly in the direction of his daughter's voice, but his expression remained blank and stunned, as if he'd been knocked on the head. With his sparse hair, freshly washed and shaved face, and the empty, searching expression in his wide round blue eyes he looked to Victor like a newborn.

Gum sank into her chair. "Lord." She put her hand to her forehead. "I'm dead on my feet. Just standing out in that hall for five minutes, and my legs feel like jelly."

Shelby looked at her sharply. "You need to go home and lie down, old lady. I bet *your* blood pressure's sky high. Do you have your pills with you?"

Gum sighed, "Naw. I'll be all right."

Shelby came around the bed and perched precariously on the thin arm rail of the chair Gum sat in. "Gum," she said in a low, yet childlike tone. "Let's go on home. I can't spend two nights in a row here, like I'm just waiting..." She slipped off the arm of the chair, stood behind her grandmother, draped her arms around the old woman's neck and shoulders, and spoke with her face against the old woman's neck. "Daddy'll be all right tonight. Let's go home and get some rest. I just... I just want to be at home. Daddy'll be all right. I want us to go home. I need us to go home, Gum. Okay?"

Victor felt a lump rise in his throat. He knew that Shelby was not exactly acting, but rather allowing herself to need what she knew the old lady needed, some time away from the horrible strain of being helpless and yet busy in the face of death. All at once he was seized by a powerful bittersweet envy; he could imagine, as clearly as if he was watching a movie, his grandmother and Shelby leaving the hospital, driving home, his grandmother retiring into her own room after making a quick supper and a few phone calls, and Shelby ensconcing herself in her own mysterious, but more familiar room, turning on one scarf draped lamp to fill the room with soft, muted light, lighting one or several sticks of incense, turning on her tiny television, and perching lotus style in the very center of her bed surrounding herself with magazines, her sketch diary, listening to music set low so as not to disturb Gum, and maybe even weeping before she went to sleep. That was what she needed, sure enough, Victor could see it clearly, and she needed for him not to be around. "I'll stay," he said suddenly, surprising himself with his own firmness. "I feel fine. I'll stay."

"Sugar, you can't do that," Gum sighed.

"Yes I can," he said. "Why can't I?"

"What if something happens?"

"I'll call you. I know how to use the phone..."

Shelby's face was still pressed into Gum's neck, but Victor knew she was paying attention to him as well. "Please, Gum. Let Victor stay. Daddy'll be fine tonight... I know he will."

Victor looked at the dying man, whose eyes had closed halfway. There was a long, pregnant silence while the grandmother pressed her lips together in some inward debate. "Eddie," she said finally, "Will you stay with them?"

Victor's father looked as nonplussed as if he had been asked to raise his brother from the dead. "What...?"

Gum shrugged Shelby off her. "I'm not going to let this boy stay all night in the hospital all by his self. Can't you stay with him?"

"Well, Mama, I got Martha and the kids …."

"Can't she handle them for one night by herself?"

"Well, sure, but…"

"Do you want me to talk to her?"

Victor's father slumped like a batter who has just struck out. He wiped his face with his hand and sighed, "Well, I'm damned if I do and damned if I don't." He winked at Victor. "Let me call Martha, let her know," he said, and reached to his pants pocket for his cellular phone.

"Take that out in the hall!" Gum screeched.

Victor's father sighed and winked at Victor chummily, and Victor realized too late that he was in for hours of his father's company.

Both Gum and Shelby lingered by the bedside for several minutes even after Victor's father returned. It was Gum, in the end who led Shelby away. As they left the room Gum said to Victor's father, "You call me if there's any change." And Shelby, withdrawn as a turtle into its shell, followed her grandmother meekly out.

Victor claimed the recliner, so his father lowered himself into the chair by the other side of the bed that Gum had been sitting in. Finding himself within reach of his dying brother, he scooted the chair back a bit. "Well!" he said brightly after a moment, prefacing his conversation with a chummy wink. "So how have you been, son?"

"Okay."

"How's your mama?"

"Fine, I guess."

His father's smile faltered. He looked down at Uncle Buzz's placid, jaundiced face and tsk'd. Then he looked back up at Victor. "What do you think of Morehead City?"

"I like it."

This seemed to strike his father as amusing. "Isn't that something. I always hated this place..." he broke off and seemed, for a moment to be gazing into some interior pool. "Do you remember coming here when you were little? You and me? It was right before we moved down from New York, when my Daddy died. Do you remember any of that? You must have been about three..."

"I think so."

"You were crazy about the beach," his father said. "Couldn't get enough if it. Acted like you were at Disneyland, splashing around in those waves...."

"Really?"

His father nodded. "You sure did," he sighed. "I should have brought you back later. But..." His father looked almost fearfully at the dying man between them, "You know; you don't think about these things till its too late. I'm glad you're having a good time this summer, though. You been to the beach much?"

"Yeah."

"I never cared much for it myself," his father mused. "I suppose 'cause it was always just right there. Buzzy liked it." He smiled down at the dying man on the bed. "He liked going out on the boat with Daddy. Didn't you, Buzzy?"

Victor saw, or seemed to see a movement, as subtle as the wind, cross his uncle's face. There was a long silence before anyone spoke. "Why does everyone call him that?" Victor said, "Buzz. Gum only calls him William."

His father smiled. "I started that." He leaned his chair back so far that the two front legs of it raised off the floor, and he laced his hands behind his round head. "Back when we were kids. Buzzy got ahold of our dad's clippers one day and shaved a strip right down the middle of his head. I guess he was just about five or six years old. Made your Gum so mad I thought she'd smack him right through the wall. He had this bright yellow hair… we both did… and Mama liked to grow it out some. But Buzzy was always copying Daddy, and Daddy always kept his hair in a flat top. I guess that's what Buzzy was trying to do, fix his hair like Daddy's. But he looked just like an Indian had scalped him…Mama had to shave his whole head with those clippers. In the military, they call that getting a buzz, so that's what I called him. It just stuck. Everyone called him Buzz from then on, 'cept mama and daddy." Victor's father set his chair down flat and addressed his brother. "Ain't that right, Buzzy?"

As if in answer, the dying man's entire body stirred, and his fingers began to pluck at the bed sheets. "Lord," Victor's father breathed, looking across at his son, "Is he waking up?"

"He does that sometimes," Victor said. "When he's uncomfortable. Maybe we better call the nurse." He looked at his uncle's face for a long, slow moment. The dying man's eyes were almost completely closed, he did not seem to be in pain, but the insectile plucking of his fingers upon the sheets was for some reason horrible to see, and his breathing, though regular, was a bit more labored that just a moment before. Victor supposed they should be paying closer attention to the dying man. He reached for the call button on the wall against the headboard.

"Can I help you?" the speaker above Uncle Buzz's head squawked.

Victor didn't know what to say. "Can someone come check on Mr. Flowers in Room 716? He's…" Victor swallowed, "he's moving around."

"Be right there," the speaker squawked. Victor shuddered with the effort of asking for help.

"Should I call Mama?" His father reached in his pants pocket, where the cell phone made a squarish bulge.

"*I* don't know!" Victor squeaked.

154

Victor's father froze for a moment, lifted up on one haunch, his fingertips just inside his pocket. "I'll see what the nurse does."

It seemed like forever before a nurse entered, this one a man, about Victor's father's age, tall, stocky build, with short salt and pepper hair and a trim black mustache. He was wearing mickey mouse printed scrubs. "How ya'll," he said in a hurried manner that did not invite a response. His voice was deep and fluting. He went right to the bedside, lifted Uncle Buzz's arm and strapped a blood pressure cuff around it in a series of movements so efficient and ineluctable that it was like watching a wind up toy. "120 over 70," he said after a moment, unstrapping the cuff with a brisk rip of the Velcro and looping the stethoscope across his neck. He reached in the breast pocket of his scrub shirt for a pen and wrote the number on his palm. "About the same. How are his respirations?"

"Slow?" Victor suggested.

The nurse put his hand on Uncle Buzz's wrist and peered down at his face as if into a crystal ball. "He's working hard." The nurse stood up. "Does he seem comfortable to you?" he asked Victor, for some reason.

Victor's eyes widened. "Umm… I guess? He keeps picking at the bed? Like this?" Victor made a pinching movement against the wooden strip in the arm of the recliner.

The nurse's dark eyes softened, and his mouth moved to one side and puckered, then relaxed. "I'll be right back," he said.

Victor and his father stared at each other across the bed for a moment. The nurse returned with a medicine cup and a swab, and administered another dose of morphine. "That'll make him feel better," he said. He smiled at Victor and his father. "Are you his son?" he said to Victor.

Victor was dumbstruck.

"This is my son," Victor's father spoke up. "I'm his brother." He pointed at Uncle Buzz. "His daughter was here earlier. We sent her home to get some rest. Do you think we ought to call her back?"

The nurse folded his thick, quite hairy arms across his chest. "His pressure's still good." He nodded. "He's hanging in there. I'd let her rest. Just watch his breathing. If they get much slower…and they might, with the morphine… ya'll buzz the desk."

"Okay," Victor's father said, rendered docile by the other man's efficiency. The nurse left and Uncle Buzz's sheet plucking subsided, though his eyes were wide open and stared, with a disturbing intensity, at the ceiling. Victor's father looked at the body on the bed as if it might at any moment rise up and come toward him like a zombie in a monster movie.

He shuddered and crossed his legs. Victor noticed that he was wearing loafers, a kind of shoe he had always associated with his father. He tried to recall what kind of shoe Uncle Buzz wore, and found that he could not.

"Well, son…" His father said, suddenly assuming a parental air. "Tell me what's been going on at school."

Victor gave his father a blank look.

"Come on, son. What's the problem at school? Your mother told me that you were skipping just about every day before she got wind of it. You have to go to school, now."

Victor can only regard his father's round, weathered, earnest face. He was well aware that this was a maneuver on his father's part to distract himself from the very present reality of his brother's death, but Victor suddenly felt like fighting.

"No, I don't," he said. "I can get my GED."

His father blanched. "Get your GED!" He lowered his voice to a whisper, "Victor, GED's are for niggers!"

Victor laughed, scornfully, and he could see from his father's expression that he knew he was being judged.

"Well, you know what I mean." Victor's father looked furtively around. "You're to smart for a durn GED. You'd get straight A's if you tried. You're smart as a whip when you want to be, son."

Although Victor knew that this was not true, it was nice to hear. He shrugged. On the bed between him and his father, Uncle Buzz took one deep breath and moaned.

Victor's father held his breath until Uncle Buzz' lapsed again into his noiseless, slow, regular breathing. It occurred to Victor that if his father wasn't so nervous, then he, Victor, probably would be.

The disturbance passed, Victor's father once again assumed the role of a concerned and directive parent. "You've got to get a good education, son, if you're going to get anywhere in life. I leaned the hard way. It isn't easy trying to get by on just a high school diploma. And if you don't shape up, you aren't even going to have that. Think son, where do you want to be ten years from now? Flipping burgers for six dollars an hour?"

Victor shrugged. Ten years from now seemed so far ahead that it was impossible to imagine even being alive ten years from now. He tried to imagine himself at the age of twenty-seven, working in an office somewhere, coming home each day as his father had at that age, to a wife and child. It all seemed beyond the realm of possibility, a way of life reserved for the more deserving. It was easier for Victor to imagine himself dead or in prison, or even a soldier at war in some desert, than married and working in an office. How did this happen to me, he thought, as if it had already happened, as if his lonesome destiny had been lived out already.

"I'm not smart," he said.

His father huffed, "Yes you are. Don't give me that, now. You take after your mother. Got a mind like a steel trap, when you want to. Matter of fact, I used to tell your mother that you were probably gonna end up going to law school as much as you had to argue every little thing. Just like you're doing now. If one of us said black, you'd say white. It used to drive your mother crazy."

Victor shifted sideways in the recliner to get a better look at his father, who was smiling slightly as if enjoying the memory. Try as he might, Victor could not remember being the least bit argumentative with his parents, not ever. He just remembered the two of *them* arguing.

His father's smile faded. "We had a hard time keeping up with you, son. We had a hard time handling you. You had such a sharp little mind. That's why we had to get you help, son." His father looked at Victor and shrugged. "I mean, shit, I was getting to where I'd listen to you go on and on about why people shouldn't have to take baths every day, about the water supply and chemicals and what not and you were even starting to make sense to me! And you were just a kid! Now, that's not right. You needed more than me and your mother could give you. We had our own mess to deal with, too...." His father looked away, avoided the presence in the bed between them. "Well, anyway, don't tell me you aren't smart. I think you're just lazy."

Victor was astounded at his father's words. His jaw, usually clenched tight, hung loose. His father didn't seem to notice, but continued his reverie.

"Now I'm not saying *I* was some egghead. I knew if I went to college, I'd just be wasting my daddy's time and money. I had a wild streak my damn self, son, I'm not gonna lie to you about that. But my father told me, and I'll never forget it, he said that if you don't steer the boat, the boat'll steer you right out to sea. He said the best thing for me to do, before I got myself into more trouble than I could handle, was to go into the military and learn me a trade. He said things weren't what they used to be, and a man couldn't make a good living on the water anymore." Victor's father sighed again. "Your granddad wasn't perfect – he was like your grandma, you know, always on us about something, but once he was gone I realized he saw things as they were. I signed up for the Coast Guard when I was nineteen, and it was the best thing I ever did. Now, I'm not saying that's the way you should go... things have changed, and the service ain't for everybody...God knows Buzzy can tell you that... but the thing is, you can't just drift all your life. You've got to have some direction... you've got to find out, son, what you want to do in this life. You only live once, you know…" With this Victor's father looked at him, almost pleadingly. Victor hung on every word, each revealing, as never before, a fresh insight into a world from which he sprung but had forgotten as completely as the womb.

"I don't want to go back to school," he said after a long moment, during which the only sound was that of Uncle' Buzz's breathing and the distant chatter and bustle of nurses and patients up and down the hall. "I want to work."

"Work! Doing what?" His father voice jumped into the upper registers.

"I don't know," Victor admitted.

"Well, that's what school is for," his father said. "To help you figure *out* what."

Victor knew this might have been somewhat true in his father's day, but not any more. But it was pointless to try to explain. If he ever learned what his life was for, it wouldn't be in school. This was as plain to him, and as unprovable as the conviction, that now arose within him like the emergence of some sunken pirate chest from the depths of the sea, that his uncle would be dead before sunrise.

The hours passed as slowly as Uncle Buzz's steady, deep breaths. Gum called around midnight, before she went to sleep, and Victor's father answered.

"Mama," he said after the old lady had launched into an anxious barrage of questions, "It's going to be all right. Nothing's going to happen if you take your pill. You need your rest." Victor wondered how it was that his father and grandmother, who had so little to do with one another over the years managed, in the space of just a few hours, to resume the same sort of mild, affectionate hostilities that characterized the bond between his grandmother and Shelby.

"Well, just take half a one, then, for pity's sake, Mama!" Victor's father's voice was sky high with exasperation. "It's just a tranquilizer, it's not going to kill you!"

There is a pause while Victor's father rolled his eyes. "Well, can't Shelby drive?"

Another pause. "She can't? She's sixteen, ain't she?"

Another pause. "Oh. Well, I wouldn't worry about it anyway, Mama. His pressure's good, and he hasn't been doing nothing but sleeping." Victor's father glanced sharply at Victor. "They just gave him some, not too long ago."

Another pause, in which Victor could make out the agitated squawk of his grandmother's voice. "Because they wanted to, I reckon, Mama! I don't know! Good God, old lady, if you're going to get all bent out of shape about every little thing I tell you, you might as well come on back now and let me and Victor go home! I'm telling you, Buzzy's fine, and if there's the slightest change, if he so much as gets the hiccups, I'll call you, and if you think you're too damn stoned on one half of a damn Xanax to drive yourself less than two miles to the hospital, well, I guess I'll come and get you."

A long pause while Victor's father shook his head and then wiped his forehead with one hand. "All right, Mama. I know. Just do what you need to do, and I'll call you soon as there's any change."

A pause. "He's fine. He's sitting right here with me; we've been catching up on things. He's been telling me about how he can't wait to get back to school."

A wink at Victor. "Your grandma says she appreciates you staying, and to try and get some rest if you can. I reckon she don't care if I get any rest or not."

Victor's father's stocky body shook with silent chuckles. "All right, Mama. I'll holler at you later." He hung up the phone. "My God, she'd worry the black off a coon," he said. "Still acts like she's the only one in the world with any sense." He cocked his head to one side and looks at Victor. "She's crazy about you, though. You must have been on

160

your best behavior this summer, cause if she had any complaints, you better believe I would have heard 'em. But she doesn't have nothing but praise for you." Victor's father's expression became thoughtful. "I reckon it makes sense, though. She always did love Ronnie. She liked Ronnie more than she liked me, seemed like sometimes," he said this last with a remarkable lack of resentment, "they hit it off from day one. I thought Mama might have a problem with Ronnie, her being a Catholic and whatnot, and her family all hell bent on making sure we were married by a priest, but Mama never said a word about it. I reckon she was just glad to see me hook up with someone with a little bit of religion. My Daddy liked your mother, too…as much as he liked anyone." Victor's father leaned his chair back on the two back legs again, and stretched his feet out on front of himself. "Mama acted like Ronnie was her own daughter. I guess in a way, she was."

Victor became all ears, imagining his parents and his grandmother in those bygone days. His mother still thin and polished, with styled hair and make-up, his father a bit more solid in the abdomen, a bit more hair on the top of his head, but essentially the same, and his grandmother looking as she did in that picture in the living room of herself and the man who had been his grandfather. And where had Uncle Buzz been? He looked at the body on the bed.

His father followed the glance. "Buzzy liked Ronnie, too," he said. "'Course, he was only a kid, then, when me and your mom got married. He was barely nineteen. Hell, I was a kid myself- twenty-two years old." His father laughed. "Be honest, I think Buzzy had a little crush on your mama. Wouldn't call her nothing but Veronica. Which she hated for anyone to call her, but she didn't mind it from Buzz. Said it didn't sound so bad, coming from him. She said that Buzzy was a sweet kid, and didn't need to go into the service." He snorted. "Yeah, he was sweet all right. Until you crossed him, then he was about as sweet and gentle as a damn shark. Ain't that right, Buzzy?"

The dying man, as still as usual, made no indication that he had heard, but Victor, looking down at him, sensed that there was more to his Uncle's deathly stillness than met the eye.

Victor's father leaned back so far in his chair that he was facing the ceiling, his fingers laced behind his head like a man napping, or daydreaming, in a hammock on a bright summers day. "Wasn't long after that that Buzzy hooked up with Shelby's mama Tanya, and then just like that, they were married. Didn't waste no time. Couple months after that you were born, and then I guess about six months after that, there was Shelby. 'Course we were up in New York while all that was happening. I never laid eyes on Tanya or Shelby until you and me came down for Daddy's funeral." A cloud seemed to come over Victor's father's countenance, and he lowered his chair. His forehead creased and his eyes looked troubled, downcast and purplish underneath. He looked like a man waking up with a hangover. "We were really just kids, then," he said, and though he was looking warily at Uncle Buzz, Victor knew he had no more than a superstitious unease lest his brother hear him. "Except maybe Ronnie. We were all just kids who didn't know what we'd got into, getting married and having kids. We thought… Well, I know *I* thought, that things were just supposed to fall into place. Well, maybe they do, but they won't if you let your foolishness get in the way. I was mighty foolish, back in those days. It's my fault, you know, that things didn't work out between me and your mother." Victor's father looked up. "Well, mostly my fault. Ronnie could damn sure hold a grudge," he laughed, "and I could damn sure give her reason to." Victor's father looked up at Victor. "When you start getting mixed up with girls, son…"

Victor flushed and paled, the sickening memory of what happened with Dora surged in him like a wave. His father did not notice.

"…Don't think you can get away with anything. You can't. They're like credit cards, son, you pay 'em back with compounded interest, or you end up declaring bankruptcy. It took me a long time to learn…" His father sighed. "You reap what you sow. I never wanted things to turn out like they did. I never meant to have a kid and leave him." He shook his head again. "But you've got to go on living. Even when you make mistakes, you've got to go on living. Remember that, son. There's no point crying over spilt milk."

Victor had a sudden, incredibly vivid image of his Uncle, as the little boy in the picture in Gums living room, only in Victor's mind's eye the boy was crying. He looked down at his uncle and saw that his eyes, once again, were slightly open and gleaming like slivers of moon.

Victor's father was leaning forward in his chair now, bent so low that the crown of his balding head faced Victor. His posture was that of a dizzy man trying to let the blood rush to his head. Victor wanted in that moment to walk over, kneel by his father's chair, and tell him everything, share with him the humiliation and shame he felt on remembering that moment with Dora when he wanted her to resist, wanted her to panic, wanted her to fight while at the same time he wanted to be accepted. He yearned briefly to tell of his dread that Shelby would one day find out how vile he'd been to Dora, he wanted to tell his father that he already knew, already understood, how easy it was, how inevitable, to do the absolute stupidest thing possible, to hurt people, to be led into temptations far too mysterious and hidden to be avoided. He wanted to tell his father he didn't blame him for the mess he'd made of Victor's life and of his mother's. But the longer he waited in silence and cradled deep within himself the dread of revealing himself so intimately to his father, the longer he looked at his father's shining, dejected head, the clearer it became that it was not Victor from whom his father was really asking forgiveness. It was Uncle Buzz whom he knew he had wronged, more than anybody, in some still unspoken, but increasingly obvious way. He'd fucked Shelby's mother, or at least he tried to, Victor realized, and his stomach clenched and he had to turn away, to lean over the other arm of the recliner and face the reflection of himself, and Uncle Buzz, and his father in the window that looked out upon the city, the sound, and the sea.

"Son?" his father said after a moment, "Would it bother you if I turned on the TV?"

They watched the television, which his father had tuned to ESPN, for hours in silence as the nurse periodically checked in and Uncle Buzz seemed at intervals to grow restless, then calm. At one point, during a commercial while Victor's father was dozing with his head lolling to one side, his mouth open issuing short, soft snores, Uncle Buzz opened his eyes while Victor happened to be looking at the two brothers, in turn, noting that, as facial features go, Uncle Buzz looked like an elongated, narrower version of his father with a touch more sand-colored hair left on the top of his head. As he had seen his grandmother do every time Uncle Buzz showed any signs of consciousness, Victor reached over and touched the dying man's shoulder and asked him if he needed anything.

Uncle Buzz' voice was cracked and hushed from disuse. The two syllables that issued from him were not clear.

"What?" Victor said, loud enough to make his father stir and look over. "What'd you say Uncle Buzz?"

"What's wrong?" Victor's father said, and Victor held up a hand to shush him. "Uncle Buzz?" Victor said again. "Do you need anything? Are you in pain?"

Uncle Buzz shook his head. "Naw," he said, cracked but clear. His long forehead was for one moment deeply furrowed, then smooth as paper. "Just come to pick up my shit and get the fuck out of here." His thumbs and forefingers began plucking at the bed sheets in an irregular, deliberate rhythm. His eyes closed halfway. Victor reached for the call button, but hesitated, too timid, too aware of his uncle's alertness to yell into the speaker on the wall. He slid out of the recliner, stretched upon standing up, and walked down the hall to the nurse's station.

"Can someone come check on Mr. Flowers in room 716?" The nurses looked up from their charts at him as if he'd appeared from nowhere. "He's waking up."

One of the nurses nodded. "Thanks," Victor whispered, and went back to the room. His father was leaning over Uncle Buzz's body like a child leaning over a dead jellyfish on the beach, anxious to see, but careful not to touch. "Has he said anything else?" Victor drew up beside his father and whispered.

His father shook his head and reached over to touch, as one might touch a slug, his brother's bare forearm. "He's cold as ice."

"Call Gum," Victor said. All of a sudden he felt as cool and steady as an iceberg, a solid prominence in the midst of a restless sea. His father, reaching in his pocket, turned and half walked, half ran out of the room and down the hall, in his panic forgetting that there was a phone right beside the bed.

A nurse trotted in; this one female, short, fat and young, with lavender scrubs and tightly curled red hair. She strapped the blood pressure cuff on uncle Buzz, squeezes the bulb, waits. "90 over 50," she said after a moment, "heart rate 130." She gave Victor a businesslike pat on the shoulder. "Do you need me to call someone?"

"No," Victor said.

"All right," she said. "Would you like us to call the chaplain?"

"No."

The nurse nodded. "Is his mother here tonight?"

"My dad is calling her right now." Victor reached over to touch Uncle Buzz's strange, cool, yet unmistakably living flesh. The dying man's breaths were becoming slower with each inhale, and with each exhalation there issued from deep in the man's chest a faint cooing sound, like the call of a dove. The nurse did not seem to hear it, but to Victor it filled the room. The melancholy sound was, in fact, nearly unbearable, but Victor grasped the dying man's hand, and the steadying sense of being an iceberg returned to him. "Oh my gosh, I need his chart," the round little nurse said, and she bustled out of the room.

Victor was alone, now, with the gradual diminishment of that subtle yet maddening dove's call. When this faded into silence the dying man gasped and opened his mouth as if to yawn. His mouth was open so wide that Victor could see the dark fillings in his back teeth, but there was no yawn, only a brief, breathy sound like the pant of a dog. Following this Uncle Buzz's chest rose and fell a couple of times, but Uncle Buzz was gone. Victor released the still supple, but dead hand and stood up straight. The nurse bustled in with her chart, and Victor turned to her and shook his head.

"He's passed?" She sounded surprised.

He nodded.

Her eyebrows rose. "I wasn't even gone a minute!" she said, as if Uncle Buzz had done nothing more alarming than get out of bed and go to the bathroom by himself. She looked up at the clock beside the television. "We'll say 3:36 am." She smiled slightly at Victor. "You okay?"

Victor sat down in the chair his father had been sitting in. At that moment, his father rushed back in, and over to the bedside. "He's dead," Victor said, and his voice was flat.

"What?"

"He just died." Victor said. "At 3:36."

Victor's father bit his bottom lip and his broad chest swelled. He took a deep breath, held it, and then released a sob. "Oh, Buzzy…" he said to the body on the bed. "Come on, now. Come on." Victor was reminded of how his father had often tried, with exactly those words and exactly that desperate tone, to palliate Victor's mother after one of their many fights. The iceberg feeling melted, and Victor had to leave the room. He brushed past the nurse and stood outside in the hall until he heard the ring of the elevator down past the nurse's station and his grandmother came running down the hall, with Shelby walking like a convict in tow.

As soon as she saw Victor, Gum stopped short and slumped as if she'd been deflated. He nodded his head slowly, in confirmation. "Oh My God!" she said, and with her hand over her mouth, she pushed past him into the room. Shelby, moving as if she was weighted down by some invisible yoke, brushed past Victor without a glance. He followed them into the room. Gum staggered over to the side of the bed, stood beside Victor's father, wailed, and bent over the dead body of her son. Victor, still standing in the doorway, could see her reach up to touch his face. For a moment her shoulders, her entire body, shook, then the shaking stopped. "Oh me," she moaned, "Oh me."

Shelby attached herself to the wall just to the side of the doorway. From the corner of his eye Victor looked at her as best he could. Her face was pale and still, her eyes wide. The palms of her hands pressed flat against the wall as if she were trying, like a child who does not want to be where she is, to sink into it.

After a few moments Gum turned away from Uncle Buzz and held out her arms toward Shelby, who just stuck like a moth against the wall.

"Shelby..." Gum's voice was an urgent, choked whisper, "Shelby, come here, honey. Come over here to Gum."

Shelby didn't move. Victor stepped a bit further towards her, and she warded him off with a look of pure, impersonal fury. He sheepishly avoided her eyes and walked over to stand behind his father. He gazed down over his father's shoulder at Uncle Buzz. Someone had closed the dead man's eyes. Victor wondered if his father had done that. The nurse was in the tiny bathroom, emptying Uncle Buzz's catheter bag.

When she came out, she walked over to Gum, and put her hand on the old lady's shoulder. "Mrs. Flowers," she said, "I'm so sorry. "

Gum's reply was warm but distant, as if she'd rehearsed it. "Thank you, honey. Y'all have been a blessing, you have no idea. I appreciate everything you've done."

The nurse embraced her in a formal way, as if they had just run into each other at church. "I've put a call in to Dr. Patel. He's going to come in the morning to sign the death certificate, unless you need to see him tonight."

"No, there's nothing he can do now, it's all in the Lord's hands now."

The nurse made a murmured, wordless sound. "I just need to know what funeral home ya'll are using..."

Gum paused. "Mason's, in Beaufort." On the last word her voice broke. "I just can't believe it," she wailed.

Victor's father turned to her and wrapped his arms around her in what was as much a restraint as an embrace. "You did all you could, Mama," he said. "He's in a better place now. He ain't suffering no more."

Gum's back heaved as if she were vomiting against Victor's father's chest. The heaves subsided after awhile and she broke away. "Shelby," she said, in a voice of sudden strength and clarity, "come here, child."

The nurse bustled out of the room and Shelby, unwilling but helpless, approached the bed, winced, then turned away and pressed against her grandmother, with a gasp and a shudder. She moaned while the old lady stroked down the length of her back. They stood pressed together in this way for a long time, until Shelby, her face wet with tears and her teeth clenched, broke away and bent over her father's body. "This isn't right," she wailed, and tears sprung to Victor's eyes. "Oh, Daddy..."

Shelby pressed her cheek against her father's face, now lifeless and unresisting. She sighed, and Gum took her by the shoulders, and murmuring into her ear, led her to the door. But at the doorway, it was Gum herself who could not pass through on her own strength. She returned to the bedside and looked down upon the body for a long time, the clear plastic bag containing Uncle Buzz's personal belongings, his pajama bottoms, the wallet that he called his billfold, his toothbrush, and his key chain with its AA chip, hung like a teardrop from the crook of her elbow. Minutes passed and she did not move a muscle; it was soon obvious that she couldn't. Victor's father walked over and led her away, just as she had led Shelby away. Victor was the last one out the door, the last one to look back at the dead body, and he was astonished by the sudden amber glow that filled the room through the window as the sun began to slowly rise way out of the sea beyond.

They filed past the unit desk, from which the nurses whispered goodbyes. Once in the elevator, Shelby, who had been moving along with her forearm covering her eyes, lowered her arm, straightened up, tossed her hair out of her face, and took a deep breath. "That was hard," she said, like someone who had just finished a set of exercises. Everyone looked at her, then looked away. Victor recognized, in her voice and her words, the echo of a clinician somewhere in Shelby's past, some social worker or therapist, or maybe even just a teacher. Someone removed and obliged to be supportive, commenting on some anguishing ordeal that a younger Shelby had to endure; someone who's real concern, in spite of their professional distance, had come through and made an impression; someone who, deep down, Shelby wanted to be; someone to take the place of her crazy mother, her drunken, unreliable father, and well-meaning, bigoted grandmother. Victor wondered if he will ever know whom that person had been, if Shelby even knew from whom she inherited her self possession, her determination.

In the lobby Gum said to Victor's father, "I don't know why you didn't call us sooner."

To Victor's surprise, his father accepted that responsibility. "Because I don't have ESP, Mama!" he snapped. "One minute he was doing fine; the next minute his pressure was dropping. We got the nurse in there every time he so much as twitched his little finger. What more was I supposed to do? Why didn't they have him on any monitors or something, so we could have known?"

"They don't do that with no code patients," Gum said stiffly.

"Maybe they ought to," Victor's father said.

"I knew I should have had him at home," Gum said then to no one in particular. "God knows I was only trying to do what was best..."

"All right, Mama," Victor's father said as they approach the revolving door. "No point in all that, now. Buzzy was taken good care of right up to the end, and that's what's important."

"I'm his mother. I should have been with him." Gum came to a standstill before the motionless gigantic revolving door, bringing the rest of them up short behind her.

Shelby tool the old lady by the shoulders and looked her dead in the eye. "Gum, he's your son. He should have had to be the one to be with *you* at *your* deathbed." She gave the old lady a gentle

170

shake. "Nothing about this is how it should be. Let's get out of here, Gum. Come on." She put her little hand between her grandmother's shoulder blades and prodded her forward. They followed her out into the parking lot, which the slow sunrise had not yet reached, and they parted company at the flagpole to go on to their separate vehicles, Victor to ride with his father, Shelby with Gum.

"I wouldn't mind stopping at Denny's for a bite," Victor's father said as the two of them got in the car he led them to. Victor didn't recognize the vehicle as his father's, and once he was settled in the front seat he could tell from the dirt-scuffed flyers on the floor mats that it was a rental. He was so preoccupied with this triviality that he did not reply to his father.

"I guess we better not," his father said, and Victor was at once relieved and sorry. He could tell his father wanted to talk, but Victor needed to be alone.

"Lets' go tomorrow," Victor said.

By the time Victor's father dropped him off at his grandmother's house, the day had dawned and the pale morning light and the fresh song of invisible birds was like a reproach to Victor's urge for solitude and sleep. When they pulled into the driveway, Gum and Shelby were standing on the front stoop waiting for them.

Victor's father did not turn off the engine, but idled while Victor climbed out. Gum came over and tapped on the window of the driver's seat. "Don't you want to come in and lie down for a little while? You've been up all night."

Victors father rolled down the window and shook his head. "Martha'll take the kids to the beach after they get up and have their breakfast. I already called her. I'll be over later."

"Well…" Gum's hands gripped the ridge of glass where the window was lowered. "I appreciate you coming up, son. It means a lot to me."

"Well I'm not just going to turn around and go right back home, Mama. I'll be over later today. We've got to make arrangements."

"Well, I've taken care of most of it. But I'll have to call Mason's and fix a time to go out there. I guess we have to do it today, sometime."

"Make it around three," Victor's father said. "I'll be by around two."

Gum reached in and squeezed his shoulder. "Get some rest, son," she said. "You too, Mama," Victor's father said. "Take your pill." And with a tired smile and a half wave to Shelby, who looked bleakly, sullenly down upon them from the front stoop like a gargoyle, he shifted his car into reverse, backed out of the driveway, and drove away.

Back in Uncle Buzz's room, Victor immediately pulled the curtains to so that the room was cast into an unnatural daytime darkness. Exhausted as he was, he was too restless at first to even consider getting into bed. He wandered about the periphery of the room; he paused for a long time before Uncle Buzz's chest of drawers, gazing without thought at the collection of trophies and the painting of the ship on the stormy sea. Presently he became aware that there was music coming through the walls from Shelby's room, faint music of the jangly, rather discordant, yet poppy type she liked. He could imagine her sitting on her bed, lotus style as usual, her tiny television muted and flickering, incense sticks issuing their constant, evanescent curls of smoke from every corner of the room, her journal open before her as she chewed on the end of a pen. 'My father is dead' she would have written, for she knew that in years to come she would have reason and desire to bring back this day.

Hard as it was to tune out the sound of music seeping through the wall from Shelby's room, it was harder still to ignore the sounds of the neighborhood awakening outside, birds chirping, dogs barking, cars humming along nearby roads, lawnmowers roaring. To cool his alert, exhausted nerves, Victor lowered himself to the floor and did twenty pushups, with great difficulty, then stood up panting. He broke a sweat in the cool room, so he stripped off all of his clothes and climbed into bed, moaning with pleasure at the cold comfort of the sheets. Sleep came then like a great wave, submerging him in itself for hours until it broke with the sound of the toilet flushing across the hall. He rolled out of bed, momentarily shocked to discover himself naked, and walked over to look at the watch that he had laid on Uncle Buzz's dresser. It was almost two o'clock.

While he was in the shower his father arrived, and the four Flowers, rested yet bleary, went in his father's rented car to the funeral home.

The funeral home man greeted Gum warmly and held her hand in his for a long moment while he murmured sympathies. Victor noticed that he called her by her first name, Thelma. He was a very large man, very wide around the middle, obese yet neat, with flawlessly combed and sprayed steel gray hair and an expensive looking business suit. He wore a Masonic signet ring on one of his ham colored fingers and his nails were manicured. He greeted Victor's father with much the same warmth, not holding his hand, but rather slapping him a few times on the back; Victor's father responded in the same spirit and all in all it was as if they were long lost friends at a high school reunion. Victor could sense Shelby's growing impatience as he stood beside her in the plush lobby of the funeral home, and he was relieved when the pleasantries ended and they were led out of the funeral home lobby into an office where they were asked if they would like coffee or tea.

After the funeral director entered some information about Uncle Buzz into a computer, they were led into a labyrinth of coffins in a large showroom, where Gum and Victor's father, after some disagreement, settled on a burgundy-plated casket with an eggshell satin lining. "I had a 68 Mustang that color, and Buzzy loved it to death," Victor's father said. Shelby offered no comment regarding the casket even though she was repeatedly consulted. The price of the casket, $6,500.00, boggled Victor's mind. The funeral director then took them into the chapel where the funeral was to be held. To Victor it was indistinguishable from any protestant church, though there was no sign of a cross. Here Shelby perked up a bit, walking up and down the aisle between the rows of pews, looking out over the lectern. "There'll be plenty of room," she said drily, and Gum glared at her.

The arrangements made, the family once again split in two, Shelby and Gum went home, and Victor and his father drove to the shopping mall in the center of town to buy suits for the funeral. Victor couldn't remember the last time he wore anything other than shorts or jeans, and he was dumbfounded by the amount of money his father had to spend just on him, almost two hundred dollars on the suit, which was black and of a light material that made Victor feel naked; another seventy dollars on black wingtip shoes, a narrow belt, a tie which Victor, after several attempts, still could not figure out how to knot; a shirt, and even dark socks, as Victor had brought none from home. When Victor came out of the dressing room in this get-up, minus, of course, the tie, the salesman, and his father laughed at him. "You look like a hippie in court," his father said. "We're going to have to get that hair cut."

Victor shook his hair, the bangs of which were long enough now to be parted and tucked behind his ears for better vision. He had not had his hair cut since he was in the psych ward.

"No," he said. The salesman, a thin, obsequious middle-aged fellow wearing too much aftershave, looked discreetly away.

Victor's father frowned. "Son, you can't go to the funeral looking like that! Your grandmother'll pitch a fit."

Victor shrugged. Defiance swelled in his chest like a wave. In the deep pockets of the new slacks, his hands clenched into fists.

His father's eyes narrowed as well. They stared at one another for a long moment, until finally his father slumped a bit, and attempted a smile. "Well, I tried," he said, winking at the salesman. "Maybe his grandmother'll have better luck. I think he listens to her."

She listens to *me*. Victor thought, and decided then and there that he would let Shelby put some of her gunk in his hair to keep it out of his face, but as for cutting it, his father was asking too much. Victor's sympathy, for the first time in his life, careened toward his mother, and he shook his hair into his face again and went back into the dressing room.

They left the store and drove across the bridge and halfway down the length of the long southward facing barrier island to the Ramada Inn where his father and his wife and children were staying. His father had taken a suite with a small sitting room set apart from the sleeping area. The baby was napping in her carryall while the little boy, ignoring Victor, watched television and his father and Martha sipped their cocktails and talked around, sometimes to Victor, as they waited for the little boy's suppertime, at which point all of them went down to the lounge to eat.

It still seemed early in the afternoon when they started their meal, though it was past six o'clock in the evening. They were placed in a booth scarcely large enough to accommodate them with the baby's carryall, so Martha was obliged to shove the carryall under her seat and hold the baby on her lap. This seemed to irritate Victor's father, who reiterated that he knew the manager and that as a party of five they should have been offered one of the spacious corner booths that could accommodate up to eight.

"Oh, this is fine, honey…We're fine," said Martha in her weary drawl. Her pretty, thoroughly made up face looked small and lost amidst her stiff cascading blonde locks. One of her arms cradled the grizzling baby while the other patted her husband's shoulder. He grunted and slid into the booth beside her and looked around for the waiter. Victor looked at little Jason, who crawled in to sit across from his mother, his little chin barely reaching the edge of the table. When Victor sat down beside him the little boy gave him a narrow, suspicious stare and drew his calves up under his bottom to boost himself up a bit. Victor scooted on the furthest edge of the seat they shared, which seemed to relax the child, who looked at him and then at his mother and reached for the packets of sugar and artificial sweetener set against the wall with the salt and pepper shakers. He tore open one packet and poured the contents into his water glass, then another, and then another, forming a cloudy mound at the bottom.

Martha shook her head at the boy, who continued unabated with his messy and absorbing project. Victor's father, directly across from Victor scowled at the cocktail list. A dark tension seemed to emanate from him, and Victor felt an unaccountable fear. He looked over at Martha, who was reaching over to wrest a packet of sugar from Jason's small grip. A waitress arrived and Victor's father ordered a gin and tonic and three cokes. When the drinks arrived his mood changed. He leaned back against the booth and put his arm around Martha's neck. She smiled, but Victor noticed that along with the baby on her lap, her husband's arm between her neck and the booth forced her head to bow. "Did ya'll get everything done this afternoon?" she said.

"Just about." Victor's father sipped his drink.

"When is the service?"

"Sunday at two," Victor's father said. "Announcement'll be in the paper tomorrow."

"I hate that I can't go." Martha said. "William seemed like such a nice man. He was always so sweet." She looked at Victor. "Of course I didn't know him like you all did. But he seemed real nice."

Her attention made Victor shy. "I didn't really know him either," he said.

Victor's father took a swallow of his gin and smacked his lips. His round face assumed a shrewd, lofty expression. "Buzzy never cut the apron strings," he said. "That was his whole problem."

"Oh, now," said Martha.

"It's true!" Victor's father's voice was high with insistence. "Mama favors him." He said this as if his brother was still alive. Martha tsk'ed to hush him, for the waitress arrived to take their order. Little Jason took the opportunity, while they were distracted, to sprinkle pepper into his water glass. When the waitress left, Martha took the peppershaker and the glass of water away from him. "Look at the mess you're making," she said.

The little boy reached for his coke, slid it towards himself, and sipped it from the straw, his eyes the whole time on his mother.

Victor's father's drink was finished; the ice diminished at the bottom of his tumbler. His gaze was off to the side, surveying the lounge, as if he was looking for somebody. Presently the waitress noticed him, wended her way over, and he ordered another drink.

Jason being appropriately occupied with his coke, Martha tried to revive conversation. "How old was William?" she said.

Victor's father thought a moment. "Just turned 42, I believe..." he said. "Three years younger than me." He sipped his drink.

"So young..." Martha murmured. "His poor little girl."

Victor smiled inside to think of what Shelby would say about this woman who was not more than ten years older than herself referring to her a poor little girl.

"Where is Shelby's mother?" Martha continued.

Victor and Martha looked at his father, who sampled his drink before he answered. "Off God knows where," he said shortly. "She's worthless. Gave custody over to Mama when Shelby was about four or five. She was one of them wild Indian girls from down in Lumberton. Ran around with Buzz after he got out of the Coast Guard, got him all mixed up in going to bars and whatnot, got pregnant, he married her, then she just up and disappeared for three years, doing god knows what. She turned up again when Daddy died; she brought Shelby here to Mama's, made a lot of trouble, then disappeared again. Not too long after that she dropped Shelby off in Mama's front yard one night and told her to ring the doorbell, then just drove off without a word. Mama said Shelby said they'd been driving around for days without stopping with a couple of guys she didn't know who they were." He sipped his drink. "Muling drugs, I'd bet. I don't know, tell you the truth, if anyone's heard anything from her since then."

Martha's mouth hung open. "She just left her little girl on your mama's doorstep and drove off?"

Victors father nodded. "Sure did. Like she was dropping off a dog. Probably the best thing she ever did, too. She was bad news, that Tanya. Real bad news. She liked to stir up trouble, that's for sure." Victor's father stared off into the air above Victor's head. A grimace appeared on his face, as if his drink had left a bad aftertaste. "She was something." His grimace turned into a smirk.

Victor's stomach turned as their food arrived. His father, already tipsy, was peering into some distant, delicious, furtive recollection like a peeping tom through the blinds of a woman's bedroom window, savoring without shame the memory of his shabbiest moment.

Victor looked down at the plate the waitress placed in front of him and picked up his fork. The steam from the broiled fish wafted into his face, and he put the fork down again. He reached for his water and took a tiny sip. "What's wrong?" his father said, with real concern. "Isn't that what you wanted?"

Victor could only nod. Beside him little Jason, gripping a hush puppy in his hand, fidgeted and moved his legs out from under himself and slumped so far down in his seat that his chin was pressed against the collar of his t-shirt. He began to kick his legs against the upholstery of the booth, making a rhythmic muffled thump.

"Sit up," Victor's father said to the little boy. "Eat."

The thumping continued unabated. Martha sighed and rose up as far as she could and reached over to wrest the now crushed and greasy hush puppy out of his grip. "Sit up like a big boy, Jason. Why are you acting like this in front of Victor?"

The little boy said nothing but continued to thump. "He's been like this all afternoon," said Martha with another sigh.

The thumping became more insistent and defiant. "Someone wants a spanking," Victor's father remarked darkly.

Victor looked down at the little boy, whose forehead, under his dark brown bangs, was furrowed so that his hair hung into his eyes. Victor wondered who and where the kid's real father was, and how he would feel about Victor's father threatening his son with a spanking.

"Someone doesn't want to go swimming tomorrow," said Martha.

The thumping became gradually slower, then stopped altogether. Then the little boy slid off the vinyl upholstery of the booth to disappear under the table. Martha emitted a little moan and handed the baby to Victor's father, who took her and held her awkwardly against his chest.

Martha bent to the left to try and peer underneath the table. "Jason, get up and sit in your seat and eat your dinner that Daddy Eddie has bought for you! You're acting just like a little baby today!"

The baby Madison squirmed in her father's arms and Victor's father swore under his breath. "Just leave him there, Martha," his father snapped. "For Christ's sake just leave him so the rest of us can eat in peace. If he wants to act the fool, let him and he'll see what it gets him when we get upstairs. Just leave him." Martha straightened and Victor's father handed the baby back to her. The tired young

179

woman smiled apologetically at Victor. "Jason's a good boy," she said. "He's just worn out. We were in the car almost six hours yesterday, and he doesn't sleep good out of his own bed."

Victor smiled at his father's wife, his contempt of her dissipating like the morning fog. She was young, that's all, for all of the fact that she was older than him, that she was the mother of two children; she was younger than he ever was or ever would be. She was exactly what his father needed, Victor thought. But what did *she* need? Not his father, Victor thought. He gazed at the baby, wide eyed and slobbering as she rested imperiously in her mother's lap. "She's pretty," he said, indicating the baby.

"Isn't she?" Martha cooed and nuzzled the child. "She's got her daddy's big blue eyes."

Again Victor, who did not have his daddy's big blue eyes was struck by the fact that this infant was actually related to him. After seventeen years of being an only child, it seemed almost preposterous that he should all of a sudden have a sister. He certainly did not feel like a brother, not to that helpless, tyrannical creature. Victor marveled at how parasitic the baby seemed, always attached to her mother. How can someone love such a burden?

There was a long silence while they attempted to eat. Within this silence, Victor suddenly experienced a pressure on his foot that was at once heavy and subtle, as if a cat had curled up on it. He wiggled his toes and the pressure lifted. Suddenly Victor felt a deep inward warmth that slowly grew to fill him; a warmth which then lingeringly receded into itself without ceasing to be, a warmth such as some women are said to feel at the moment of conception. He took a bite of broiled fish. After a moment the pressure returned to his foot, and Victor held it still. He realized that the little boy, bored under the table but determined not to come to the surface, where he was sure to be reprimanded, had decided to rest his head, and was using Victor's foot as a pillow. Victor held his foot still for the remainder of the meal.

It was the baby, having grown restless and loud, who determined the end of their time together. Martha, who had eaten almost one of the two crab cakes she was served after her salad, sighed with feigned resignation and smiled at Victor. "She wants to lie down. I guess I better take both the kids upstairs."

The disgruntlement visible on Victor's father's face dissipated like mist. "Yup!" he said. "It's getting to be bedtime." He knocked on the surface of the table. "Hear that, J.C.!" He called, addressing the boy underneath. "Bedtime. And no ice cream, neither. You didn't touch a thing on your plate, wasting good food and my money."

The little boy under the table did not respond, his head shifted slightly, but did not move off of Victor's faintly tingling toes.

"All right, now," Victor's father said. "If I have to reach under there, there won't be no waterslide tomorrow."

Victor wiggled his toes. Left to himself, he knew, the kid would blow it, out of nothing but stubbornness. It would be a shame for him to miss going to the waterslide, whether he realized it right now or not.

The little boy's head lifted and he crawled slowly out from under the table onto the carpeted floor of the lounge. "Stand up!" Victor's father hissed, and the boy stood up, his dark little eyes hooded with spite. Victor's father rolled his own eyes, then grunted as he slid out of the booth to let Martha and the baby out. "I'll be up in a bit, honey," he said as Martha struggled her way past him. She nodded at him and turned to Victor.

"I'm sorry the kids were like this tonight. But it was good to see you."

"Nice to see you too," Victor mumbled.

"You come down and see us as soon as you can," she said, and reached for the little boy's hand. "Jason, can you say goodbye to Victor?"

Jason's expression of solemn petulance did not change, but he regarded Victor for a long moment before tugging his mother away. When they have disappeared through the glass double doors of the lounge into the hotel lobby, Victor's father winked at him, signaled the waitress, and ordered another drink. When it arrived he pushed it toward Victor. "You'll have to help me with this one," he said. "I forgot I have to drive you back to Mama's."

His father's gin was strong and bitter, like medicine, and nowhere near as palatable as the wine he'd drunk with Dora, but it had that same warmth, so he sipped it obligingly a few times before sliding it back across the table to his father. They talked easily, as they shared this drink, of the funeral the next day, of the restaurant where the reception after the funeral was to be held, and his father talked about the house he and Martha were having built in Florence, South Carolina, the four-bedroom house where, his father asserted, there would be room for Victor any time he felt like coming down. After awhile a man walked over to the booth, Victor's father having called across the room for him, and slid in next to Victor's father, holding out his cuff-linked hand for Victor to shake. It was the manager of the lounge, a co-owner of the hotel, a man named Jack with whom, it turned out, his father had played baseball on the high school team. "This is Victor, my oldest, my son," Victor's father said. "He stays with his mother in Raleigh."

The two men slapped each other on the back. "So what brings you to this dump, Ed?"

Victor's father's expression became appropriately grave. "Had to come see to things," he said. "Don't know if you know, but Buzz has been pretty bad off for awhile now, and he passed on just this morning."

The hotel managers' hairy, pale hand with its wedding band and cufflinks and Rolex watch covered his mouth in an almost feminine gesture. "Oh, Ed. I had no idear. Damn, I'm sorry, buddy."

Victor's father nodded. "Just turned forty. Got a little girl not barely in high school. It's a shame..."

The hotel manager, whose blue eyes stood out like polished stones in a weather burned face, placed his hand on top of Victor's fathers. "Well, I can't believe it. Damn, I hate to hear that. I think I heard he had some liver trouble, but...." He sighed. "Well, you just never know, do you? How's your mama holding up?"

"We'll, you know Mama. She's strong. She's been raising Buzzy's little girl, oh about ten years now. So she won't be by herself."

"Mm, mm, mm." The hotel manager lifted his countenance to the wooden rafter of the lounge, and to the heavens beyond. "Well, I am sure sorry to hear that. Old Buzzy Flowers. Best shortstop in the history of East Carteret High."

"Ain't that the truth." Victor's fathers grin was wide and his eyes were moist. A lump arose in Victor throat at this unexpected sign of real grief on his father's part.

A series of musical notes issued from the hotel managers waist, he unclipped a cell phone and peered at it before putting it back. He stood up. "Listen," he says, "it was sure good seeing you, Ed. Your dinner's on me, hear? I'll let the cashier know."

"Jack, I can't let you do that..."

"I don't want to hear it." The hotel manager backed away. "It's nothing but money. You give your mama my love, hear?"

"I'll do it." Victor's father lifted his hand, lowered it, slumped and sighed. "Well I'll be," he said. Suddenly he looked very old. He rubbed his hand over his face, then turned to Victor. "You 'bout ready?"

Victor's father drove the rental car slowly and boozily across the bridge and into the city to his mother's driveway, where, without cutting the ignition, he told Victor to tell his grandmother that he would meet them at the funeral home about an hour before the service. "You gonna be all right tonight, son?" he said, as Victor stood waiting for him to stop talking so he could close the passenger door.

"Me? Yeah…" Victor said. He stared at his father, who gripped the steering wheel of the rental car hard. It was as if, in the space of the ride, his father had gone from being tipsy to being very drunk. "Dad, are *you* all right?"

His father closed his eyes for a moment. "I'm just tired, son," he said. "Tell Mama to take her pill."

Victor was torn between concern for his father and his own longing to get away from him and into his grandmother's house. "You're drunk, Dad," he said.

"No, I'm just tired," his father said, with such an absence of defensiveness that Victor could not argue with him. "I'll see you tomorrow." He shifted the car out of park.

Victor watched as the rental car backed out of the driveway and disappeared around the corner of the intersection. He thought of Dora, whose own father died in a wreck. He imagined how he would feel if his father were to die tonight, driving drunk across the bridge, when Victor could have stopped him. But Victor didn't believe that he could have stopped him. He won't die, he decided, and he went into his grandmother's house without giving it another thought.

Stepping into the cool, lamp lit living room, Victor found his grandmother on the sofa, talking on the cordless phone. She nodded and lifted her gnarled hand to him and he looked down the hallway to see that Shelby's bedroom door was closed tight, with a line of light underneath that indicated she was in there awake with at least one of her shawl covered lamps on.

Gum stood, phone in hand, and held one finger up. "Ronnie," she said into the phone, "Victor's back. You want to talk to him?"

Victor's eyebrows shot up. "Your mama," Gum whispered, covering the mouthpiece. "All right. You take care, Ronnie. Here he is." She handed the phone to Victor and discreetly scuttled into the kitchen, where she could hear every word that Victor said without obviously eavesdropping.

It had been such a long time since he'd talked to her that his mother sounded different, actually younger. "How are you doing, hon?"

"All right." He dropped his packages from the shopping mall onto the sofa and sat down beside them.

"Are you sure?" his mother said. "Your grandmother says that you were with Buzz when he died last night."

"Yeah." Victor was intentionally abrupt. He did not want to talk about that. His mother is silent for a moment. "You're so young," she whispered. "I'm proud of you, hon." Then she assumed a more familiar, directive tone. "The service is at two tomorrow?"

"Yeah," he said. "Are you coming?"

"No, babe, you know I can't do that drive with my back. No, I'm going to send a wreath. Poor William. How is Shelby holding up?"

"Okay, I guess."

His mother clicked her tongue. "She's probably in shock. What a shame..." She broke off. "Your grandmother is worried about her. Listen, is your father staying there for a while? To keep an eye on them?"

"I don't think so. They're staying in a hotel on the beach."

His mother's voice was like a needle. "Oh, so he brought *her*." There was a long pause. "Well, he's made his choices. But it's a shame

185

he can't see to it that his mother and Shelby get the support they're going to need."

Victor suddenly felt drowsy.

"Anyway, you know school starts in a couple of weeks," his mother continued. "Can you believe we're into August already? Now, I don't think it would be right for you to leave right away, but you need to have some time to get settled back at home before school starts, don't you think? If you get a jump on it, we can even start making arrangements for some tutoring to help you catch up on everything you missed last year. I worked with a girl whose son goes to –"

"I'm not going back to school," Victor blurted. "I'm going to get a job."

The silence on the other end of the line was like the silence after a thunderclap, ominous and resounding.

"Victor, what the hell are you talking about?" his mother said.

"I'm going to get my GED," Victor said quickly. "Look, I can't talk about it now. I just don't want you to think I'm going to go back to school next year. I'm not, Mom. I've already talked about it with Dad."

"Oh, you have, huh." Her voice is like a dull saw. "And he thinks it's a good idea for you to be a dropout? That's just gorgeous…"

"No," Victor felt like a car skidding into an intersection, "Wait… He doesn't like it either. But I have to do it."

"Oh you have to do it, huh." His mother's voice became slick and treacherous, more Long Island than ever. "So you want to tell me what's going on down there, Victor?"

Victor sighed. She suspected he was on drugs, of course. "Nothing," he said. "I just like it, that's all."

"You're going to school, Victor. You can't just decide you can do your own thing at seventeen…"

"I know that," Victor said. "But why should I go to school if I can get a GED? It doesn't make sense, Mom… eight hours every day, when I could be working. I *like* working –"

His mother's cut him off. "I've ordered your return ticket for next Friday," she said. "I figured that'll be enough time for you to," she paused, "wrap things up."

He smiled wearily, rather relieved that she had decided not to listen. She would never listen, so he'd eventually just do what he had to do against her now quite resistible will. "Okay." He says.

His willingness to drop it seemed to mollify her. "You've been through a lot," she said, meaning his presence at his Uncle's deathbed. "We can talk about all the rest of this later. Did you find something nice to wear to the funeral?"

"Yes."

"What about shoes?"

"Yes."

"All right." She sighed. "Well, give your grandmother my love. And Shelby, too. I'm proud of you, son," she said. "Call me if you need me."

"All right."

They muttered goodbyes and hung up. Victor took the phone into the kitchen where it's base was, and found his grandmother sitting at the kitchen table, spaced out and surrounded by a cloud of cigarette smoke like a tired old dragon.

"Thank you, honey." She said obscurely, as if from a great inward distance. Victor imagined that he wouldn't have to tell his grandmother to take her pill even if he intended to, which he didn't. He was willing to bet she'd taken more than one, considering the vague glazed look in her eyes. He bet his mother talked her into it. "Have you had supper?" She said.

"Yes, Gum. With Dad and Martha, remember?"

"Oh, that's right." She turned upon him a drugged smile. "I'm a little tired," she said.

He nodded. "How's Shelby?" he asked.

"She's alright right now." She inclined her head in the direction of Shelby's room. "Wouldn't eat no supper, but now she's in there with that Dora, and they came out a little bit ago and got them a bag of that microwave popcorn."

It was a long moment, during which a band of alternating warmth and nausea gripped Victor's gut, before he could move or say anything. "I didn't see Dora's car," he said, in a voice higher than usual.

"I believe her mama dropped her off," his grandmother said. "She's staying over tonight. Shelby wants her to ride with us tomorrow in the limousine." His grandmother tiredly lit another cigarette with her fish house matches.

Victor had a brief mental image of himself melting into a slick, dirty puddle and evaporating into a foul mist, then dissipating. He would have, in that moment, given his soul not to exist in the same world as Dora.

His grandmother, oblivious, seemed to have lapsed into some tranquilized reverie. "'Night, Gum," he said.

"'Night, honey." She said, from far away. He took a deep breath and made his way down the hall to Shelby's room, where he paused, one foot firmly on top of the other, before raising his hand to tap and be admitted into what once had been the only room where he felt welcome.

Shelby opened the door after an excruciating moment and stood slightly back from the doorway in an attitude that could have suggested either welcome or challenge. Her red framed glasses were on, and her hair, usually so untamed, was pulled back into a tight, round little bun. This made her head look surprisingly small and naked, as if she'd been shorn like Joan of Arc. Behind her the incense was smoking, the television was flickering, and Dora was resting on her front, her face forward like a sphinx on the bed. Victor forced himself not to look at Dora, but he could feel that she was staring straight at him.

"I just wanted to see how you were," Victor said, trying, without being obvious, to speak loud enough for Dora to hear.

"I'm fine," said Shelby, as if that should be obvious. "We're planning a part of the service," she added, going back to climb up on her bed. She did not invite Victor in, but he took a small, exploratory step forward, anyway.

"The preacher came over while you were with your dad," she said, settling herself flat onto her bed with her head propped against the headboard so that her chin rested firmly against the collar of her shirt. This gave her words a mumbling, lock jawed quality. "Too bad you weren't around. Gum volunteered you as a pallbearer. Did she tell you?"

"No." This was alarming. Victor hadn't expected to have any part in the service. How was he supposed to know what to do?

"Yep," said Shelby, grinning at his aggrieved expression. "You and your dad. And Oliver and a couple of guys from Daddy's church. It's going to be short and sweet. Daddy didn't have many friends," she adds, without emotion, as if she were saying that her father didn't have many teeth. "People who are sick for a long time tend not to."

This last comment made the skin on Victor's arms prickle. He stole a glance at Dora, whose aggressive gaze was fixed upon him.

"I'm going to sing," said Shelby. "They want me to sing the hymn. You didn't know I could sing, did you?" she said to Victor.

"No."

"I used to sing in the church choir. So I know all those hymns. So Gum's preacher asked me to sing. I was going to whether they wanted me to or not. Daddy loved to hear me sing."

There was not much to say to say to that. The silence became long and oppressive. "What's the matter with you?" said Shelby, looking Victor up and down with her chin tucked in. "You look like you've shit yourself."

Victor shoved his hands in his pockets. "Nothing." He looked from beneath his hair at Dora. He knew now she hadn't said anything.

By looking down at the floor, and backing towards the doorway, he tried to signal to her his thanks, his acknowledgement of how much they both cared for Shelby, his promise that he would keep his distance, his absolute assumption of guilt and sorrow. "I'm just tired," he said.

Victor awakened the next morning to a flurry of female voices and footsteps as the three women made no effort to hold down the noise of their scramble to prepare themselves for the funeral. By the time Victor was able to get into the shower the water ran lukewarm, then ice cold. Though the funeral was not set to begin until 2 p.m., it seemed like there was no end to the details that must be taken care of. All morning long the telephone rang; calls from relatives giving excuses as to why they couldn't attend, calls from out of town relatives needing directions to the funeral home, several calls from Victor's father who was already at the funeral home setting up the chapel, and calls from the waitresses at the restaurant who were setting that place up for the wake afterwards. Gum, having slept off her tranquilizer, was as alert as a squirrel, and looked like a stranger to Victor in her shapeless navy dress with black velvet collar and cuffs, her freshly sprayed hair, and her made-up face. Shelby, as well, looked like a different person, like a grown woman almost, in her long black dress of some heavy material gathered by a trailing sash at her waist, a long necklace of large amber beads, her glasses off, and her curls held up off her neck and above her ears with jeweled combs. Dora looked as she usually did, in a black dress, stockings, and dark eye make-up stark against her pale face.

Victor put on his suit and managed to knot his tie after six tries. He wet his hair with gel and combed it off his face and looked with dismay at his reflection in the bathroom mirror. With nothing to hide his face, he looked awfully young and tired to himself.

Once dressed, they all gravitated to the kitchen, where someone had put on coffee. There was a box of doughnuts on the counter. "Have a couple," Gum told them. She was utterly composed now as if she was going to any old church service in her fancy dress and shoes. "It's a long time before you'll have a chance to eat again."

Realizing that in fact, he did have an appetite, Victor reached for a doughnut, and so did Shelby and Dora. They all munched in silence, but it was not an uncomfortable one. Victor would have thought that the prospect of the ceremony ahead would have everyone on edge or in tears, but for the moment it was as if they were going to a potentially tedious, but meaningful event, like a graduation or an award ceremony. Someone, probably Shelby, had brought Lily into the house, and she sat watching them eat their donuts, every few seconds licking her chops in envious sympathy. They lingered, sitting around the table after their coffee cups became empty or grew cold, watching Lily as she scratched and nipped at herself before settling down to doze in front of the humming refrigerator. Gum peered at the dime-sized face of her watch and said they better go now so that Victor's father wouldn't get worried. Victor felt like a secret service agent sitting silent and all in black as his grandmother maneuvered her enormous sedan though town. In the backseat, Shelby and Dora whispered like schoolgirls on a field trip.

When they arrived at the funeral home, the same man who helped them pick out the casket met them, and he directed them to the chapel where Victor's father was waiting, forlorn and fidgety, in the furthest back pew. He greeted them as if he had not seen them in years, hugging Victor, kissing his mother on her powdery cheek, and beaming at Shelby. He looked curiously at Dora, whose smirk as she regarded him was faint but supercilious until Gum introduced her to him as Shelby's friend. "They've been thick as thieves all summer," she added.

The funeral director backed discreetly away and they all turned as one toward the front of the chapel and the casket there, which was open. "How does he look?" Gum asked Victor's father.

"They did a good job," he said. "Suits a little tight."

"Oh, they didn't let it out?"

"Probably," he said, "but there's only so much to let out, Mama. That suit's twenty-years-old if it's a day. He got married in it for Pete's sake!"

"I know," Gum sighed. "But that's what he wanted on him. Does it look real bad, Eddie?"

"Naw. Just a little bunched at the collar. Ain't no one going to notice."

"Well, I just hate to think of him…." She shook her head. "Well, let's go see."

She reached for Shelby and looped her arm through the girl's. Victor's father led and Victor and Dora followed behind Gum and Shelby, careful not to look at one another, a full yardstick of distance between them. At the coffin, Victor's father stepped aside and Gum and Shelby, arm in arm still, stepped up. Shelby grasped the edge of the coffin with her free hand as if to steady herself, then stopped to bury her face against Gum's shoulder. Gum patted her back, bearing her up like a pivot then they staggered together, like the Willis twins, to rest on the front pew. As if pushed forward by some invisible hand, Victor stepped up to the casket and looked inside. The corpse, dressed in a pale blue suit that was indeed tight about the shoulders and neck, seemed not so much dead as inanimate, like a doll or a statue. The face was chalky with makeup, and but for the receding hairline and placid, closed expression, it would be unrecognizable as Uncle Buzz. The fine root-like network of broken veins in his nose and cheeks were covered by makeup, leaving his complexion as smooth, pale, and impersonal as the silk pillows he rested upon.

Victor was glad that he had seen Uncle Buzz before the embalmers did their work. Still, there seemed to be something there of the man who had shared his room with Victor. Something about the way the man had hung around the house those first few days of Victor's visit shuffling about in his robe, pajama bottoms, and ever-present can of Ensure made Victor smile now, made Victor feel peaceful. At the same time, he felt it wasn't right that his life, gentle and resigned if wasted in the eyes of most, should already be over.

After a moment Victor became aware of some movement in the back of the chapel and turned to see a group of people filing in. He stepped aside and he and his father took their seats in the front pew across the aisle from Gum and Shelby.

After a brief look into the casket, Dora slid in beside Shelby and squeezed her hand. For the next half hour or so a steady stream of people, most of them indistinguishable white women of Gum's generation, filed in, paused over the casket, then stepped over to where Gum received them with nods and a brave smile. Many of these women stopped to embrace Shelby, who submitted to these formalities, over and over, with a blank expression before resuming an ongoing whispered conversation with Dora. As the pews behind the family filled, Victor could not resist twisting around to have a look. There were plenty of people, mostly old men, who had not approached the casket or the family; these were dispersed among the predominant women like weeds in a garden. Within the congregation, there was one black face, an older man with iron-gray hair and a serene expression, dressed in a dark brown suit and a tan and gold striped tie. Victor's gaze remained on this man longer than upon any other unfamiliar face, but the man did not appear ill at ease, or even to notice Victor's attention. All around him chattering old ladies stole glances at the black man and whispered speculations, but if he noticed, he did not seem to mind. Victor turned back around and wished he could ask Shelby who the man was.

Having been handed an order of worship by the funeral director when they arrived, Victor turned his attention to that, smoothing it out on his thigh, as he had unconsciously bunched it up in his hand while standing at the casket. On the front, a line drawing of Jesus with a crooked pole in one hand and a drunk looking lamb in the crook of his arm was captioned by a slightly slanted legend that read "Memorial Service for William Emmett "Buzz" Flowers 1963-2005" Inside, on the right-hand page, there was a schedule and a listing of pallbearers, among which he saw his own name, inaccurately given as Victor Andrew Flowers.

As he was reading this his father nudged him, and Victor turned. The chapel had filled almost all of the pews near the front, while the ones in the back remained empty. Behind these, framed by the doorway like a caged bird on its swing, a woman in a short-skirted black dress stood, a large black purse held in one hand, the other hand shading her eyes. Her hair was short and the color of buttered popcorn and her skin was the color of honey. When she lowered her hand from her face, Victor could see, even at such a distance, that her eyes were bright green, like Shelby's. "Look what the cat drug in," Victor's father said under his breath. "Tanya, for Pity's sake."

Victor's father leaned forward and caught his mother's eye, then tilted his head to indicate the back of the church, where the woman was beginning to advance down the aisle. Shelby and Dora were still head to head in some whispered conversation. Gum looked back, puzzled, then her eyes widened. She turned upon Victor and his father a stricken expression. Victor could hardly sit still; he was so curious. He watched as the woman in the short black dress made her way forward with small, unsure steps on her high-heeled black shoes. The closer she got to Victor the clearer the woman's resemblance to Shelby became, despite the artificial color of her hair and the slightness of her frame. Her eyes were identical to Shelby's in shape and color, and her skin, while a bit darker than Shelby's, had the same rose-copper quality. Her lips, like Shelby's, were full and painted a dark, earthy red that was almost brown. Even in her high-heeled shoes, she was clearly much shorter than Shelby, perhaps even the same height as Gum. Form the distance she could have been mistaken for a high school girl, so self-conscious was her demeanor. But, as she advanced, it was easy to see that she was a woman of middle age; the roots of her yellow colored hair were gray at the part above her right temple; her neck was corded and the skin of it was loose, and there were deep purplish circles underneath her eyes that no amount of make-up could hide. Still, she was a striking woman; her features, particularly her full mouth and her large, bright, catlike eyes retained an arresting beauty. In the same manner that Shelby radiated intelligence, her mother projected a kind of sultry feistiness. Looking at her, Victor realized later, was like looking at Shelby and Dora all rolled up into one.

The woman who was Shelby's mother approached the casket. Victor saw his grandmother stiffen and purse her lips, and then beside her Shelby, sensing Gum's distress, looked up. She looked up and after a moment of incomprehension, her relaxed smile melted, and her brow lowered so that if she had bared her teeth and slobbered she would have looked exactly like the Tasmanian Devil on her nightshirt. By the time Shelby recovered enough from the shock to look over at Victor, her mother, having leaned far down into the coffin to plant a kiss on Uncle Buzz's dead face, stood and turned to face the gathering. Shelby shuddered and looked down into her lap. Gum stared straight ahead at the round stained glass design set into the wall behind the coffin, and Shelby's mother gave the congregation a brief, nervous yet strangely triumphant smile before she walked, chin up like a proud but jilted bride back down the aisle.

"God Damn," Victor's father whispered to Victor. "She looks like hell. I wonder if Mama called her people, and they tracked her down and she decided she better come and make a scene. You'd think Mama would have known better, but…"

Tuning his father out, Victor hunched down in his seat and turned to see whether or not the woman left the chapel. She did not; she took a seat in the furthest pew from the coffin, on the same side of the aisle as Shelby, Dora and Gum. Victor's father nudged him and he turned around to look at the coffin again, but not before stealing a glance at Shelby and Gum. Shelby had her eyes closed as if she was in the middle of some furious prayer, and Gum looked simply embarrassed, as if she'd just farted and was hoping against hope that no one else heard it.

Victor, for his part, felt helplessly sorry for the woman, who after all, had at least made the gesture of sending Uncle Buzz off with a kiss. Uncle Buzz would have appreciated that, he thought. Restraining himself from taking another look toward the back pew, he sat up straight and told himself that he would introduce himself to the shunned woman if he got the chance. It is at that point that a tall, broad-shouldered man in a dark suit and a youngish, florid face strode down the aisle to the lectern. "Friends, let us pray," he said, in a supplicatory drawl, and the entire congregation rose as one, with Victor a beat behind.

The sermon was prefaced by a direct address to Shelby and Gum, to keep in mind that, as Jesus in the Gospel of John said to Martha of Bethany, "I am the resurrection and the life, He that believeth in me, though he were dead, yet shall he live:" Gum received this offering of comfort with a frozen smile and Shelby with a raised eyebrow. Victor was so preoccupied with the presence of Shelby's mother that he himself received of the sermon only a general intimation of unreality as the Preacher described the life of a man unrecognizable as Uncle Buzz, a brave guardsman, a devoted churchgoer, a loving father and son, and an expert deep sea fisherman. There was no mention of either the dead man's alcoholism or of the baseball triumphs of his youth, and when the preacher ended his eulogy with another command to the congregation to rise and bow their heads in prayer, Victor made no attempt at prayer, but looked boldly around the room to see if anyone else felt as uninspired as he did. Shelby's head was unbowed, and she did not look Victor's way. Beside her Gum dabbed at her eyes with a tissue. After a moment the preacher said, "Please be seated." But Shelby remained standing. The preacher nodded at her with an unctuous smile and backed away from the podium.

"You can stay there." She directed the preacher. "I don't need the microphone."

But the preacher just smiled and nodded and continued to back away. As Shelby mounted the steps up through the altar rail, the preacher hurriedly stepped down and went to take a seat in the front row just a few feet to Victor's right.

Shelby made her way to the podium and rested one elbow upon it. In her simple black dress draped about her and her wild curls bunched together, stacked on top of her head, she looked taller and slimmer than usual, and majestic, like priestess. Every eye was on her as she smiled a small smile to herself. Victor was amazed, he would have never imagined that she would be so self-possessed after having her mother show up from out of nowhere. But she seemed as comfortable now as she always did behind the register at the restaurant. She cleared her throat, adjusted the hem of her dress and clasped her hands together in a ladylike way just below her belt.

"When my grandmother and Reverend Jacobs asked me to sing the hymn today, I said I would. I said I would because, like Reverend Jacobs says, my father was a Christian, and he loved to hear me sing his favorite hymns, but also because I love to sing, and I loved to sing for my father, and I'm going to miss singing for my father, at least singing for him and hearing him join in with me, because even though he thought he had a voice like an old crow, he never could resist singing with me when he heard one of his favorite songs. It's something that my father and I shared and will always share, among other things, love of music… a love of the way that music can say for us some things we can't say without it."

Here Shelby paused, and looked down at her grandmother, who looked back up at her with an expression at once proud and wary. Victor smiled. Shelby bit her lip, as if considering her next step, and took a deep breath.

"So, just as much as my father was a Christian, he was a musician. Maybe not a whole lot of the rest of you know how much talent he had and never developed while he was busy living his life. My dad had a gift for music, just like his gift for baseball, and he could pick out a tune on a guitar or a piano just from hearing it once, even though he never had any formal lessons. And he had a sense of the power of music, and I know this because there were some songs he never got tired of hearing, from me or from the radio, or whatever, songs that meant more to him than he ever said, songs that touched something in him that he couldn't reach on his own. Some of these were gospel songs, and some of them weren't. There's one in particular that I'd like to sing for you today. It was a song that my father would listen to a lot, especially during those times when he needed—" here she paused again and looked down at Gum, "to know he wasn't alone. It's a song that some of you know, and maybe some of you don't know. I'd like to sing it by myself, though, if that's all right, and then after, I'd like everyone who wants to join me in singing his favorite hymn, *Softly and Tenderly, Jesus is Calling*. Okay, Gum?" Shelby was grinning. Gum shook her head, but she was smiling.

"All right," said Shelby, and she closed her eyes. Standing with them closed, as if only by closing them could she truly sing for her father, she began. It was a song Victor had never heard before but the words, formed and shaped by Shelby's surprisingly strong, pure, and rather haunting contralto, were as clear as a bell and echoed in his mind like the peals of a carillon, leaving him spellbound by a performance that was as much a curse as it was a song, and impressed him as never before with a sense of the pain and rage that his uncle must have lived with every day of his life on account of his brother and his wife's betrayal.

"I fed your pride with my foolish love
I quit and I hoped that you would starve for more
Our greedy love burned me
Like salt on a sore…"

…. Now you're with another
that's how the worm turns
Like salt on a sore
His greedy love burns.
It burns me. It burns me up inside…"

When the song was through, Shelby hung her own head for a moment as if in prayer, then she lifted it again to gaze out upon the small and stunned congregation. "Amen, Daddy," she murmured, just loud enough for Victor and perhaps the rest of the family on the front row to hear. Then she nodded at the woman sitting at the piano to her left, and after a few false notes, and another song began, which a smattering of voices waveringly sang, led by Shelby, who's expression and low, gentle notes were painfully beautiful as she sang of a gentle and patient Savior in whom she did not particularly believe.

The family graveyard was forty-five minutes from the city in a tiny, still unincorporated village called Atlantic near the end of a jetty of what was mostly marshland that jutted far out into the sound and from which the shadows of one of the barrier islands of the Outer Banks could be seen. It was in this sleepy, sunlit outpost, with its weathered houses lining the banks of the Core Sound, that four hundred years of Flowers and related families had lived, mated, and died, and where Victor and Shelby's grandmother and grandfather had grown up before marrying and moving to Morehead City. Victor stepped out of the cool limousine onto the gravel driveway that led into the small graveyard and followed his grandmother, his father, Shelby, and Dora to where a canopy stood over a freshly dug grave near the wooded edge of the cemetery. Shortly Rev. Jacobs and a number of other people joined them. Everyone gathered around the coffin, which now sat suspended above the grave.

Perhaps on account of the heat, the burial service was mercifully short. Rev. Jacobs repeated some of the banal sentiments of his sermon, droned the necessary prayers, and ended with the ashes to ashes and dust-to-dust speech that even Victor knew enough to expect. Only half of the congregation of the funeral had followed the limousine out to the cemetery, and Victor found himself looking around for Shelby's mother when he was supposed to be praying. As soon as the customary clod of dirt hit the shining lid of uncle Buzz's coffin, signaling the end of the service and hence his centrality to the gathering, a kind of relaxation broke out among the crowd, and the old ladies who made up the majority of delegation from the funeral home turned to one another and began chatting, and not a few descended like seagulls upon Gum.

Now that it was all over, Victor felt oddly out of place. Shelby and Dora were standing a bit away from the canopied gravesite, deep in conversation. Victor's father was chuckling away among a group of dark suited old men whom, disengaged from their wives, coalesced as naturally as oil separates from water in a container. Gum was at the center of the wives, accepting condolences, hugs, and hand presses with the weary grace of a dowager. Only Victor was unattached, hanging close to the coffin like a child too shy to leave his mother's side. He wanted to talk to Shelby, to tell her how well he thought she sang and how brave he thought she was for singing, but now that the service had ended and the air of solemnity had somewhat dissipated, he was afraid to be too near Dora. So he kept to himself until his grandmother noticed him and beckoned him over to her.

"Victor," she said, reaching for him as he approached, "this is my Aunt Glenna, that I was telling you about. Remember the picture on the living room, of my granddaddy? Well this is one of his daughters."

"Well, hey there, Victor." The old lady named Glenna shouted. The old lady was almost a half a foot shorter than Gum herself, so bent was she by age and what seemed to be a small hump on her back underneath the cheap-looking, dark blue dress she wore. The loose skin of her face and throat seemed transparent and fragile as the pages of an old bible, and she trembled from top to toe like a withered leaf in a breeze with palsy. Yet her eyes, black as those of a bird, were bright, and her bird claw grip upon his forearm was strong.

"Hi," said Victor.

"He said hey, Glenna." Gum whispered to Victor, "You have to speak up." Turning, Gum raised her voice, "Victor is Eddie's oldest boy," and after a moment the old woman nodded as if she understood. "He's about a year older than Shelby."

"He don't look a thing like Eddie," the old lady crowed.

"Oh, now!" shouted Gum. "Look at his ears, Jessie! Well, you can't see them under all that hair. But they stick straight out like Eddie's and Buzz's. Least they did when he was a little boy...."

"He looks like my brother Ace," the old lady's voice was like the horn on an eighteen-wheeler, "that died in the war. Over in Italy." She tightened her grip on Victor's forearm and looked up into his face, tilting her head to the side like a sparrow. "Just as handsome as he can be."

Victor felt his skin crawl and looked about for some excuse to break away. Some feet away his father was handing out a business card to an old man with a bandage over one eye. Shelby and Dora had turned their backs and were walking toward the fence that surrounded the graves.

Gum followed his gaze. "Now what are they up to?" she said. "We've got to be at the restaurant in an hour. We don't have time for those girls to lollygag."

"I'll tell them," Victor said, his arm still held fast by Glenna. "It was nice to meet you!" he shouted.

She stared at him blankly for a moment, then nodded. "You come see me," she said, without relaxing her grip. Gum reached for her hand and interposed her own fingers between the old lady and Victor until Victor was finally freed. "Let's get you out of this hot sun," she said, patting the old woman's lumpy back. Victor shuddered and loped off to where Shelby and Dora were standing amongst a collection of weathered and crooked marble gravestones. "Gum sent me," he said, avoiding Dora's gaze. "She says we have to be at the restaurant in an hour."

"Tell Gum to keep her drawers on," said Shelby. She squinted through the sunlight at him. "How'd you like old Glenna?"

Victor grimaced. "She's creepy," he says, and immediately felt not only guilty, but hypocritical. How could he, who had behaved so nastily to Dora, call a lonely old lady creepy? He could feel Dora's eyes on him like pinions. He turned to Shelby and hung his head. "I shouldn't have said that," he said. "It's just that she... she seems so lonely."

"She is creepy," said Shelby with gusto. "She was a real bitch back in the day. She used to set poison out for the fish house cats because they would come into her garden at night to mate. Until they got too smart for her. All of her kids are either crazy or in jail. She was never right, Gum said, ever since they found those two little girls..." she paused. "I'll show you what I'm talking about. Come here."

She stepped lightly over the mound of an old grave and led them toward the center of the cemetery where a monumental marble stone rose up in the middle of a row of smaller stones, drawing attention to itself through sheer size. The three of them stood in front of this stone and read the time, worn but deeply etched and still legible lettering that announced the entry into heaven of Sallie Ann Fulcher born May 16, 1938 and Nina Polk Scarborough, born December 20, 1937, both of whom departed this life on August 15, 1949. *"Cousins"* proclaimed a banner held at each end by somber, standing angels across the top edge of the gravestone.

"They drowned," said Shelby. "The way the story goes, they were swimming in the sound way out off some sandbars out there and somehow either one or the other of them went into a trough and got in over her head. I guess the other one went in after to try to help her, and then a little boy found them later when they washed up behind the oyster beds down by Glenna's house. Glenna was just a kid then, but she remembers it, and so does Gum. It was Gum's brother Jack that found them. He said it was the worst thing he ever saw, and he had nightmares every night for weeks after he found them. He said that they were all wet and pale as death and covered with seaweed, and that they had their hands around each other's throats, and claw marks down their faces. Can you imagine?" Shelby crossed her arms against her chest and gave a shudder. "That would be the worst way to go, I think. Drowning. And taking your own flesh and blood with you, just because you can't fight the instinct to latch on to something to keep yourself afloat."

The three of them stood in silence for a while, gazing at the shared marker for the separate graves of the two cousins who died so long ago, clinging to one another and struggling. After awhile Shelby nudged Victor. "They're related to us, of course," she said. "Gum's mother was a Scarborough. Gum was just a few months younger than Nina and used to play dolls with her. Just think, if Gum hadn't been doing something else that day, she might have gone along with them. She would have drowned, too, and we wouldn't even be here. It makes you think…"

Victor looked across the graveyard over to where the funeral party was still gathered around the canopy raised above Uncle Buzz's coffin. A line of people trailed like ants toward the cars lined up along the graveyard fence. He could see his grandmother, still shouting into the ear of her aunt Glenna, and his father, standing in the midst of a group of dark-suited old men, pointing to some dilapidated house along the waterfront. Soon they would have to join the adults and head back to the restaurant. He would be sorry, he discovered, to leave this little place, this graveyard and this tiny village, each populated exclusively with his own blood relatives. How odd that he had never known that such a place existed, a town at the very edge of the continent, tucked away between swamp and sound, known only to those who proceeded from it, and abandoned by most of them. More than half of the markers he'd seen in the graveyard bore his last name. Maybe, he said to himself, they could bury me here. It was a somber but somehow uplifting idea.

He turned to Shelby. "Is our grandfather here?" he asked.

"Yeah," said Shelby. "Over here…" She stepped forward and to the left, but then froze as if seeing a ghost. "Oh, shit!" she breathed.

"What's wrong?" said Dora, stepping up beside Shelby. Victor's stomach clenched. He'd forgotten, for a moment, that Dora was there.

"God Damn it," said Shelby. She pointed past the canopy to the open gate of the fence that surrounded the graveyard. Moving against the stream of people who were filing out of the cemetery to their cars was a figure wearing a short black dress, high-heeled open-toed shoes, and a crown of spiky yellow hair. "My fucking mother."

Shelby turned her back and folded her arms.

Dora and Victor look at one another, then at the approach of Shelby's mother, who as she approached Gum and Glenna, threw open her arms and almost knocked Gum over with the suddenness and unsteadiness of her embrace. Gum staggered under the younger woman's weight for a second, and then took her by the shoulders and pushed her away. Victor searched the crowd for his father, who was watching the scene open mouthed.

Shelby's mother shaded her eyes with her hand and scanned the cemetery until she spotted Victor, Dora, and Shelby's broad back. Like an eager child she made her way toward them, determined and unsteady on her little spike heeled shoes which stabbed the tender, sandy turf covering the dead with every step.

Shelby turned to face her just as the woman was about to throw her arms around her neck. Shelby kept her own arms folded against her chest as she submitted to her mother's embrace and a flurry of kisses against both of her cheeks. "Hello, Mama," she said dryly, once her mother let go. "Nice of you to make it."

Victor and Dora, as one, backed away, then looked at one another. There was an unmistakable odor hovering about the dark little woman, an invisible cloud of whiskey, perfume, and nicotine. Victor was shocked to see tears glinting in Dora's eyes.

"Baby, I can't believe it!" Shelby's mother cried. She reached for Shelby's hand, and Shelby let her take it. "I had no idear your daddy was so sick! No idear! You're Gum didn't tell me till it was too late! I can't believe he's gone! I can't believe no one told me he was so bad off!"

"There's nothing you could have done," said Shelby, as calmly as if her mother was upset over a spilled drink. "How have you been doing, Mama?"

Shelby's mother lowered her head. She was so much smaller in every way than her daughter that to see the two of them so close together it was impossible to imagine that the mother ever gave birth to the daughter. "I'm doing good, baby," she said. "Real good. I'm taking nurse's aide classes at Robeson Community. I'm staying with your Aunt Birdie; you remember her?"

"No," said Shelby. "Have you seen Tina and Hunter?"

"I saw them on Mother's day." Shelby's mother let go of Shelby's hand. "Baby, I've missed you so much. I never hear from you...."

Shelby just looked at her mother, and folded her arms across her chest again. The older, smaller woman looked over at Victor and Dora. "Who are your friends, baby?"

"That's Victor," said Shelby. "You know. Eddie's son. He's been here all summer. And my best friend Dora. They both live in Raleigh."

"Victor!" Shelby's mother shrieked as if she'd been pinched and gave a little hop of surprise. "This can't be little Victor! I ain't seen you since you were this high! My Lord, you're a lot taller than your daddy!" And she pitched herself forward to throw her arms around him. As if sensing his distress, she let go of him quickly, then gave him a wink and a smile that promised the moon and the stars. "You tell your mama I said hey," she said. Her accent was as country as any Victor had ever heard in person, it was so flat and nasal and drawling that in comparison Gum sounded like the Queen of England.

"Mama," said Shelby. "I appreciate you're coming. I know it means a lot to Daddy."

"Oh, Baby…" the little woman said, and tears welled up in her eyes as quickly as if she'd turned on some internal spigot. "I wish I'd known he was so bad off. I wish your Gum would have told me. I know I've been a terrible person, but–"

"Mama." Shelby closed her eyes and seemed to back away, though she did not move. "I don't want to hear all that. I'm glad you came, Mama. I hope you're taking care of yourself."

"I am, baby, I am. I'm going to church, going to meetings… I'm blessed honey, I sure am. But this has been hard on me, finding out about your daddy so sudden, and…"

"I'm sure it has been hard," said Shelby wearily. Then, out of nowhere, like lightning, her anger and resentment flashed. "So hard you had to have a shot or two between the funeral and the burial. For Christ's sake, Mama! Why couldn't you just stay away!"

Shelby's teeth gritted on the last two words, and her green eyes, so much like her mother's in shade but larger and rounder, blazed. She walked away in an arc and headed toward the gathering at her father's grave, a gathering which was slowly making its way toward the line of cars parked along the gate of the cemetery. Victor looked at Shelby's mother, whose own green eyes were now dry and hard in her tense and dark and tearstained face. The woman shouted toward Shelby, in a hot nasal voice loud enough for every living being within the confines of the cemetery to hear. "Your daddy wouldn't appreciate you talking so ugly to me!"

Victor watched, covered in prickly heat, as Shelby stopped short and her hands clenched at her sides. For a moment her broad shoulders sagged and her head, heavy with combs and curls bowed, but then only a second later she drew herself up and moved forward again, away from where her mother, like a spoiled child, stamped her foot and as a result sank her heel into the soil that covered some ancestor's final resting place. The dwindling group at the graveside looked toward the commotion, then looked quickly away, as if they'd seen someone expose herself. Victor, torn between contempt and helpless sympathy, gave Shelby's mother a brief glance, then followed Dora towards the rest of the family.

The gathering at the restaurant was even smaller than at the graveyard, consisting of the family, the employees of the restaurant, Dora, the tall old black man who had sat behind Victor and his father in the chapel, and a few other people that Victor couldn't place. Martha, Jason, and the baby were there too, and Gum spent the entire time cooing over the for once smiling and docile infant.

There were a bunch of platters laid out on the bar, and the older waitress Dottie served drinks. Oliver was there, looking out of place among the somberly dressed crowd in the jeans and t-shirt and stained apron that he washed dishes in, but Victor was glad to see him and greeted him in Spanish, realizing how much of all of that language that he'd absorbed from Oliver had seeped away since Uncle Buzz went into the hospital. Dora watched from the booth as Oliver seized Victor in a tearful embrace, nearly lifting Victor off the floor. Dora sat in a booth with little Jason, sharing a paper plate loaded with hushpuppies and ranch dressing. Victor smiled at her, smiled at the warm and unlikely image of the glamorous young woman and the silent, wary little boy; Dora smiled back, but her smile was quick and soon vanished, and afterwards she turned her attention completely away from him to wipe the crumbs from his stepbrother's fingers.

Victor asked Dottie for a beer, which she drew for him and handed him with a wink. He walked with it over to where Shelby was perched in her usual place behind the register, talking to the black man from the funeral. "This is my cousin Victor," she said as he approached. "Uncle Eddie's son. Victor, this is Allen. Allen was daddy's sponsor."

The man smiled broadly and held out his hand, which Victor shook. It took Victor a moment to recall what a sponsor was, and when he did he blushed helplessly, for he was still holding his beer.

"Allen's a preacher," Shelby said.

"A minister," Allen corrected her. His voice was low and roughly textured, as if he was hoarse from shouting. "I do quite a bit more than preach." He scratched a spot on the crown of his head and nodded at Victor. "Shelby tells me you live in Raleigh. Are you still in school?"

Victor nodded and forced himself not to hide the beer behind his back.

"I have a godson in eleventh grade at Leesville High."

"I'm at Sanderson," Victor said.

"How do you like the beach?" said Allen, the favorite question, it seemed, of those who lived on the coast year round.

"I love it," Victor said simply.

Uncle Buzz's sponsor laughed. "That's pretty straightforward," he said. "Maybe after you graduate you can come down east. Or do you have college plans?"

"No."

The minister raised his eyebrows. "No?"

"Victor wants to be a dropout." Shelby informed the man.

Victor looked her in the eye. "I want to work."

"You can do both." Shelby said. "I do."

"I'm not you."

The minister looked at them in turn as they went back and forth, a smile on his dark, deeply creased face.

"I'm going to be a *psychologist*," said Shelby, with all the pride and assurance of a little girl announcing that she is going to be queen. Victor felt suddenly extremely world-weary, and, forgetting that he was in the presence of an alcoholic in recovery, he took a deep swallow of his beer.

The minister seemed unperturbed. "A psychologist!" he said to Shelby. "That's a lot of school to pay for. Better not tell your grandma!"

Shelby's set her chin. "I'll get scholarships," she said.

Victor finished off his beer. "I think you should be a singer," he says to Shelby. "You could be famous. You really can sing, Shelby." He presses the hard flat heel of his first time worn dress shoes into the top of his foot, and looked down. He couldn't seem to express how good a singer he felt she was.

"I don't want to be a professional singer." Shelby waved her hand languidly, as if she was turning down an offer of dessert.

Victor looked at Uncle Buzz's sponsor. "She's crazy. She could be famous."

The sponsor laughed. "Well, Shelby, the Lord does tell us not to hide our light under a bushel."

Shelby lifted her eyebrow. "And look what that got him."

Victor looked to the minister for a horrified reaction, but he only threw back his head and laughed so freely that the entire funeral party turned to stare at them.

Uncle Buzz's sponsor pressed Shelby's hand, shook Victor's and went over to speak to Gum, leaving Shelby and Victor at the register.

"I wanted him to do the eulogy, but he said he couldn't," Shelby said. "He and Daddy were too close. And he knows Gum can't stand him."

"Because he's black?"

Shelby gave Victor a weary look. "Because he's tough. He speaks his mind." She lowered her voice, "One time, daddy got so drunk after we moved in with Gum that he came into my room in the middle of the night while I was sleeping, opened the door of my closet, and puked in there."

Victor's mouth gaped. Shelby nodded. "Yep. On my clothes and my toys and everything. And he woke me up, too, hollering about my mother to the thin air."

"Jesus!"

Shelby shrugged. "That's nothing compared to some of the things my mom did. But the point is, after that was the first time Daddy ever really tried hard to stop drinking. He went into AA and met Allen, and he was sober for about a year and a half. And even when he'd relapse after that, he never came into my room when he was drunk. Allen never let him forget that he'd puked all over my things."

A swift succession of images flashed through Victor's mind, of Dora, the drifter named Shorty, pornography, his father rubbing his hand over his face. He can see clear as day his Uncle, muttering and cursing and vomiting into his own daughter's closet. Victor set the beer he was holding upon the glass beneath the register.

"Gum thought daddy should be able to forget that, since he doesn't remember doing it. But Allen thought he should remember."

"Yuck," said Victor.

An odd, rather wistful smile crept onto Shelby's face. "It's not as bad as it sounds. I knew he didn't know what he was doing, and I knew he'd be sorry. That's the difference between him and my mother. That's the difference between just about everyone and my mother. She's never really sorry, even though she *acts* sorry."

"Then how do you know she isn't?"

"Because she's always the same." Shelby waved and smiled as the minister, Allen, passed by them and out the door. "Daddy changed. He may have relapsed, but he changed. He was never nasty like that again. My mother's the same whether she's on drugs or off. She doesn't care about anybody but herself."

Maybe that's why she's still alive, Victor thought, but he didn't say it. Shelby could explain everything, and it made him feel all alone. Behind them the rest of Uncle Buzz's funeral party scraped chairs and clinked silverware as they ate. Victor went back to the bar for another beer. Dottie didn't hesitate to serve him, and he felt wonderfully warm and special as he straddled the barstool and took the first few swallows of the sharp, cool fresh beer. With every sip he felt his sudden loneliness at once expand and dissipate. No one would ever know how lost he felt, yet as much as anyone else in this room, he was part of this family.

Victor was on his third beer when people began to leave. His head felt light and the small thoughts that crossed his mind struck him as being supremely clever. He sat at the bar, empty but for himself, and secretly relished the knowledge that he really liked feeling drunk. It seemed to him that he had never felt better, stronger, safer, and at once as innocent and wise as at that moment. And, dare he even think it? He even felt charming! He leaned forward over the slick glossy wooden bar and let his hair, stiff with gel but no longer plastered back, fall over his face. He took a gulp of beer, stifled a small belch, and wiped his wet lips with the sleeve of his brand new suit. He swiveled around on the bar stool, and the movement was exhilarating. The gathering had thinned considerably. His father, Gum, Martha, and the children had all stuffed themselves into Gum's favorite booth, and Martha and Gum nattered over the baby while Victor's father looked above them at the TV over the end of the bar. The waitresses were clearing the buffet table of plates and left over food, and Shelby and Dora were nowhere to be seen. Victor caught his father's eye and smiled at him, the full, happy smile of a child. His father smiled back before his attention returned to the football game on the television.

A cigarette! Victor thought. That's what I need. That would be perfect. Now where the hell is Shelby? He watched as Jean, the middle-aged waitress carried a bus pan full of dishes through the swinging doors that closed off the kitchen. It seemed logical that Shelby, since she was not here, would be there. So, he slipped off the barstool and made his way with a carefree new unsteadiness through the gaily swinging double doors in search of his cousin and, he could not help but smile, maybe Dora, too? The way he felt, blunted and warmed by alcohol, he would not be afraid to face Dora, to take her by the hand and look her in the eyes and apologize sincerely, in front of Shelby, in front of God and everybody. After all, it wasn't like he'd raped her. Things just got out of hand, and he'd lost control because, well, to be honest, because she was toying with him, she knew she was. But he would tell her it was because she was so beautiful, for she *was* beautiful, in her silly way, with those red painted lips and those nice round soft breasts and those crazy seamed stockings…

The lights in the kitchen were off, but the dishwashing area was brightly lit up, and Jean jumped when she turned around after slamming the buspan onto the stainless steel countertop that led to the machine and saw Victor standing behind her. "God almighty Victor, you scared the shit out of me!" She laughed, holding one hand to her chest. She was a tall woman with long, slightly bowed legs, waist length hair that she kept in a braid at work, and a long, pleasant face with large teeth. "What are you doing back here? We told your grandmaw we were gonna clean everything up; it's the least we can do. Are you doing all right? I just can't believe he's really gone. Do you think your grandmaw's gonna be okay? Shelby says the doctor gave her something…" It was Jean's habit to jump from question to question in conversation, always answering herself before giving anyone else a chance. In this way she was nice to talk to when you didn't feel like talking. She went on in this fashion for a while before noticing the mug in Victor's hand.

"Oh, my god, Victor what is that, beer? Holy shit, don't tell me Mama's been serving you!" The waitress Dottie was the Jean's mother, as Jean was the waitress Kelli's mother. "I'm telling you, one of these days she's gonna get us busted by the ALE and then we'll all be out of a job. I guess it's all right though, since this is a closed party. But still, you shouldn't be drinking, boy, good lord what are you? Sixteen? Seventeen? I know you're not no twenty-one. You're too young to be drinking, but I guess it's all right if you know how to handle it. I was drinking when I was thirteen, my boyfriend was nineteen and back then eighteen was legal, I guess I shouldn't have been drinking that early, but there sure wasn't much else to do around here, especially back then. Mama would have killed me if she knew though, and you better believe I would have killed Kelli if I'd ever caught her doing such at that age. I guess that's kind of messed up, though, huh. Listen, does your daddy know you're drinking? I guess he must, you've been sitting at that bar just about all afternoon, haven't you, but it just didn't cross my mind that Mama was giving you beer. I'm gonna wear her out. Don't you ask her for any more Victor, I can tell you've had enough; your little face is as red as it can be. But listen, you didn't have to bring that mug back here, we're doing all the bussing today like I told you it's the least we can do. Go on back out to the party, drink all you want, I guess you only live once."

The party's over," Victor said. "I was just looking for Shelby. She's got our cigarettes."

"You and Shelby and your cigarettes." Jean smacked him smartly on the shoulder as she passed by him with an empty buspan. "When you all are dying of cancer, don't come crying to me. She's out there puffing away, I think..." Jean tossed her braid to indicate the area outside the service entrance, which was propped a bit open by a pickle barrel. Victor stepped deftly over the pickle barrel, reveling in the slimness which allowed him to noiselessly pass from inside to out, and he looked around for Shelby and Dora but they were nowhere to be seen. He leaned against the heavy metal door and peered out into the brightness of the afternoon at the dumpster set in the center of the gravel parking lot behind the restaurant. The lot was empty but for three cars, Dottie's Buick, Jean's pickup, and a very dirty white Mazda that Victor recognized as Oliver's. Oliver! Victor's eyes lit up as he thought of his friendly Spanish buddy. Was Oliver still around? Victor swiveled his neck to peer back into the kitchen but did not see anybody. He looked back over at the dingy Mazda, parked in the shade of the dumpster. Was he crazy, or was the car running? He stood up, once again unsteady, and approached the vehicle. Sure enough, the engine *was* running, but no one was inside. At least that was how it seemed until he got right up to the driver's side window and saw his friend Oliver inside, his shirt tossed over the headrest of the driver's seat as he writhed on top of a fully clothed but nevertheless uninhibited Shelby. Shocked into absolute stillness, it was a long, moment before Victor could turn away. Backing away and shaking his head wildly as if he'd just seen a vision of hell, he crouched in the gravel like a cornered animal, threw up a handful of pebbles and sand toward the car, then ran off toward the highway as Shelby and Oliver bolted up in the backseat, their passion interrupted by the gravel pelting the roof and windshield of the car like a hard and filthy rain.

Victor didn't get far, being too drunk to run very steadily. He came to a staggering stop just a block or so down the road from the restaurant. Cars slowed as they passed him and it occurred to him that he must look ridiculous if not mad, running down the street on such a blazing hot afternoon wearing his dark funeral suit. The giddiness of his first real alcoholic buzz was now violently eclipsed by disproportionate misery and a deep physical discomfort. He had no idea why the sight of Shelby and Oliver making out in Oliver's backseat made him so angry, but it did. Thinking about it now, he became aware of the urgent need to urinate. He turned off the edge of the highway onto a dead end street, at the end of which was a chained off wooded area. He stepped over the chain and into the woods, unzipped and pissed, moaning with relief and misery.

When he was through he walked back down the highway towards the restaurant. He was fairly sure that Shelby and Oliver had risen in their seats too late to see him dash away, and even if they had seen him, he figured he can play it off now like he was joking, trying to scare them. He wasn't mad anymore, just weary, weary of himself and everybody else, weary of a life so full of unpleasant twists and turns. Why should it matter to him that Shelby had turned to warm and cheerful Oliver for comfort? Shelby and Oliver might have been fooling around for months, and Victor, so absorbed with himself and so blinded by his own cousinly vision of Shelby as pretty, but heavy and too incorrigibly strong minded and brusque to ever possess that simple appeal that brings people together for better or for worse, would never have noticed. The truth was that as at home as he had come to feel in his grandmother's house, he was really only a guest, and seeing a side of his cousin that she had not shown him made him feel as if he'd left already, as if he'd never really been an important addition to her life in the first place. He'd thought that he'd kept his attraction to Dora a secret from Shelby out of pity and consideration, but in the end he was only protecting himself. It wasn't Shelby who felt left out when other people were happy, or belonged to one another, it was Victor himself.

When he stepped back into the restaurant through the customer entrance, they surrounded him. Where had he been? They'd looked all over the place, what in the world had he been doing? His father, Martha, his Grandmother, Shelby, Dottie, Jean, and Kelli, all of them stared at him and blurted their questions in rapid fire, and he just smiled and shrugs. "Too much beer," he said. "I had to take a walk."

"You should have said something," his grandmother said. "We've been ready to go for fifteen minutes. We've just been hunting for you."

Shelby gave him a long, diagnostic stare. Only her hair, now loose from it's combs and springing about her head in it's usual fashion like a tangle of vipers, suggested that she'd been up to anything. Oliver was nowhere to be seen and Dora was still sitting in one of the booths with Jason.

"Leave him alone, mama." His father stepped forward and clapped Victor on the shoulder. "He just needed a little fresh air. We all ready to go?"

Once outside, the family all waved at Jean, Dottie, and Kelli, who were staying behind to open the restaurant for the supper crowd, and then they piled into their separate cars, Victor's father and his brood in the rental, and Victor, Gum, Shelby, and Dora into Gum's sedan. After the cars started, Victor's father rolled up beside them, rolled down the passenger window, and shouted across Martha. "We'll be by tomorrow on our way out. Okay?"

Gum nodded.

In the backseat of the rental, Jason strained upward to peer out the window. Dora waggled her fingers at him and he ducked away. This made Victor laugh for some reason, and Shelby and Dora, who were strapped into the backseat, peered forward at him. "Are you still drunk?" Shelby said.

"Hush, Shelby," said Gum. "Nobody is *drunk*, for pity's sake."

"Yeah," said Victor, though he didn't feel drunk, just tired.

"I don't think you should drink," Shelby said. "You get weird."

"Shelby!" Gum snapped.

"I'm not drunk," said Victor, contradicting himself.

216

"*I* think we all need a nap," said Gum.

Victor closed his eyes and leaned back into the passenger seat, as if obeying.

As usual it was some time before he could fall asleep in the dead man's room. It was only late afternoon, and the daylight just beyond the curtains made relaxing a challenge. He tried the old trick of pushups, but this only made him feel overheated. He no longer felt drunk, just unsteady and slightly ill. He propped the pillows one atop the other against the headboard and leaned his back upon them, crossed his arms over his chest, and sat and stared into the corner of the room where the wall that faced out into the front yard met the wall that separated this room from Shelby's room. In this corner there was nothing to look at, but his gaze remained fixed there for a long time as his arms crossed against his chest and his brow lowered and creased over his open eyes as if he were thinking hard; but he was not really thinking at all, just letting his mind drift, numb and detached, over the events of the day. He felt nothing, now, except a slight embarrassment over having seen Oliver and Shelby in Oliver's car. He didn't know why, now, it had upset him, and it seemed a waste of time to wonder. It seemed so trivial beside the fact that he would be leaving soon. His mother's will was inexorable, and he knew that he was going to have to return to her home to at least attempt another year of high school.

Even as he scowled into the corner, he knew it wouldn't be so bad. He could imagine now, going back to school, walking the halls alone, sleeping through classes, and enduring eight hours of isolation among the crowd as long as he had work to do afterwards. He would find a job as soon as he got back to town, hopefully in a restaurant like his grandmother's, a small, family owned one, and he would stick with it and save up money for a car. And with his car he would drive down over the holidays and visit Shelby and his grandmother, and God willing, he would never be far from the dim, stuffy, wise and wry comfort of Shelby's room. He smiled and his brow relaxed, because with the thought of that room, just on the other side of the wall, came a memory of himself within that room, a memory, from the otherwise forgotten time he had come here with his father from New York, when Shelby's room was still just his father's childhood bedroom, and he had been put to bed there for that reason. He'd not been able to sleep then either, for it was a room in a strange house, full of strange adults; his mother had stayed in New York. He knew that he was with his father's family, but this meant little to him in the midst of being touched and cooed over by unfamiliar adults and then dispatched to a strange bedroom where he was expected to go immediately to sleep. He remembered crying, then screaming, then calling for his father, because all at once his feelings of homesickness and abandonment had coalesced into the form of a grinning, fur covered monster in the dark corner of that strange room. But his screams brought no answering presence, and in fact had the effect of amplifying his distress. Before long he jumped out of the too large bed and was running down the hallway in search of his father, unsure as to whether or not he would find him; so complete was his sense of having been abandoned. But of course his father was there in the brightly lit living room amongst all the other unfamiliar people, so transformed by his familiarity with them that Victor hardly recognized him. Victor had run to him nonetheless, and buried his damp and wailing face into his father's soft chest. Not heeding the humiliating oohs of sympathy proceeding from all the strange old women in the room, Victor let himself be gathered up by his dad and taken back into the room where an invisible menace crouched in the dark corner.

"What's wrong!" his father had said, laying Victor back in the bed and tucking him in like an expert. "What's all this crying about? You miss your mama? We'll be back home soon."

Victor, immobilized by the sheets tucked all around him, could only gaze wide-eyed up at his father's calm, round face. "There's a monster," he said, matter-of-factly, as if the presence of a monster were no more extraordinary than that of a spider, but nonetheless something to be dealt with by an adult.

"A monster!" his father exclaimed, gamely. He sat up straight and looked around the room. "Where at?! I don't see any monster in here! There better not be no monster!"

Not sure whether or not his father was making fun of him, Victor struggled to free one of his arms. He pointed to the corner. "There," he said, summoning what was left of his fear. His father turned his head.

"Him?!" his father said, looking the corner up and down as if in dismissal. "You mean *that* monster? Shoot…" He leaned close over his son and winked, "He ain't nothing. Don't you worry about *him*. All that monster can do is sit there looking ugly. Best thing you can do is just go to sleep. Then you can't see him, and he gets mad and pouts. Why, he's been around ever since I was a little boy." Victor's father reached over and ruffled Victor's fine dark hair. "Don't you know this was my room when I was your age? That monster never got me, and he sure enough ain't gonna get you!"

Victor, having been seen to, already no longer feared the monster and already was beginning to dismiss the very existence of any monster, but he wasn't ready for his father to leave him yet. "I want to go home," he said.

His father reached over and tickled Victor's little belly. "Home!" he exclaimed. "Home! Boy, why would you want to go home?! This is fun! Tomorrow after the service for Granddaddy we're gonna go to the beach. You're gonna love that. Then later on maybe we'll go to the waterslide, and after that we'll get us some shrimp…" Victor's father sat up and yawned. "Now, look what you've done. Just thinking about all we've got to do tomorrow, I'm worn out! Listen, I'm gonna go to bed. You settle down and don't you worry about that old monster.

Monsters like that aren't bad unless you mess with them. If you let them be, they'll let you be. And if you're good, and quit worrying about them, they'll sit right there and look after you and make sure nothing really bad comes to get you. That's what monsters are for. They keep you safe. They can't help they look so ugly. That's just how they work."

Throughout this speech Victor's father had been speaking with his eyes half closed, as if talking in his sleep. Victor stared up at him in wonder. Without looking to the corner, where he knew no monster could be seen, Victor could nevertheless see it in his mind's eye as clear as day- a hideous thing, squatting on skinny legs that ended in clawed and hairy feet, it's mouth open and slobbering through a lolling blood red tongue, black lips and silver fangs, bulging, bloodshot eyes and a matted fur coat of a bright purple hue, altogether like a monster from Sesame Street. "What's his name?" Victor asked.

"Gertrude," Victor's father said, without hesitation, and with that Victor, all but his head swaddled by the sheets, burst into giggles. His father chuckled, bent, and planted a beery kiss on Victor's forehead. "Go to sleep, now, son," he said. As he walked rather unsteadily out of the room it was as if a part of himself he was hardly aware of stayed behind to keep his son company. Victor wiggled away some of the closeness of the bed sheets and sat up in bed for a while, staring into the empty corner that harbored his guardian monster. All he could really see was darkness, mitigated a bit now by a sliver of light from the hallway beaming through the door that his father had drunkenly failed to close completely. "Good night, Gertrude," little Victor had said to himself before he closed his eyes. It wasn't long before he was fast asleep.

By the digital clock on the bedside table it was almost eleven. Victor cursed and sat up and rubbed his face. As much as he hated to wake up, he hated even more to sleep away the morning as he has done today. His father, and perhaps Martha and the children, if they were not here already, would be here soon before getting in their rental car and heading back to South Carolina.

He listened at the doorway for any activity before opening the door and bolting to the bathroom. After a horribly loud and liquid bowel movement that made the air around him reek, he shamefacedly showered and brushed his teeth and afterwards realized that the time was now utterly past when he had the ability to take refuge and a spiteful comfort in being dirty. He went back to uncle Buzz's room to dress and then into the sunny kitchen for coffee. Shelby and Gum were there looking through condolence cards.

Here's one from Aunt Patti," said Shelby, "and here's one from the Mason's. We got one from Helen Willis… that's the Siamese twins mother." Shelby said this last to Victor, by way of a greeting.

"How come they don't separate those twins?" Victor said. He'd wondered this, on and off ever since he saw the two Willis'.

"Because they're Jehovah's Witnesses," Shelby said. "Didn't I tell you that?"

"Maybe," said Victor. "But what does that have to do with separating Siamese twins?"

"To *separate* them," said Shelby with exaggerated patience. "They would have to *operate*. And to have an *operation*, they would have to give them *blood*. And Jehovah's Witnesses aren't *allowed* to take blood transfusions."

"Oh," said Victor. "Why not?"

"Because it's in the Bible somewhere. You aren't supposed to eat blood. I think it's in Deuteronomy or something."

"But getting a transfusion isn't eating," said Victor.

221

"Tell them that," said Shelby. Abruptly she put down the card. "Hey Gum," she said, "I showed Victor that big grave for those two little girls that drowned."

Gum pursed her lips and shook her head. "Nina and Sallie Anne," she said. "Lord, that was a sad day. I never will forget that day. Nina Scarborough was my cousin," she said to Victor, "my aunt Rhoda's oldest girl. Aunt Rhoda never got over it, neither. My brother Jack found them, washed up on a sandbar. Nobody had even known they were in trouble. They'd just gone out swimming, just like any other day." Gum sighed and rose and took her coffee mug to the sink and rinsed it before returning to the table to stand behind Shelby, looking down over her granddaughter's shoulder at the handful of condolence cards. "That one's pretty," she said, reaching for it. She opened it, sniffed, and set it down. "But you know, I always said…" The old lady hearkened back to the tragedy of the past. "…at least they were together. I can't think of anything worse than dying alone. I'll never forget," she said again, "my brother telling us how they looked when they washed up ashore, with their arms around each other. At least they weren't alone. God never sends us more than we can bear." Absently, the old lady scratched a spot under her breast. Across the table Shelby and Victor exchanged a long look.

"He's sent us more sappy cards than I can bear," said Shelby after a minute. "Here's one from the Budweiser distributor." She reached back and handed it to Gum. "Isn't that ironic?"

And so Victor learned, without having to ask, what irony is.

His father came to the house and left in less than five minutes, leaving his wife and children in the car running in the driveway. "Well, you could at least bring that baby in to see me," snapped Gum, brushing past her only surviving son as he stood in the screen door.

She slapped her slippers on the pavement as she ran out to the car and smiled at Martha in the passenger seat. Victor's father shook his head in amusement and winked at Victor and Shelby before holding his hand out to Shelby, who ignored it. "Shelby, honey," Victor's father said, "We're sure going to miss him, aren't we?"

Shelby cocked an eyebrow. Victor's father, not to be denied the benefit of his gesture of fellowship, lowered his outstretched hand to leave it resting, palm out at his side as if to convey helplessness. "He was a good brother to me," Victor's father said, looking up to the ceiling. "Better than I deserved. All I can say is that I know he's gone to a better place. He's up in heaven with our Daddy."

Victor's father's smile was faint and, could it be...a bit bitter? "And they're probably fishing. It's the living who feels the pain."

"That's true," said Shelby.

Victor's father stood silent for a moment, as if in prayer, and then he reached out and clapped Shelby on the shoulder like a man, which made her start and jump back and give Victor a wide eyed look of absolute outrage.

"Now, you let me know, little girl, if you need anything. We're just a phone call away, you hear? And look out for Mama for me. She's not as strong as she thinks she is."

Shelby could only stalk down the hall to her bedroom. Victor's father, oblivious to his niece's undying contempt, beamed down at his son and reached for him. Victor submitted to an awkward, manly embrace and ducked his head. "Well son," he said, "I sure wish we had more time. But the baby's already getting fussy."

"Yeah," said Victor. "Bye, Dad. It was good to see you." He followed his father out into the driveway, where his grandmother, bending into the backseat of the car so that only her bottom and legs, in their lavender sweatpants were visible, could be heard baby-talking to Madison.

"Mama," said Victor's father. The old lady reluctantly emerged from the backseat. "We gotta go now. You come on down and see us as soon as you can, I mean it."

Gum pursed her lips and suffered her wrinkled cheek to be kissed. "Well, I wish I could," she said. "But I don't know how. With Shelby starting school in a few weeks and all these bills to take care of, I don't know when we'll be able to get away. But I appreciate it Eddie. Maybe around Christmas."

Gum sighed like a languishing bride. "We'll see. Drive careful, Eddie." She waggled her fingers at Martha and blew kisses to the baby, who, strapped in her carryall, was indeed fast asleep. Victor looked through the windshield at Jason, who looked back at him with a blank expression, his index finger fully one joint deep into his nose. Victor was overcome by an upsurge of love for the sullen, wary little boy like a tidal wave in his soul. "I'll come see you soon, Dad," he said.

And he would.

Victor remained with his grandmother and his cousin for about another week, during which he worked at the restaurant, practiced Spanish with Oliver who was so happy to have him back at work that it was impossible for Victor to continue to resent whatever it was he resented about the secret sharing between Oliver and Shelby. He did, however, begin to feel a certain reserve now, that he had never before felt with his cousin, a shyness and a sense of wonder as if by some trick of time Shelby had suddenly become years older than he. He saw no more of Dora, who right after the funeral flew with her mother and stepfather, according to Shelby, to some kind of convention in the Virgin Islands, and who would not be returning to Morehead City until next summer, her real home being, like Victor's, back in the capital city. Shelby suggested, teasingly, that they might run into each other. Victor couldn't imagine anything more unlikely or awkward.

But the night before he was scheduled to board the bus, after they left the restaurant and dropped off the money at the bank overnight deposit, Shelby asked Victor into her room, where, with incense lit and her strange, jangly music playing, she handed him an odd shaped package. Victor blushed and shook his head as he accepted it, ashamed because he had not thought to buy her, or his grandmother anything.

"Don't be that way," said Shelby, as if she'd read his mind. "Just take it, dumbass. Open it up."

Still shaking his head, Victor perched on the foot of Shelby's bed and unwrapped the gaudy silver and metallic green paper. Inside there was a carton of cigarettes and a picture in a frame. Shelby, sitting beside him, leaned to the other side and tilted the shade of her bedside lamp to cast a better light upon these gifts.

It took Victor a moment to recognize the figures in the picture as himself and Shelby, as the image was at once abstract and impressionistic, the figures having pale green skins and features that were at once vague and singular. It was a painting, adapted he assumed, by Shelby, from a photograph taken by Gum of the two of them right before they left for Uncle Buzz's funeral, a moment Victor had completely forgotten and never would have remembered had not Shelby given it back to him. In the photograph the two of them stood in the doorway of Shelby's room dressed in their fancy clothes, with Victor's arm around his cousin's, Shelby's shoulder and Shelby's head against his shoulder. Shelby was smiling broadly, her eyes squinting behind her red rimmed glasses, which she had put on to check the camera battery for Gum, who wasn't good with such gadgetry and then had forgotten to take them back off; and Victor smiled slightly, but enough to show a row of his teeth and a crease in his cheek. In the painting, which looked like a watercolor, all features but their smiles were blurred into the greenness of their skins, giving their faces a mysterious underwater quality that was at once both eerie and comforting. Also in the painting, their black clothes simply merged into one irregular black shape out of which their faces and hands emerged, so that they looked as if they were as connected as the Willis twins. In both photograph and painting one of the several posters of James Dean in Shelby's room peered out over Victor's shoulder as if it was not merely an image, but a presence in the room itself, an approving presence with an everlasting melancholy and tender half smile. "Now let me get a picture of you two looking so nice." Victor remembered Gum saying, and Dora had stood behind the old lady to observe. Looking at the painting now, Victor was struck by the chance perfection of its composition. The darkness of their clothes, the green hue of their faces, the poster of James Dean on the far wall of Shelby's room adding dimension. It was an image that lent itself well to the watercolor's indistinct rendering. "Wow," said Victor, looking with wonder at Shelby. "You paint like this, on top of everything else?"

Shelby gave him a long look, then a smile, then shook her head. "No. I can't even draw that well. Dora did it. For you."

Victor looked down at the picture and the figures blurred into clouds of green and black as tears welled up. Every picture tells a story he heard his grandmother say, and maybe all could be forgiven.

About the Author

David L. Carter holds degrees in Theology, English Literature and Library Science, and is the author of the novels *Familiar* and *Lustration Rites*. He lives in North Carolina.

Apprentice
House Press
Loyola University Maryland

Apprentice House is the country's only campus-based, student-staffed book publishing company. Directed by professors and industry professionals, it is a nonprofit activity of the Communication Department at Loyola University Maryland.

Using state-of-the-art technology and an experiential learning model of education, Apprentice House publishes books in untraditional ways. This dual responsibility as publishers and educators creates an unprecedented collaborative environment among faculty and students, while teaching tomorrow's editors, designers, and marketers.

Outside of class, progress on book projects is carried forth by the AH Book Publishing Club, a co-curricular campus organization supported by Loyola University Maryland's Office of Student Activities.

Eclectic and provocative, Apprentice House titles intend to entertain as well as spark dialogue on a variety of topics. Financial contributions to sustain the press's work are welcomed. Contributions are tax deductible to the fullest extent allowed by the IRS.

To learn more about Apprentice House books or to obtain submission guidelines, please visit www.apprenticehouse.com.

Apprentice House
Communication Department
Loyola University Maryland
4501 N. Charles Street
Baltimore, MD 21210
Ph: 410-617-5265 • Fax: 410-617-2198
info@apprenticehouse.com • www.apprenticehouse.com

CPSIA information can be obtained
at www.ICGtesting.com
Printed in the USA
LVHW04s1953031018
592296LV00005B/24/P